PRAISE FOR
THE ENTITLED

"I wish it were longer, and that's something that I've rarely said about the baseball games I've covered in 30 years as a sportswriter. But it's how I felt while reading *The Entitled*."

—Tony Pluto, *Washington Post*

"More than a terrific baseball book. It's a terrific book, period."

—*Sports Illustrated*

"Deford scores another hit with this novel of athletes behaving badly...Deford tackles timely and provocative issues without flinching."

—*Publishers Weekly*

"Frank Deford is not just an immensely talented sportswriter, he's an immensely talented American writer. *The Entitled* is his wise and pleasurable portrait of a Willy Loman-like baseball manager finally getting his chance in the Bigs late in his career."

—*David Halberstam*

"Readers are exposed to a richly textured understanding of baseball and, no less, of estrangement, ambition, mendacity, and the search for one's destiny—notwithstanding the cost in human or financial terms. The outcomes of the many subplots will generate surprise, delight, and disappointment and will sharply divide the members of any reading club—as one would expect with a story that is so true to life."

—*Library Journal*

"*The Entitled* is a baseball masterpiece, like *The Natural* and *Field of Dreams;* the difference is the plot and the characters depict the true inside world of baseball. Frank Deford writes like he played in the majors for ten years. If you have a passion for baseball, this is a must read."

—Mike Schmidt, Baseball Hall of Fame

"While it contains all of the keen insider knowledge one expects of America's premier sports journalist, it also displays his gifts for dialogue and intricate plotting and his poignant grasp of character. It proves once again that Deford can play at the highest level in any league."

—Michael Mewshaw, author of *Year of the Gun*

"In men like Traveler and Alcazar we find the beating heart and struggling soul of baseball; and in their story we rediscover the redemptive power of the game's simple magic and moral order...Another great American read by America's greatest living sportswriter."

—Jeff MacGregor, *Sports Illustrated*;
author of *Sunday Money*

THE ENTITLED

A TALE OF MODERN BASEBALL

THE ENTITLED

FRANK DEFORD

SOURCEBOOKS LANDMARK™
AN IMPRINT OF SOURCEBOOKS, INC.®
NAPERVILLE, ILLINOIS

Published by Sourcebooks Landmark, an imprint of Sourcebooks,
Inc.
P.O. Box 4410, Naperville, Illinois 60567-4410
(630) 961-3900
Fax: (630) 961-2168
www.sourcebooks.com

Library of Congress Cataloging-in-Publication Data

Deford, Frank.
  The entitled : a novel / by Frank Deford.
      p. cm.
  ISBN 978-1-4022-0896-6 (hardcover)
  1. Baseball managers--Fiction. 2. Baltimore Orioles (Baseball team)--Fiction. 3. Baltimore (Md.)--Fiction. 4. Baseball stories. I. Title.

PS3554.E37E57 2007
813'.54--dc22

                                        2007010914

Printed and bound in the United States of America
VP 10 9 8 7 6 5 4 3 2 1

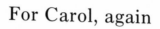

For Carol, again

THE ENTITLED

THAT NIGHT

So, for Howie, it was, at last: neither resignation on the one hand, nor anger on the other. No, it was simply awful, horrible disappointment that tore at him. That it all must end this way. No, not *this* way. *Anyway* it ended would be a calamity, because despair would follow, and Howie understood himself well enough to know that he didn't possess the creative resources to really ever overcome that despair.

This is the way he put it, over the phone, to Lindsay: "I'm a dead man, sweetie. I know I won't get outta Baltimore alive."

Howie was, after all, a practical man. Whenever one of his regulars would go onto the disabled list, all the writers would flutter around him, asking how the team could possibly manage until the wounded star returned.

"I don't deal with the dead," Howie would reply. That concluded the discussion. Ask me about the ones who could suit up. You play with what you had. And now it was he who was the dead man, because he was positive that he was going to be fired in Baltimore, and that would mean the end of his life in baseball, which was the only existence he had ever known.

There was a singular blessing. Because his demise was so clear-cut, he had, for the short term, found a certain calm within, so by the time he got to Baltimore he was concerned mostly with how, when the inevitable happened, he must display dignity upon his leave-taking. There would be no grousing. He would, in fact, thank the Indians for giving him the opportunity to manage in the major leagues. He would wish the team and the organization well.

There would be no backbiting. Of course, yes, he would, in passing (only in passing, you understand), recall how well the team had done under his aegis his first year on the job. He would not embellish that fact, but he would mention it (in passing) so as to remind everyone that just because Howie Traveler was a busher, he had shown that he could damn well manage a team in the big leagues. He had proved that. It was important to leave the media bastards with that. Especially the talk radio bastards, those who spewed venom for a living, and those amateur venom-spewing bastards who just called in.

When he got to Baltimore and found the time, Howie was going to write down what he wanted to say, and then commit it to memory so that he would display extemporaneous eloquence in his last public appearance.

In the meantime, he tried to pretend that he was not dwelling on what everyone knew. The pallbearers were assembling. Not only the columnists from the *Plain Dealer* and the Akron *Beacon Journal,* but, as well, the lead columnist of the Columbus *Dispatch* had signed onto the press manifest this trip, ready to dress up his obituary on the spot for the enlightenment of central Ohio fans. After all, a road trip offered the kind of timetable general managers preferred for these proceedings. Fire the manager away from home. Let an interim manager—in this case, the team's trusty old reliable, Spencer "Frosty" Westerfield, the bench coach—handle the next series, in Chicago, and then have the new man on hand, prepared to assume command— "take the helm," as the papers would have it—when the team returned to Cleveland, ready to start fresh, turn a new leaf, salvage the season, restore the damage that he, Howie Traveler, had indisputably done.

Never was anything so pat. So Howie just waited for Moncrief to fly in from Cleveland and fire him. Of course, everybody knows that baseball managers are, as it is written in stone, hired to be fired, but this was cold comfort when you were the manager in question and this was your time to be eighty-sixed.

O'Reilly, one of the newspaper beat men who liked Howie and drank with him sometimes, told him that Diaz was already in Cleveland, working out his deal. Nobody could locate Diaz, but O'Reilly said they knew he was there. This figured. Even when the Indians had hired Howie, the season before last, there had been a lot of speculation that Diaz would get the job instead. Diaz was surely Jay Alcazar's man, and if Juan Francisco Alcazar, El Jefe—The Chief—could not put out his best for Howie (which this season he evidently chose not to) then it would be just a matter of time before Diaz was brought in. So this is where it stood, Diaz working out the details of his contract, whereupon, that buttoned up, Moncrief would pop over to Baltimore, via Southwest Air, and, with the saddest, most sympathetic expression he could manage to put on, basset-faced, he would tell Howie that he was toast.

Once there was a basketball coach named Cholly Eckman, and when he got a call from the owner, who told him he was "going to make a change in your department," Cholly said "fine." Then, as Cholly recalled, it ruefully occurred to him that he was the only one in his department.

Nowadays, though, what general managers tell managers when they fire them is that: "We have decided to go in another direction." Unsaid: that direction will be up, whereas you, you dumb sonuvabitch, have been taking us in a direction that is most assuredly down.

So now, Howie put on the best smile he could manage, of the sort he assayed when he had to take a staged photograph at a charity auction or some such thing. "I wish I could think to say something really clever wise-ass when Moncrief tells me that," he said.

He had arrived in Baltimore and was eating dinner (as best he could) with his daughter.

"Don't, Daddy," Lindsay said. "Just be classy, like always. Everybody with any sense knows it's not your fault. Go out with style, and that'll help you get another chance."

Howie took his hand off his Old Grandad, reached over and laid it on hers. Lindsay was his only daughter, only family now, really. How adorable it was of her, how thoughtful, that she had come up from Washington, where she worked as a lawyer for some arcane House subcommittee, to see him. She had just showed up, knowing what an incredibly difficult time he was going through. She had been standing there when Howie came out of the clubhouse after the game tonight. The Indians had beaten the Orioles, 6-4. Alcazar had gone three-for-five, with a monstrous home run and then a two-run double in the ninth that won the game. He'd been dogging it all season, it seemed, but now that he knew Howie was shit-canned, he was suddenly a hitting fool again.

And then there was Lindsay, standing outside the clubhouse. Howie almost cried. Funny, too. He didn't instantly recognize her, for she was there, amidst a covey of other women, who were there to consort with his ballplayers. Howie could forget sometimes that Lindsay was a grown woman now, and more than that: as pretty (well, almost so) as the sort of women ball-players would take out on the road. Lindsay Traveler had more style, though, than those sort of women. Howie didn't himself necessarily possess style—for one thing, to his eternal despair, his legs were too short, and he had a lumpy face—but he recognized style when he was within its penumbra.

Somehow, Lindsay—she, a lousy minor league ballplayer's daughter—had learned to dress in that way chic ladies of fashion do, with the ability to choose clothes that manage to work so perfectly that they count twice—once for how they look and then again because they proclaim to the world: this lady *knows* what's best, what's right, what's stylish, so don't even try to put one over on her.

Howie just wished she would let her hair grow longer, have it tumbling down, the way she did when she was younger. That was his only real complaint with her.

"No, honey," he said to her now. "Guys like me just get the one shot."

"Maybe not," Lindsay said.

"Nah, and now I'm pegged, too. Traveler can't get along with the big star. I'm old school. A hard ass. I thought Jay could work with me, and he did last year, but—" Howie shrugged. He didn't want to go over it anymore. These last few days, he had constantly had to talk with the writers about the possibility of his getting fired, and everybody else avoided him, so, effectively, for some time now, he hadn't talked about anything else. So he asked Lindsay about her job and her iffy boyfriend and anything else he could think of, so he didn't have to talk about himself getting fired. He also asked: "How's your mother?" and Lindsay told him, obliquely. Howie said to give her his best, and Lindsay said of course she would.

Thank God, Lindsay hadn't gotten his stumpy legs. She could stand with the best of them. She had her mother's wonderful green eyes, too. This occurred to Howie now. Also, better boobs. This was a terrible thing to pay attention to, your own daughter's boobs, but it did cross his mind—but only relatively, you understand, only as they compared to his ex-wife's boobs. He went back to focusing on her eyes.

Then there was no more to say, and so he called for the check. They had gone to a restaurant in Little

Italy, which was just far enough away from the hotel, at the Inner Harbor, and far enough off the beaten track that nobody was liable to find him there. "Are you sure you wanna drive back to Washington?" he asked. "I think the couch pulls out." Managers got suites. So, alone among the Cleveland players, did Alcazar. It was in his latest contract. Not enough he got seventeen and a half million a year, he got perks, too. He had incentive clauses. Excuse me, Howie thought: seventeen-five with five zeroes wasn't incentive enough?

"No, Daddy. I'll go back. I'm taking next week off and goin' down to the beach in Delaware, so I've gotta finish a lot of stuff."

"Last chance to use your old man's manager's suite."

But she said no again, and dropped him back off at the hotel, where she gave him a big hug. "I'm very proud of you," Lindsay said, and Howie knew she was starting to cry. She hadn't cried the whole time, up to now.

"I'm prouder of you," he replied, reaching across the seat, holding her as best he could, behind the steering wheel. Had he been feeling particularly guilty, he would have added: *All you managed without a father.* Her whole life, he had been away so much of the time, being a player, being a manager. But he was feeling so down in the dumps right now, there wasn't space in his battered old mind to review the familiar old guilt, too. He just held his daughter a little tighter, and then pulled away, got out of the car and went through the lobby walking quickly, dead on toward the elevators, looking straight ahead, praying there was nobody there to ask him about whether he'd heard anything new about his own impending demise.

As it turned out soon enough, too bad there hadn't been somebody there to delay him.

On his floor, he hurried down the hall. And then the door just ahead of him to his right flew open. If only Lindsay had come up with him. If only he'd arrived here a minute earlier or a minute later. Just that, either way. Seconds. The one thing Howie knew, whenever he looked back on it, was that he did not want that door to open before him. But it did, and even before Alcazar came up behind the woman, and grabbed her roughly and slammed the door shut with his foot—almost as quickly as it had opened—for just those split seconds, Howie saw it all clearly. And he remembered exactly what he saw and what he heard. It was not much, but then, after all, it happened so quickly that there was not enough for his vision of it to be blurred.

No, however much Howie was taken by surprise, however much that made him freeze in his steps, it emblazoned the scene in his memory: the woman, pretty (if in no special way) but built rather nicely, her blouse pulled out just a bit from her skirt, her hair out of place some, her face creased with shock as Alcazar's strong arms came up behind her, wrapped round her waist, yanking her back as she tried to get away, even as his foot reared up and violently slammed the door shut. And that last moment before she disappeared as she caught sight of Howie in the hall and her mouth seemed to open just enough to cry out to him. But there was no sound, just the pretty enough face, aghast, and then the door slamming shut before him.

Howie had paused there, listening, pondering whether he should knock. But he heard nothing—certainly no scream, no struggle—and, at last, he only turned and went down the hall to his suite. There he poured himself another bourbon, a nightcap, but it didn't help, for all he could think about was that he hadn't had the nerve to intrude. It was too late now. Whatever Alcazar was going to do with that woman, he had done it. No, it wasn't any business of his who his players were screwing, but this seemed to be a different kettle of fish, completely.

Had standing there in the hall like some dummy waiting for a bus given Alcazar the chance to rape her? Had Jay actually done that? Rape? Jay Alcazar—tall, dark and handsome, rich and clever, the veritable idol of millions, who could get most any piece of ass he wanted anywhere on God's green earth anytime he wanted it—what the hell would he be doing forcing it on some woman? Sure, a stiff dick has no conscience and all that, but...But the goddamn door had flown open and she was obviously trying to get away, and Jay had grabbed her roughly and wouldn't let her escape from him.

There were not many times in his life when Howie felt that he had failed for lack of trying. Failed, yes—of course he had failed. After all, he had failed as a ballplayer; he had failed at the thing he wanted most in the world. But he had tried his damndest. But now, when he was tested by a moment, by that exquisitely raw instant when a man either grabs the grenade and throws it back or dives for his own safety, he had found out who he was. He knew he had failed himself, and, in a very real way, he realized that, above all, he had failed his daughter; he had failed Lindsay, too.

He reached for the other bourbon in the mini-bar, but put it back. No. One was a nightcap; two was escape, a scaredy-cat, a drunk. So then he just got into bed and hoped that he could sleep, and he did, at last, at least for awhile. But not much. He was wide awake at eight o'clock when the phone rang. It was Moncrief. Well, at least the waiting was over. He even hoped Moncrief would tell him right now, over the phone, that the Indians had decided to go in another direction. For Christ's sweet sake, he didn't need a face-to-face to tell him what he already knew. But no, Moncrief didn't even want to talk about Howie's job, let alone about making a change in his department.

Instead, it was another urgent matter. It was about what had happened behind the door that had opened and closed in Howie's face, while he had stood there stunned and lacking.

HOWIE

WHAT YOU HAVE TO REMEMBER, Howie would remind people in whatever organization he was part of at that time, what you have to never forget, is that everybody who made the major leagues used to be a star. Probably from the first day they played the game as kids they could hit a ball or pitch it—or probably even do both—better than everyone else around them. At each level some of the best ones would drop off. They didn't care enough. They didn't want to work hard enough. Or there was, perhaps, just one thing they couldn't manage at this next step up. Usually, for batters, they couldn't hit a breaking pitch. Or, for pitchers, they couldn't learn to throw a breaking pitch. At a certain point, it didn't make any difference whether you could hit a fast ball four hundred-some feet or throw it ninety-some miles-an-hour, because if you couldn't hit a ball that curved or make a ball curve over the plate, then you were finished.

So a lot of the players who were stars as kids fell by

the wayside. But the point was that the boys who made it had all been hot-shots. "You gotta understand," Howie would say, "because in a way, all these guys were so good that it frustrates them when they get to a point where somebody is better than they are." Most old managers, holding forth like that, would have said "fucking better than they are." But Howie never said fuck, nor variations thereof, and he never said shit. It was not that he was a prude or he had promised his mother this when he went off to play ball. It was just something he had decided himself, after a couple of years in the minors, that if he was going to stay in this all-male jock subculture, he would never be totally beholden to all its habits and mores.

Probably no one ever even noticed that Howie Traveler didn't ever say fuck or shit. He never substituted anything asinine like "Oh, sugar" when he meant "Oh shit." And he said hell and goddammit and asshole and prick and sonuvabitch. It even amused some of his players when he screwed up, because then he would often say, "I got my tit caught in a wringer," which was an expression that had mostly gone the way of white buck shoes.

No, Howie was always and very definitely one of the boys. He reveled in the camaraderie that came with being on a team. He drank whiskey, and, when he was younger, he chased women and chewed tobacco. The latter he had given up for good some years ago. It was found to be as unhealthy as it was ugly and hence had mercifully gone out of style, so that dugouts were no longer little more than live-in cuspidors. The former he had given up most of the time after he got married, to have resumed it, on a select basis, after Suzie left him. Well, he had never been a whoremonger. Howie was, in fact, a man of moderation and some erudition. He read newspapers and the occasional book, and he had even made it a point of going to the opera and a concert when his team, visiting New York, played day games there; however, he didn't enjoy either the one or the other, so he never felt any compunction about not going back. He was simply rather pleased with himself that he had tried it at all. Also, he was pretty damn good at cross-word puzzles.

It irritated Howie, though, that outside of baseball nobody much wanted to talk to him about anything except baseball. Yes, yes, he understood that people talked to doctors about their ailments and to preachers about God and to pilots about airplane food, but, still, it pissed him off that everybody just naturally assumed that all he knew and cared about was baseball. As a matter of fact, it occurred to him once in a fit of guilt—rationalization?—that the reason he had cheated on Suzie every now and then wasn't on account of the sex, but because if he was with a woman instead of some men, she wasn't going to ask him about squeeze plays and when to go to the bullpen for middle relief.

Well, at least it wasn't *entirely* to do with the sex.

But, from another point of view, he never got enough of baseball. Howie loved it so. Otherwise he would have left it years ago, when he realized that, even if he had been a star in Little League and high school and college, he was one of those who wasn't quite good enough. Water found its level for Howie somewhere between Triple A and the majors. It was plain as day. He wasn't a spectacular outfielder, but he was a right-handed hitter who didn't have much power. Every scouting report said the same thing.

Howie Traveler had been a prospect. But he turned out to be an almost, a fill-in, a 'tweener. God, what he would have given just to have been a journeyman. In the vernacular, in fact, he would have given his left nut. He was certain that he could have ascended to that estate, too, if only he had been a left-handed batter. Left-handed athletes are like blondes. They get a second look, even if they don't deserve it.

The message never seemed clearer than that one time he went to Lincoln Center by himself, determined to try a concert. The first piece was a symphony by somebody named Prokofiev. Just Howie's luck—not a composer he's heard of, like Beethoven or Mozart or Brahms (the lullabies), but one he can't even pronounce. It was pretty nice music, though, easy listening, live Muzak. Then, though, a pianist takes the stage, and can you believe this: he plays only with his left hand. First Ravel, then Strauss. Who would believe this? Who would have known that there are actually major works written just for left-handed piano players? Goddamn southpaws always get the edge. Even with pianos.

As it was, Howie spent eight days in the major leagues. That was when he was twenty-seven years old, in the Detroit Tigers system, and the big team suffered a slew of injuries. He played in five games, starting two in left field. He came to bat eleven times and got one hit, a line single up the middle off of Dave McNally of the Orioles, who was a very good lefty. That was a point of pride with Howie; he didn't get his one major-league hit off a humpty-dumpty. McNally was so good, in fact, he even could have made it as a right-hander.

Unfortunately, though, figure it out: one-for-eleven: an .091 batting average. There in the record books, .091, forever and a day, for as long as men play baseball. Howie would say: "I hit in double figures. If only I woulda been in basketball with double figures, I'da been a star." It got a laugh, whenever he would use it, such as on the winter dog-and-pony shows Howie would make for the Indians down deep into Ohio, or when he had been a minor-league manager, trying to scare up ticket sales at Rotary Clubs and the like.

But you know what? Three years in a row he hit over .300 in Triple A, at Toledo and Syracuse. The organization didn't even bother to protect him, though. Right-handed outfielder, not enough power. "If we have a boy," Howie had told Suzie, with a good degree of seriousness, "I'm going to make him a left-hander. Even better. A pitcher. A left-handed relief pitcher is worth his weight in gold. There'll be a spot for him into his forties." He tried, too, to make Davey a southpaw, but it didn't take; the boy didn't have the slightest bit of interest in that alchemy.

Yet for all his complaints that nobody accepted him as anything but a baseball man, Howie knew for a fact that he was truly a full person only when he was around a diamond. And if, despite all the years, the decades that had gone by since he had failed as a player, he still was twinged with the pain of nearly—still, nothing satisfied him so much as to watch the players who did possess the talent he had almost had. Even more, perhaps, than the joy Howie had gotten out of playing the game, he loved watching it being played well. Secretly, he could not even help but be pleased, deep somewhere within his soul, when some magnificent opponent achieved something magnificent—even if it was against his own team. When it came to the game of baseball, Howie was a connoisseur as much as he was a competitor.

Perhaps his favorite part of every day was batting practice, when he would sit in the dugout, talking to the writers and others of the fraternity. Handling the media, public relations—that was as much a part of the manager's job nowadays as filling out the lineup card. Howie was good at it, too—the kibitzing, telling stories, lying a little, dropping a few benign inside pearls to make the writers think he trusted in their confidence. When the Indians went to the West Coast and the regular newspaper guys from the Cleveland and Akron papers would have a tough time making a deadline, Howie would call them into his office before the game and give them two quotes: one to be inserted if the team won, the other if the Tribe lost. Now whoever would've thought of that? The beat guys loved Howie for it.

There was an old Yankee pitcher named Waite Hoyt, who remembered the ancient days of all-day-game ball in this fashion: "In the daytime, you sat in the dugout and talked about women, and at night you went out with women and talked about baseball." It hadn't changed a great deal, except maybe now with all the night games, it was harder to fit the women in. On the other hand, they made themselves more available now, women did. Women had become more of a convenience than they had been when Howie had started off. That, Howie understood, was an offshoot of the women's movement, dovetailing neatly into the predominance of night games. In the full scheme of things, it was a fair trade-off.

So Howie would sit there before the game, chewing the fat, imagining that he was still chewing tobacco, laughing, entertaining, commanding his own dugout salon. Invariably, though, when one of the best players would step into the cage, Howie would divert most of his attention away from his visitors and watch the man swing away. Of course, he had seen Jay Alcazar play before he started managing him, but especially when he first got the Indian job and wasn't used to the man's achievements, game in and game out, Howie would pause at whatever he was doing and just gaze at Alcazar when he took his cuts—left-handed, of course. Howie would simply marvel at him.

One evening, early in the season, at the SkyDome in Toronto, as Alcazar laced practice pitch after practice pitch, all so graceful, all so effortlessly, all so absolutely perfect of motion, Howie jumped up in the dugout and dipped at his knees, swinging his right arm back behind him. "What's that? What's that called?" he asked of the assembled members of the diamond press.

"What's *what* called?"

"You know, like in the Olympics where they throw that Frisbee-type thing. The famous sculpture."

"The discus thrower," one of the more learned writers said.

"Right. I'm tellin' ya, if the sonuvabitch who made that statue, if he was around today, he wouldn't do the discus thrower. He would do Jay Alcazar swinging a baseball bat because that's the prettiest thing in the world."

"Prettier than a pair of tits, Howie?"

He smiled, but only a little. "Prettier than any pair I ever saw," he replied then, declaring that so stoutly that it came off as an absolute statement of fact.

He turned then to watch the last pitch thrown to Alcazar. He caught it waist-high and drove it on a line—but a rising line—way up into the right-field stands, where young boys with gloves scrambled over the hard seats to retrieve it. "Amazing," Howie said. "*Fucking* amazing."

Sometimes, in the face of such beauty, a man just could not be expected to hold to the promises he had made to himself.

TY

AFTER HOWIE GOT THE INDIANS JOB, he rented a condo in a high-rise downtown—the operative word here was *rented,* as in: not bought—and spent the next few weeks at the offices with Moncrief and the chief scouts and Frosty Westerfield, going over the roster. Being new to the Cleveland organization, it was important to analyze all the reports, even though, from his past experience as a coach with Seattle and even back when he was managing in the minors, Howie was familiar with just about everybody on the team (which, in fact, was one of the reasons he got the job; he laid that on thick in the interviews).

Westerfield generally agreed with Howie, but he was in no hurry to emphasize concurrence, otherwise what was the point of having him around? Westerfield was the team's bench coach, which was a relatively new position in the baseball hierarchy. Previously, managers tended to look to their pitching coaches or their third-base coaches for comradeship, but now the job of bench coach had been created to formally give the manager someone in the nature of middle management to sit next to him and spit with him, offer him advice and consent.

Westerfield had been with the Indians since, as he described it, "Christ was a corporal." He had been a back-up catcher, widely recognized for being canny. It irritated Howie some; had he been a catcher, he thought, he could have made it in the majors. Next to being left-handed in baseball, being a catcher was the best thing to overcome a lack of talent. The shortness of legs didn't matter so much either, squatting. Westerfield was not, by any lights, a bad guy, but it was the fact of him, rather than his personality, that Howie disliked. He wanted to hire his own bench coach, but Moncrief wouldn't permit that. Howie could bring in Rogers as a pitching coach, and he could name the rest of his staff, but if he was going to take the manager's job, he had to accept Westerfield as his right-hand man.

And he had to settle for a two-year contract. Howie would've killed for three. As he told Lindsay: "It takes three seasons to really turn a team into your own. Then it's yours." But that was not negotiable: two years and the team's option for a third. It was Moncrief's way of saying that the Cleveland manager Howie may be, but the front office still held him to a tether. One time years ago, after the front office of the Reds had failed to promote him, Suzie asked: "Why do they always call it a front office in baseball? Why isn't it just like the plain office like it is everywhere else?"

It was the one baseball question Suzie asked that Howie couldn't answer.

But, anyway, the Cleveland front office was adamant: Howie would only get a two-year contract, and Frosty Westerfield would be at his flank the whole time. You see, the Indians weren't quite sold on such an untested quantity. Howie did not have to be told he better rent the condo. He wasn't a big name. And, of course, he had to keep Alcazar happy.

So, right before Christmas, Howie set out to meet with his star personally, to make an effort to bond.

For appearance's sake, so as not to make it seem as if the mountain was going to Mohammed, Howie visited two other team stalwarts as well. Wyn'amo Willis was the slugging first-baseman. Jesus, Howie thought, why had black people started giving each other all these crazy made-up names? What the hell was the matter with Tom, Dick, or Harry? Hadn't they served the Republic well enough down through the years? Or even Sean or Shawn or Jason. And now, some of these black guys' names weren't just a bunch of letters strung together; no, they even had apostrophes. D'Rondo Williams. Mali'qi Tolliver. Not even the basketball Muslims went that far—just Jamaal and Ahmad and Rasheed. But soon as they get equality, they go out of their way to be different. Why would they do that? What the holy hell kind of name was Wyn'amo (except that because he became a slugger, he was re-christened as Wyn'amo the Dyn'amo. Still…)?

Ty Baggio was the number-one pitcher, the bellwether of the staff, one of the two or three best left-handed starters in the majors. He was smart, not at all goofy like southpaws are supposed to be. "He's a left-hander who thinks like a right-hander," Howie had said. "And that's the most dangerous kind." Baggio was almost forty years old, but he still studied batters, endlessly watching tapes. Never did anyone who got a hit off him see that same offending pitch again. And never, never did he make a mistake over the plate. "A man can make a good living on the outside corner," he liked to proclaim, as if the remark had originally appeared in *Poor Richard's Almanack*.

Actually, Baggio was indeed a man of wicked wit—although he generally managed to conceal that talent from the public, to whom he preferred to present a wise and sensible facade. Specifically, he did an on-target imitation of Stu Percival, the beloved Indians play-by-play announcer, who, like a lot of sports announcers, often spoke his sentences backwards, *i.e.,* "Plays a shallow center field, does Humberto Miranda." "Set for his southpaw slants, is Ollie Jorgenson."

Sitting in the dugout between starting assignments, Baggio would often critique the surroundings that way. "Over the Angels' dugout, shines one great duo of big tits." "Unable to call a pitch on the outside corner, is senile veteran arbiter Mike O'Leary."

At some point, Baggio had also taken to employing the terminology TV weathermen used as references for baseball. Thus were hot streaks "heat waves," a bad inning "a cold front blowing through," a weak relief appearance (particularly in relief of him) a "lake-effect storm," and, whenever the manager was angry, it was "the wind-chill factor." Baggio also christened a few players likewise. Keichi Ohura, a relief pitcher who seldom smiled, became "lingering showers," Wyn'amo Willis, the optimist, was "sunshine, punctuated by rainbows," and poor Humberto Miranda, who was not very bright, became "partly cloudy." (It stuck, but Miranda didn't know enough English to understand it.)

Baggio's arm never seemed to age. When he was a kid, in the minors, he babied himself. They even called him "The Judge" back then, because with the slightest pain, he'd rule he'd had enough and take himself out of a game. Baggio, though, could see the big picture, the long-range view. He wasn't going to use himself up throwing too many innings to win games in the bushes that didn't mean jack-shit. His first team, the Cardinals, dropped him out of their system. They called him a pussy then and said he didn't have any heart, but Baggio got the last laugh, because he was still throwing hard for 9.6 million a year when he had kids in high school.

Of course, none of this might have mattered if he also hadn't taken steroids for a number of years.

In any event, Baggio was properly advertised as the brightest, most sophisticated guy on the team, and, in a display of that sagacity had moved to Cleveland year-round. He came from Southern California, but he didn't bitch publicly about the cold weather or the fact that now he couldn't play golf in the winter. Instead, he made an effort to fit in, to be a local presence. Baggio did bank commercials, was accessible, and he and his absolutely gorgeous wife, Aimee, were chaircouple of a big, society charity ball. Cleveland was crazy about the Baggios. Some people thought he might even have a future in Ohio politics if he set his cap to that.

Naturally, when Howie called him up and asked if he could meet with him, Baggio immediately invited him to his house in Shaker Heights. The meal was like a catered affair, soup to nuts. Really. Soup, salad, quiche, a peach cobbler, with wine. And cashews were on the table.

"You like living in Cleveland?" Howie asked.

"It's important to be part of the community. This *amigo* isn't going to last forever." He held up his trusty left arm.

As long as Howie had been in baseball, he never really understood pitchers. They were different from hitters in that pitchers didn't seem to Howie to be whole people. They were just one thing, an arm, attached to the corpus. Pitchers were sort of like ordinary girls who got by because they had big boobs. Some pitchers, like Baggio, also used their heads, but even thinking was not requisite on the mound. Pitchers had catchers to advise them what pitches to throw. In fact, Howie would disparage pitchers who wouldn't pay attention to catchers and tried to think on their own; he called them "impulse pitchers." In a way, even, pitchers were inexplicable freaks. Normal-sized people like Sandy Koufax or Nolan Ryan or Pedro Martinez could throw bullets. Or, that is: the arms God gave them could. Anatomically, it made no sense.

Anyway, it didn't much matter what Howie thought of them—or what they thought of him—because managers really had very little to do with pitchers. They were merely necessary evils. Pitching coaches, who were ex-pitchers, handled the pitchers. It was tribal. Sure, when it was time to take a pitcher out, Howie himself had to go to the mound and "ask" for the ball, but that was only like ships crossing in the night. One thing Howie had learned early on: he, the manager, had to decide when the pitcher had to get the old heave-ho. Pitching coaches were great for coaching pitching, but they could not be trusted to decide when a pitcher should be yanked. That was because all of them had been pitchers themselves, and thus it was cauterized in their consciousness how awful it was to be yanked. A pitcher could be getting walloped, knocked all over the lot, but ask the pitching coach: take him out? And he would say: no, let 'im have one more hitter. Always one more. And that was the one that jacked it outta the park. No, Howie had to make the call.

Predictably, as Howie expected, at lunch, Ty Baggio didn't seem to have all that much interest in him, in his new manager. No, mostly he just wanted to know about Connie Rogers, the pitching coach Howie was bringing in from Colorado. As a consequence, it was late in the colloquy before Alcazar's name came up in any substantial way.

Baggio introduced it himself. "You know Jay?" he asked.

Howie shook his head, but said he was going down to Miami to see him. "How will I do with him?"

Baggio took another sip of his cappuccino from the beautiful Limoges China cup that the maid had brought him. "I got no idea, Howie. You never know about Jay. Oh, he wants to win. He's not just in it for himself. I've seen him play really hurt. But he's not a team guy, if you know what I mean."

"Not really," Howie said.

"I mean he doesn't really identify with the team. It'd never occur to Jay to get on another player, kick somebody's ass. He's no lead dog. He plays hard, but the way Jay figures it, he just has to do his own shit. And what the hell: when you come right down to it, his shit is better than anybody else's."

Howie said: "That's the God's truth."

"I remember the first time he came up. Rookie. Up at the end of the season. Tommy Wister is pitching for the Rangers, and you can see Tommy's looking in, thinking: Like who the fuck is this, Alca-what, another beaner. Jay steps in, all coiled the way he is, and then he gives that little hand motion of his."

Howie nodded. What Alcazar did, before every pitch, just as he got ready, he took his bottom hand, the right one, off the bat, and kind of reached out toward the mound, opening his hand wide, almost as if he was grabbing a fistful of air. Then, just as quickly, he would bring the hand back on the bat—set, ready to hit. He'd always done that. It was just his way of getting set, but the first time anyone saw it, it looked almost as if he was gesturing like some punk boxer—*come on, bring it on,* he seemed to be saying.

"I'm sitting in the dugout, and I see Wister see this, and he's a mean cocksucker under any circumstances."

"Altogether," Howie said.

"And, I remember, out loud, I said: 'Pissed off big-time is the volatile Tommy Wister.' And sure enough, he busts one way inside, right on the wrists—like, hey Chico, keep your hands to yourself. Jay doesn't faze. He just gets back in, gets all coiled, throws that goddamn hand out again, and this time Wister tries to throw it past him, and Jay sends that sonuvabitch right back up the middle. Almost took Wister's head off. And I just said: 'Storm warnings are posted! Don't drive unless you absolutely have to.'"

"So I just let him be Jay Alcazar?"

Baggio laughed. "Well, you got that right. Jay Alcazar. Don't ever—ever—call him Chief. Phillips did that one time—you know, in the excitement of the moment. Jay won some game in the tenth inning or something, and Phillips called him Chief, and honest to God, I think he was dead meat from that moment on."

"Okay, I don't call him Chief."

"Or *Jefe*. Not Chief in any language." Baggio chuckled, then massaged his chin. "This between you and me?" he asked after a moment. Howie nodded. "Sometimes I don't think Jay really knows who he is. Yeah, sure, he's Hispanic, but he didn't grow up in any barrio. He came over from Cuba early, I guess. But you hardly ever hear him speaking Spanish much with the other Latinos. I mean, I know Jay can speak it. I heard him one time with this kid just in from Venezuela who couldn't speak a word of American. Jay is sitting there, helping him learn the ropes. Very nice. But most of the time, around, he just says *bueno* and *vamos* and *uno mas* and shit like that that even I know."

"That doesn't altogether surprise me," Howie said. "Those Spanish guys aren't just peas in a pod. I've had teams where the Puerto Ricans and the Dominicans didn't want anything to do with one another."

"Yeah, I seen that."

"The Puerto Ricans are more educated. And they're Americans, you know. The Dominicans always think we don't like 'em. I always find I gotta baby 'em more."

"Yeah, but you see, Jay doesn't fit into any of that. Matter of fact, he doesn't hang much with any of 'em. It's not just that he's Cuban. Hell, the other Cubans who just got over here—all they wanna do is eat. Jay's different from them all. Ollie's his only real good friend, and what the fuck is he? A Swede or some shit from Minnesota. The girls Jay takes out—all beautiful, but like his own United Nations." He sipped his coffee again. "You know what he is—his religion?"

Howie just shrugged.

"The sonuvabitch is an Episcopalian."

"He's not Catholic?"

"No, that's what I'm tellin' you, Howie. I don't know if he goes to church or anything, but he's a Cuban raised an Episco-fucking-palian. He's a white guy with brown skin, and he's a Spanish guy who's really Anglo. You see, Jay really doesn't know who the fuck he is."

WYN'AMO

ONE THING HOWIE KNEW (besides baseball) was domestic geography. It was occupational. He had, after all, played and coached and managed all over the United States of America and even one season up in Canada. It amazed him how ignorant modern players were about geography. Of course, it also amazed him how ignorant many modern baseball players were about the game of baseball, and they played baseball for a living, so perhaps he shouldn't have found their lack of geographical erudition so astonishing.

Still, for example, a number of them could simply never understand why the hotel and the airport and the stadium in Kansas City were not in Kansas. Of course, there were some who didn't know that there was a state of Kansas, so that idiosyncrasy was of no conflict for them. Others were generally unaware of how the various states aligned; they just got on team planes and flew to hotels. Oregon might as well lie cheek-by-jowl with Arkansas. For two seasons, Howie managed at Norwich, Connecticut in the Yankee chain. That winter, working with rookies in Florida, when he told the team's number-one draft choice, a slugger from Arizona, that he lived in Connecticut, the boy asked him: "What state is that in?"

It is well known, of course, that many baseball players come from the Caribbean, but it's also true that an inordinate number of American players come from the Sunbelt. Simply, this is because, growing up, they can play more games in their warmer climate. They can swing at more pitches, field more grounders than the kids up north who sting the hell out of their hands, hitting balls in the chilly spring weather. Howie grew up in Nebraska. Sometimes, when he was making excuses for himself, he thought if maybe he'd only been raised in Texas or Mississippi, he'd have been better. Or he thought: he should have been a pitcher. The weather isn't so important for pitchers. Sixty-feet-six inches: you can throw in the school gym even if it's a blizzard outside. But, of course, God didn't opt to give Howie an arm. Goddamn pitchers. They're just arms.

And then, ever since Suzie left him, Howie really didn't live anywhere. His driver's license was still from the State of Washington, because he'd been the bench coach there, with the Mariners, for two seasons, before he got the Cleveland job. But he'd put most of his stuff in storage. What was he to Seattle or Seattle to him? Howie Traveler was, basically, a displaced person. Baseball had cost him any sense of home. After his career was over, after no one would hire him anymore, he'd have to go somewhere to live year-round, but for the life of him, he couldn't imagine where that might be. He was scared to move to Florida, because then he knew he'd just play golf and drink, like so many old ballplayers did. Well, like so many old people of any stripe did. Maybe he'd go back to college and finally get his degree. He'd left after his sophomore year to sign with the Reds.

No, who was he kidding? Go back to college? Pushing sixty. No.

Most of all, what Howie hoped was that Lindsay would marry and have some kids, so he could live near her—Washington, DC or wherever—and be the grandfather he never was up to as a father, because back then, of course, he was always someplace else with the National Pastime.

If—when—Lindsay did marry, he hoped it would not be Atlanta where she settled down. Howie hated the Atlanta airport so much that he had transferred his antipathy from the terminal to the whole city. It was easy to do that when you traveled a lot. He hated Pittsburgh just because he'd always had to fly USAir to get in there. So, he started hating Atlanta all over again, for no good reason, as he rode the little airport subway in from Concourse B with the recorded announcement telling him over and over about what concourse was next and hold on to the rail and here we go, on and on.

He tried to remember what it was like when he grew up in a world that was sometimes actually silent.

He rented a car. Wyn'amo lived a good ways out of town, as everybody seemed to in Atlanta. His house, which appeared larger than most Wal-Marts, was in a gated community, ironic—inasmuch, Howie knew, since most gated communities were built with the express purpose of keeping black people at bay, on the lee side of the gate. And here was one family of them in the largest house in the whole shebang. Wyn'amo soon enough revealed to Howie how many square feet his house encompassed, too, but the figure was meaningless to Howie. He'd just never gotten into house square footage, which seemed so important to everybody else. He knew acres pretty well and he could relate to the number of rooms, but the square footage of a house didn't mean anything more to him than earned run averages did to sensible people who didn't know baseball. Maybe if he ever had a house again himself, Howie would learn to appreciate the values of residential square footage.

Of course, he gasped with proper admiration when Wyn'amo exclaimed the specific number. "Wow!" Howie gushed, "this is magnificent, Amo."

The house had been done by a decorator. Except perhaps for the waterfall in the living room, it was too perfect and didn't have wall-to-wall carpeting. Ballplayers thought wall-to-wall carpeting was the surest sign of opulence and taste; they learned otherwise only through decorators. The Willis residence also bore some resemblance to a seminary, inasmuch as both Wyn'amo and his wife, Jatesha, who had been a professional gospel vocalist, were devout evangelical Christians. Renderings and statuary of the Lord Jesus were prominent.

Howie was prepared for this. He was well aware that Wyn'amo led Sunday services before Indians games. Baggio called him "El Nino." Yet unlike some of the more officious worshippers in the majors, he did not have a reputation as a scold. Amo Willis was accepted by all groups—white, black, Asian, and Latino—as a spiritual man who did not force his religion upon others. Indeed, he was quite a respected leader—very much like the sort of fellow that Baggio said Jay never could be. Nevertheless, as soon as he and Howie sat down in the den, underneath a painting of Jesus in a boat with some of his disciples on the Sea of Galilee, Wyn'amo gently inquired: "If you don't mind my asking: are you a Christian, Howie?"

"Amo, no, I don't mind, Amo. The answer is yes, I am. I'm a Methodist." Howie could tell, though, that Willis was disappointed. He knew he would be. Just being a Methodist or a Catholic or a Lutheran didn't really mean you were a real Christian to ballplayers like Willis. You couldn't just start off as a Christian, in a denomination, to be a real one. So, Howie sagely lowered his head as a sign of unworthiness. "Only I'm afraid I'm not as devout as you."

This admission turned things on its head, the way Howie knew it would. "I only try to be devout," Willis said, humbly. "Too often I fall short."

"Don't we all?" Howie said, anxious to move onto a more worldly realm of discussion.

But Wyn'amo wasn't quite finished. "I know you suffered a terrible tragedy. Did it bring you closer to God, or make you angry at Him?"

"I think, I, I think it just, uh, kinda altogether confused me about God."

"You're still working through it," Wyn'amo declared in response, with the same assured tone of a professional counselor. Christian ballplayers were always so cocksure, which made Howie envious of them. If you were that damn certain of Jesus, you could also be pretty damn confident looking at an oh-two pitch. But as big as Wyn'amo was—and nobody had ever accused him of needing steroids to bulk himself up—he had a soft, modulating voice. Howie could understand how the other players would listen to him, even when they got tired of all the Christian crap.

Jatesha entered then, carrying a silver tray with Diet Cokes. With her were two adorable young children, a boy and a girl, who had, apparently, just come from school or a play group. They were polite and respectful and distributed coasters and napkins. The little girl even curtseyed; Howie hadn't encountered that courtliness in many years. Sometimes modern black people could be like old-time white people. Howie didn't quite get the children's names, though, as they were unfamiliar monikers, originals, as far as he knew, and maybe even had apostrophes. The two then made their departures as exquisitely as they had entered, and Howie felt genuinely obliged to offer compliments on their appearance and good behavior.

Jatesha said: "Well, that's most kind of you, Mr. Traveler—"

"Howie, please."

"Not Howard?"

"No, I've always just been a Howie. There's not many of us Howies left, but that's what I am."

"All right, Howie, Wyn'amo and I are most appreciative of you making the effort to visit with us before the season. We've never had any other manager do that."

"Well, I know I'm altogether something of an unknown, so I thought I should...I mean, I can't see everybody. I'm just seeing you"—he gestured to Wyn'amo— "and Ty in Cleveland the other day, and Jay tomorrow. The big three, I guess."

Wyn'amo nodded, pleased to still be registered in that company; the last couple seasons he'd fallen off some.

Howie went on: "I know my reputation precedes me. I'm supposed to be a"—he started to say "hard-ass," but thought better of it in this precinct, "...to be old-school." Wyn'amo nodded. "Well, all right, fair enough, I am something of a disciplinarian. You know, I never had anywhere near as much ability as players like you, Amo, and the only way I could even stay in the game was to work my tail off. I guess maybe I expect that of everybody. But I'm altogether not some kind of soldier, the way some of the papers have written it." He smiled. "I'm not any football coach."

"Praise the Lord," Wyn'amo shouted, with a big smile.

That gave Howie enough confidence to turn to Mrs. Willis. "You see, Jatesha, no matter what they say, there's only two kinds of managers...or coaches...in any sport. One is too hard on the players. If the team loses, people say the players revolted against all his rules because he didn't treat them like grown men."

Wyn'amo chuckled, rocking himself back and forth on the sofa.

"I'm right, aren't I, Amo?"

"You got it."

"And the other manager is too easy. They call him a 'players' manager.' Only as soon as his team starts to lose, the papers say that the team is starting to *get away from him*."

Wyn'amo laughed knowingly, out loud.

"That's it, Jatesha," Howie went on. "They tab you as one or the other. I'm the hard case. Look, I've known Teddy for years." Teddy Phillips had been the previous manager of the Indians. "You won't find a better baseball man than Teddy. But things went bad, so, naturally, they said he lost the team, so the front office brought me in, because I'm more in control. And if I don't succeed, they'll say the players revolted and Moncrief will hire somebody like Nino Diaz, who's a players' manager. Right?"

"Right as rain," Wyn'amo said.

"So why do you have to be one or the other?" Jatesha asked.

"You don't. They just put you in one of those two pockets. That's all. Look, I can't tell you how many managers I've had. I been in this game, just the pros, almost forty years. All these different managers—and managing myself in the minors and winter ball. I only know one thing for sure. You have to be yourself. That doesn't guarantee you'll be any good, because maybe yourself just isn't good enough to be what a good manager is. But it's your only chance. You try and be anyone else, they'll eat you alive."

The maid, an Hispanic, announced dinner, and they all rose. Casually, as they drifted into the dining room, Howie said: "How will Alcazar take to me?"

"Oh, Jay'll be fair with you."

"I heard he gets along."

"Oh yeah, everybody pretty much likes Jay. Including Jay. 'Course if I were that good, I'd like me a whole lot more, too. Let me tell you, Howie, I been in the majors going on twelve years. I been an All-Star.

Jay Alcazar does things ever' now and then that I can't even imagine."

They came to the dining room and Howie moved to the place at the table that Jatesha pointed to, on the one side of the table across from the two children. "I mean," Howie went on, "will he hold it against me that I'm his manager, but I was never any good as a player?"

Wyn'amo laughed. "You don't understand. Jay be so much better than anybody else, it's no different in his mind whether you're Howie Traveler or Henry Aaron."

Howie laughed, and although Jatesha smiled, she shook a friendly finger at her husband. "Now, Wyn'amo, that's a bad example for the children. You said: 'Jay be…'—and you know how."

Wyn'amo ducked his large head, properly chastised, but chuckling a little then, he added: "I know. But honey, the fact is: 'Jay be.' That's just it: 'Jay be.'"

Even Jatesha had to smile. "I don't want to put you on the spot," she said then to Howie, "but if you'd like to say grace, our family would be honored."

For just a moment Howie paused. The number of times he had said grace in his life approximated the number of times he had come to bat in the major leagues, which, as we know, the record book shows clearly to be exactly eleven. But Suzie had said grace at dinner, when he was there, or when it was just her and the children. He knew that because pretty soon she got the children to say it in her stead when he would come back. And it was always the same one— short and sweet. Howie punched it up from the back of his mind, and, after a moment, he said: "Why, no, I'd be altogether delighted." He bowed his head. "Lord make us thankful for these and all thy many blessings," he intoned, not missing a beat. "Amen," he added with authority.

"Amen," all the Willises chimed in.

After dinner, Howie and Wyn'amo talked about the team for another hour or so, but he knew, when he left, that his being able to say grace was the one thing that had made the most favorable impression on his big first baseman. Everything else aside, people are always taken by people who share something with them. It was, he thought, one of the more important secrets of managing a team of baseball players. You talk Jesus with some guys and pussy with others. You just want to make sure the Jesus guys don't hear you talking too much pussy with the pussy guys.

JAY

ALCAZAR THOUGHT THE WHOLE IDEA was a royal pain in the ass. He didn't know Howie Traveler, and he didn't want to be his buddy. He was going to spend the next season, maybe more, with him every day, so what earthly good would it do to spend a day in the off-season getting to know one another? He never gave managers any trouble. He wasn't a clubhouse lawyer. *He came to play. He played hurt.* Wasn't that enough?

However, when he bitched about it to his agent, Montague—because that's what agents were good at, listening to you bitch—Montague dared to tell him to just go ahead and meet with Howie. "For Chrissake, have lunch with him, Jay. Everybody's convinced you wanted Diaz for the job, so you blow off old Howie, somebody'll make a big deal outta it."

Then Montague told him about some group in Fort Lauderdale that wanted to give him a brotherhood award. "I told you, Freddie, no awards. Tell 'em to get

Muhammed Ali. He'll go anywhere for an award."
The trouble was, you see, even if they paid you to
come and accept the award, you had to go to a recep-
tion and dinner and be on display for hours. "I told
you, Freddie: only awards they'll mail me."

Montague laughed, as Montague did whenever
Alcazar assayed anything even remotely humorous.

But, anyway, Jay called Howie and agreed to meet
him at the Mandarin, the hotel where he was going to
stay in downtown Miami. No, no, Howie said, I'll
come to you, to your house. Jay wouldn't have it. He
would do the driving. Of course, he didn't say it, but
that way, he was in control. He could make his excuses
and leave whenever he'd had enough. He'd give
Howie the time for one sandwich. How much more
time did they need? What were they going to do, talk
about signs for the double steal?

So, after a late breakfast that day, Alcazar walked
Ashley out to her car. Her's was a sunshine yellow
Saab convertible. Ashley was in marketing in Fort
Lauderdale. Or anyway, she had been when Jay had
first met her. The subject hadn't come up on this occasion. Ashley was cagey enough to understand Jay
didn't ever want to talk baseball, or about himself, so
she didn't talk about herself either. Actually, they
didn't talk a whole lot about anything. "I'll give you a
call," he said, when they got to the car.

Ashley reached up and pinched his cheek. "Sweetie,
you said that last time."

"And I did."

"Well, yeah. Three months later. Hey, that passed
my sell-by date."

Alcazar had to laugh. He pinched her cheek back. Ashley smiled. She was an older woman, at least thirty-two or –three. Jay liked the aging ones, the grown-ups. There was less posturing with them, and he knew that nobody that much older than he was would be ridiculous enough to imagine anything serious could come of this.

"Hey, I had a baseball season to play."

She clicked her door lock, and he opened the door for her. "Well, there's that other thing you do as well as you play baseball, so I guess it's worth the wait."

"Dancing?" he said, coyly.

"That too, sweetie. You're fun to be with, Jay. You're not like what you're supposed to be."

"Yeah. What am I supposed to be?"

"You're supposed to be like an asshole ballplayer."

"And I'm not?"

Ashley shook her head and reached up and kissed him quickly, before sliding down into the driver's seat. "No, you're too much like a gentleman. I feel like a lady with you, Jay. Even when I'm in bed with you, I feel like a lady. A naughty lady, but still a lady."

"That's nice. My mother always told me, don't be common, Jay."

"Well, your mother raised a good boy." She turned the ignition on and flipped the convertible hooks.

He reached into his pocket and extracted some hundred-dollar bills and gave them to her. "I was gonna getja something."

"But you forgot again."

"Well, I'm no good at picking stuff out, anyway. You know what you want."

"So do you, Jay, so do you," she said, laughing, as she started to send the convertible top down. "Okay. Anytime you wanna dance again."

"Stay by the phone," he said, winking at her.

Ashley wasn't the kind of woman who would have taken this kind of treatment from anybody else, but now, she just laughed and tossed her head. She had a fabulous head of hair. Then she roared away around the circular drive.

Alcazar watched her go. He liked her better than most. Next time he wouldn't wait so long. But only then did he really remember that he had to meet Howie, and so he walked back to his house, which instantly put him in a bad mood. Goddamn managers would drive you crazy. Wasn't Howie supposed to be a tough guy, toe-the-line, and all that bullshit? Isn't that why they fired Phillips, because he was too easy on everybody? Now, what's this old guy doing, trying to be palsy-walsy so he'll be my buddy when he starts to bust balls?

I know one thing, Alcazar thought, as he got into his Porsche, if he starts in on how the team has got to be like a family, I'm outta Cleveland next year when I'm a free agent. Nobody says an insurance office is supposed to be like a family, or the local Burger King. Just do your job. Show up ready to play. It's always the fringe players, the guys who make all the noise with their mouths instead of their bats, who play up the family crap. And those are the guys who end up managing. They get the last word. They get to push the buttons of the next generation of the guys who can do things they never could themselves.

Alcazar especially hated it when other players called the manager "Skip." That was for Skipper, which was some ancient half-assed synonym for manager. He literally rolled his eyes every time he heard that. Oh well, it was better than the other sports where all the coaches were called "Coach," like it was a title, an honorific, like they were doctors. At least in baseball nobody ever actually called a manager "Manager."

But Alcazar would never voice his opinion on a subject like that. You wanna call him Skip, go ahead. You wanna call it family, call it family. He might not like it, but he just went on his way, mum. That was the good thing about baseball. It was a team sport, sure, and sometimes you had to give yourself up and hit it to the right side, move the runner up, that type thing, but by and large, four or five times a game it was you and only you standing in against the pitcher. Once one of his managers in the minors was carrying on because somebody screwed up, and, quite seriously (as if this was original with him), he said: "Remember, there's no *I* in 'team.'"

Yeah, you asshole, Alcazar muttered under his breath, *but it's no team in the batter's box when heat comes in at you over the top ninety-some miles an hour. Don't tell me it's not me—I—then.*

Alcazar was fifteen minutes late meeting his manager. But then, he was always late. It wasn't, the way some people imagined, that he was late on purpose, to show he was a big star. It was more the other way round, that since he was a big star, no one ever called him to account, so Alcazar just naturally didn't pay rigorous attention to appointments or promises to get back to you. Hey, he knew Ashley would be there whenever he got back around to her. He knew people would wait on him; he knew they wouldn't even mention it. You might lose your privacy being a big star, but in consolation, one of the perks you got is that time belongs to you. It's a wonderful thing to own, time. That and your own airplane—well, anyway, a time-share jet, like Alcazar had—are about the ultimate luxuries today.

Alcazar passed through the tables at the hotel restaurant, outdoors, overlooking the water. The diners cleared a path for him with their eyes. Almost subconsciously, waiters leaned away from him, giving him the floor. Howie watched in admiration. He'd always heard the phrase "cut a swath." He never really understood it till right now when Jay Alcazar strode through the tables, cutting a swath. Exactly; whatever it meant, he was seeing it. Howie stood up. After all, he wasn't sure that Alcazar actually knew what he looked like. Alcazar did seem to recognize him, though, and smiled a benediction on him and shook his hand. However, right away, he said he didn't want to eat anything, maybe just have something to drink.

Here was the thing Jay had considered: food would take awhile to be prepared, and then it would have to be consumed. Don't get trapped.

So Alcazar ordered an iced tea. Howie really was hungry and wanted a big meal, but he settled for a cobb salad, as if that had been what he had in mind all along.

From the first, Howie understood that Alcazar only suffered his presence. He had no interest when Howie told him about his plans for the team. He didn't ask any questions. Howie even quickly recognized the way Alcazar treated him; it was like those times when he himself had to do an interview with some reporter, and he just robotically mouthed the standard answers—all the while thinking about whether he needed to pick up his cleaning on the way home or when he was getting a haircut. Now he knew the feeling of being on the other side. It wasn't that Alcazar was antagonistic or rude. If he had been, it would have encouraged Howie more, because at least he would have felt then that Alcazar was engaged, that perhaps then he could win him over.

But, sitting there, sipping his own iced tea, stabbing at the salad, he felt so impossibly removed from him. He grew certain that there would never be anything between them, that he would manage the Indians and Alcazar would play for the Indians, but they would never really intersect *on* the Indians.

"What's he like?" Lindsay asked him over the phone later that day.

"I don't know what he's like because I don't know anyone like him," Howie replied. "Maybe you don't have to be *like* anyone if you're that good."

"And you know you're that good yourself," she said.

Well, Howie interjected, one thing: he didn't think Alcazar was as handsome as everybody always said. When describing him, in fact, invariably they wrote: "movie-star handsome."

"Aw, come on, Daddy, he's one good-looking dude."

"Hey," Howie cried, in mock seriousness. "You stay away from him."

"Don't worry," Lindsay said. "I don't want to sleep with him. I just wanna get out of the government and be his agent. Do they have any women agents?"

"No. It's altogether a man's world, agents."

"Well, I'm a woman, and trust me, Daddy: Jay Alcazar is a hunk."

"All right, *nice* looking," Howie said. "If you're a star, they always say you're smarter and better-looking than you really are. If some star just lets on he knows what country Paris is in, he's played up like some international expert."

As lunch had continued at the Mandarin, a man had come over to the table and nicely, almost obsequiously, asked for an autograph. Politely, Alcazar replied: "I'm sorry, but I'm meeting with this gentleman now. When I leave, I'll be happy to sign."

The man backed away, embarrassed, but understanding. Howie said: "You handled that very nicely, Jay."

Alcazar shrugged. It was something stars learned. It was like they had to tip more, too. That was another surcharge on fame, a celebrity tax. "The cocksuckers never leave you alone, wherever you are," he declared.

"Yeah," Howie said. And, taking advantage of this one register of emotion, he said: "I'm thinking of maybe switching you and Wyn'amo, batting him ahead of you. Whatdya think?"

This was as sensitive as Howie was going to get. Always before, Alcazar had batted third, Willis fourth. In the diamond argot, this way Willis "protected" Alcazar. That is, the pitcher throwing to Alcazar couldn't get too cute with what he threw, couldn't risk walking him because then he'd have to face another good hitter, but with a man on base to boot. The pitcher was therefore more obliged to throw strikes to Alcazar, which, of course, gave him a better chance to see a good pitch to hit.

Alcazar rubbed his chin. He didn't answer directly. Instead: "We gonna get Casagrande?" Casagrande was a free agent, a good hitter.

"We're trying like a sonuvabitch," Howie said. "But his agent wants five years."

"He can hit better than Amo can now."

"Wouldn't surprise me."

"Get his ass and bat *him* behind me," Alcazar said. But he grinned when he said that.

Howie nodded. That, however, evidently concluded that particular line of discussion, and it was equally clear to him that Alcazar had no topic of his own to introduce. So Howie said: "I saw Amo yesterday. In Atlanta."

"Go to church with him?"

"No, just had a nice dinner at his house."

"Well," Alcazar said, "you'll find out: he's a good man. He's not the player he was, but he's a good man. I'm usually suspicious of the Jesus-this/Jesus-that guys, but Amo doesn't fake that crap."

"That's what I've heard," Howie said. He was pleased that Alcazar appeared to like Willis. It was nice that the young star approved of the old star he had superseded. That sort of thing mattered on a team. But Alcazar didn't offer anymore.

Idly then, in some desperation, like they were no more than two strangers with nametags on their lapels at a convention, Howie said: "So, you got any interesting plans this off-season?"

"Nothing much." But then Alcazar perked up, and he actually volunteered something. "One year, though, I'm gonna go back to Cuba," he said.

"Yeah? How old were you?"

"When I came over?" Howie nodded. "I was a baby. I don't remember any of it."

"Jay, maybe you'll go this year, Jay."

"No, not this year. Maybe next. It's uh—" But he stopped and shrugged. "Nah, I don't wanna go there."

"I thought you said you did."

"No, I mean, I wanna go to Cuba, but I don't wanna talk about it now."

"Oh, okay," Howie said, and since Alcazar didn't have anything else he wanted to say, this was usually the time that men would start to talk about their golf games, but Howie didn't want to go there, so he just said thanks for coming to visit with him, and he'd see him in Spring Training. They just shook hands perfunctorily then, and Howie watched Alcazar walk away.

The man who had asked for his autograph earlier pounced again now, and as soon as he did, so did some of the other more reticent diners and a red-headed waitress and a Latino bus boy, who looked up at Alcazar absolutely beatifically. Alcazar signed, and he flashed that brilliant smile of his as he did, his logo-like deep blue eyes glowing out of his khaki skin, but he never stopped walking, never even broke stride. That was the secret. Keep signing, but keep moving. Howie thought of fish. Isn't that what they said of fish—or is it just dolphins? or sharks?—that if they stopped moving, they would sink? Alcazar kept moving, signing his name, but never stopping.

Always after that, in his own mind, Howie thought that Jay Alcazar was like a shark, a big, beautiful fish that no one could ever sink a hook into. More even than that, though, as Howie got the chance to observe Jay more, he noticed how, like a fish, when he moved on, things would close up behind him, leaving no trace that he had gone before. And that, Howie knew, is how Jay liked it.

NEXT MORNING

IRONICALLY, THE FIRST THING HOWIE thought after Moncrief had called him first thing that morning in Baltimore was that maybe it would've just been better if he had fired him. This business with Alcazar couldn't go anywhere good. He wanted to talk to someone, but there was no one but Lindsay, and she was the last person in the world he could talk to about a thing like this. Jesus, he thought, he was fifty-seven years old and the only person he thought he could turn to for advice was his daughter, who wasn't much more than a kid. A smart kid, but at the end of the day a kid all the same. If he only had his own bench coach and not Frosty Westerfield. But no, this wasn't baseball. This was nothing to discuss with a bench coach, even if he'd had one who was his buddy.

There was one special woman. Her name was Margo Barnett, and there were times when Howie thought that he could love her, and she could love him, too. He thought that if he wasn't in baseball, going from pillar to post, he and Margo might have settled down, living a life in a house, having a couple cocktails in the den at night, eating in, watching TV, going out to see movies in theaters and all that. Maybe even going to church and *getting active* in local affairs. But she was in the Bay Area, where he had met her, when he had come into town when he was coaching for Seattle, and she still had two kids in high school, so they never really spent much time together. Actually, Howie only imagined that he could love Margo or that she could love him. When it came right down to it, he didn't really know, because he really didn't know her. She was very pretty and very nice, but that was about all he really and truly knew about Margo.

The trouble was, once he and Margo had put in a decent amount of preliminary time together, pretending to get to know one another, then, whenever he could see her, they spent entirely too much time together in bed. It wasn't that their affair was only about sex, but it was just easier that way. A large part of Howie's problem was that he never did learn how to talk to women. He was great at talking to men, because that's what he'd done all his life, but because he'd spent that lifetime without much being around women, in the normal give-and-take of daily life, when it came to the opposite sex, Howie remained, essentially, a teenager. A part of you never grows up when you stay in the game. This doesn't affect you so much when you're still playing, because nobody around you has grown up either. It's away from the game, where playing a child's game makes you different.

Anyway, Howie couldn't call Margo about what had happened, because the issue was sex, and whereas he could do sex with Margo, he certainly wasn't able to talk about somebody else's sex with her. Besides— and maybe more important—he felt ashamed of himself because he had seen the woman throw open the door, and then Alcazar had grabbed her and kicked the door shut, and he had just stood there, useless.

So, he met Dougie Flint in the lobby, and they got a cab to police headquarters, which was just a few blocks away, on Fayette Street. Flint was the team's PR man. Neither one of them said much on the way over, but Howie volunteered: "If anybody asks about me, you can just say I'm still the manager. Between you and me and the lamppost, Moncrief's not gonna make any changes right now. Because of this."

"Okay," Flint said. "'Course, once they hear about this shit, Howie, nobody's gonna give a rat's ass about you anyway."

"Yeah, be grateful for small favors. Is the word out yet?"

Flint shook his head, but when they went into police headquarters a reporter and a photographer from the *Baltimore Sun* were already there. Obviously, they had been tipped by one of the cops. After this would come the deluge. The shooter took Howie's picture, but he told the reporter that he really didn't know anything and had nothing to say and brushed past him.

A cop took them into a little waiting room, which was sea-green in color, bare and cheerless, where Alcazar was alone, with the lawyer. Alcazar was over in the corner, staring out the window. Howie thought he looked more befuddled that anything else—and since he had never seen the man befuddled before, it was probably an instinctively correct assessment. Alcazar acknowledged Howie and Flint, but barely.

"I'm sorry, Jay," Howie said. He wanted to commiserate with him, be on his side. Maybe, after all, nothing had happened. Maybe the woman had just opened the door because they were horsing around. Hey, it's possible. He tried to remember the expression on her face. No, who was he kidding: it wasn't giggly or full of fun. She might even have gone "oomph" when he grabbed her. Did she go "oomph?" He wasn't sure.

But he was sure she didn't shout. She saw Howie looking at her, and she could have called out for help, but she didn't. If he was attacking her, wouldn't she have screamed? Of course, it all happened so fast. And then the door was closed. No, Howie couldn't get away from it. Why would you—why would a woman—open the door if she wasn't trying to get away? With her blouse even pulled out some and her hair a little mussed up. The one thing he did know about women was that only wild horses could get them to go out with even one strand of hair out of place.

So, he didn't go over to Alcazar. He didn't pat him on the shoulder or anything like that. Part of him even regretted that he had said, "I'm sorry."

Alcazar only turned away, stared back out the window. Given Alcazar's reaction to him, though, Howie understood for sure that he had not seen him in the hall when the door had burst open. Howie really wasn't certain in his own mind, though, whether he should be relieved about that or not. Anyway, he sure as hell wasn't going to bring it up.

The lawyer, a large, shambling man with an intent manner that contrasted mightily to his appearance, introduced himself as Warren Mundy and spoke without embellishment: "All right, Mr. Alcazar hasn't volunteered a damn thing, and he's denied it all, so that's where we stand. You're Mr. Flint?" Dougie nodded. "Okay, we're gonna take Jay to another hotel—Cross Keys, way the hell uptown. He'll be registered under an associate's name in my office. No one knows where he is—got it?" Howie and Flint nodded. Mundy pointed a finger at Flint. "You—you, no one else—pick up his stuff and get it up there."

Howie said: "The cops are in the room now. When I came down the hall from my room, it had that yellow tape up and all."

"All right," Mundy said. "If they won't let us move Jay's stuff right now, you call me, and I'll get on it. Then we're gonna issue this statement. You type it up, word for word." He handed Flint a sheet of foolscap. "That's it. Nobody says anything. Whatever they ask you: you tell 'em, read the goddamn statement. That's it. Savvy?"

Howie ventured: "What about the woman?"

"The cunt," Alcazar muttered.

Mundy said: "I don't know her name, and because of the rape shield—"

"Tricia," Alcazar said loudly, even rising to his feet for emphasis. "Fuckin' Tricia. She has a drink with me, she's dee-lighted to go to my room, she has another drink there, we're makin' out, we go to bed—

now she pulls this. It's a set-up, Howie."

Mundy bit his lip. He let Alcazar finish venting before he raised his hands perpendicular before his chest and spoke very softly, chopping with his hands. "Jay, that's it. We leave this room, not another word." He turned back to Howie. "The police took her to the hospital to be examined. That's all we know now. All right? Let's go. Vamoose. I know there's a back way out here so nobody sees us."

Howie said: "Wait a minute. Jay, you wanna play tonight, Jay?"

Alcazar banged his left fist hard into his other palm. "You goddamn right."

"Okay, I tell you what. You take my office and change in there. That's yours as long as you want it. I'll dress at your locker."

Alcazar cocked his head toward Howie. Howie had noticed through the years that some of the best hitters almost seem to have a natural cant to their head, turning it just so, watching the world the way they watch a pitch come in. That was the way Alcazar looked at Howie now. And a softness came to his expression. "You mean that, Skip?"

How strange it was that he called Howie "Skip." Much as he hated that word, it just sort of came out now, the first time ever it had passed his lips. It was, apparently, some unconscious way of him being sweet.

"Of course I do."

"That would really be very nice of you."

It occurred to Howie as they left the room and ducked down the back stairs that that was the warmest exchange he had ever had with Jay Alcazar. It was such a simple thing, letting him have his office, but all the things people gave Alcazar or that he took as a matter of course were obvious things, so that he wasn't surprised by typical, quotidian generosity anymore. It wasn't that he was greedy, but he had just come to feel entitled to other people's generosity as he was to so much else that was provided for him. But Alcazar— well, nobody—had ever heard of a manager giving up his office before. Never. Howie could tell: it touched him.

NOTICING

THE FIRST TIME ALCAZAR HAD IT out with Howie had
come in Minnesota, three weeks after the season
opened that first year he was the manager. Howie had
been sitting in his baseball underwear in his office
with Connie Rogers, his pitching coach, when Alcazar
came in. "I'd like to talk to Howie," he announced,
and, dutifully, promptly, Rogers got up and left.

Alcazar closed the door and glared at Howie.
"Don't you ever do that again," he said. There was
real menace in his voice.

"Do what?"

"What you did."

"Jay, what did I do, Jay?"

"You know."

"No, I altogether don't." Howie was upset, but he
also couldn't help but be reminded that this all
sounded like some stupid conversation he'd had
with his son, when Davey was a teenager. "Tell me
what I did."

"It was in the fuckin' paper."

"What paper?"

"One of them."

"Well, which one?"

"How do I know? I don't read the goddamn papers. They're always wrong. It was just what someone told me."

"Okay, what'd they tell you?"

"That you called me Chief."

"Well, it might be in the paper. They all call you Chief in the papers, but I didn't call you Chief, because I never call you Chief. The first thing I came here, people said: 'Whatever you do, don't call Jay Chief.'"

"Well, it was in the paper."

"Okay, but you just said yourself the papers are always wrong."

Alcazar thought that over for a moment. Howie got up out of his seat and walked over and put his uniform shirt on, number thirty-nine. Managers get dopey numbers like that. Alcazar had number three. He put his one long leg up on the manager's desk and crossed his arms over his knee. "What my guy back in Cleveland read was that you said: 'The Chief is takin' too many pitches.'"

"Didn't I just say I never call you 'Chief?' Didn't I say that?" Howie spat that out with spirit, and some disgust.

"Well, what about the bullshit of me takin' too many pitches?"

"Yeah, I said that."

Alcazar loved hearing that. That admission put ammunition back in his gun. "Yeah, I know the way it works," he said, with a big triumphant grin. "You wait till we get on the road, then you knock me, 'cause you think I won't know what's written in the papers back home."

"That's ridiculous," Howie said, buttoning up his shirt, fastening it between the second *e* and the *l*. "I know about telephones, Jay. I know somebody can call you from Cleveland—which is probably exactly what happened. And, for Chrissake, it's hardly a knock to say you're taking too many pitches."

"It's only three weeks into the season, I'm hittin' three-forty, and already you want more outta me."

It was occasions like this when Howie wished he still chewed tobacco. Chewing gave a man time to think before he said something. Nobody would interrupt a man in mid-chew. It was a nasty habit, but one that was useful for cogitating—or, anyway, for appearing to cogitate. And then, in particular, this was the sort of moment when a good wallop of a spit into a can could speak volumes. Instead, by way of punctuation, the best Howie could do was kick off his shower clogs. "Let me tell you something," he said, and when Alcazar didn't say anything back, he, pointedly, asked him: "Can I tell you something?" He grabbed his pants and stepped into them. Alcazar finally grunted assent.

"I wasn't good enough, playing," Howie said. "You know that. And it drives you crazy when you're not good enough, but you're only almost good. There's guys already in the Hall of Fame—Morgan, Bench—I was almost as good as them in the minors."

Alcazar looked a little bored, but he'd sort of

trapped himself, putting his leg up, so he stayed that way and let the manager go on.

"You try to figure it out, you see. And after awhile, you realize, it doesn't make any difference. Even if you could figure out what it is you're doing wrong, you still can't fix it. You can't make a sow's ear into a silk purse."

"What the fuck is that?"

"Uh, like you can't make lead into gold. It was like Popeye said. You remember Popeye?"

"The spinach guy," Alcazar said, remotely. At least Howie had thrown so many obscure allusions at him that he didn't seem to be so worked up anymore.

"Yeah, well what Popeye said was"—and Howie screwed up his mouth like he had a pipe in it—"'I yam what I yam.' I was what I was. But I started looking altogether more closely at the other guys—especially the ones that were pretty good—and I could see stuff." He began to fiddle with the bottoms of his pants. Howie wore his pants just so, bloused in the middle of the calf, which had been the right way for generations. Now, most players wore their pants all the way down around their shoes. Howie thought that looked terrible. They looked like pajamas. Then, the ones who didn't wear their pants all the way down went the other way; they tended to blouse theirs too high, showing too much stocking. No, if he'd been a goddamn football coach, he would've told them: hey, everyone on this team wears their pants bloused one way—and the right way.

Howie stood up now, pants bloused perfectly midcalf, the way God intended baseball players to look.

He pointed to his legs. "Name me any player, any player in the whole damn league, I can tell you how he wears his pants, high or low, whatever."

Alcazar looked at him like he was crazy. "Pants?" he said. "So?"

"So nothing," Howie said. "Right. It doesn't mean jack. No, but it's what I do. I notice. I notice baseball. And some of the stuff I notice matters. It doesn't take much, but that's why I'm here, that's why I'm a manager in the big leagues, because I notice better than just about anybody. And I don't care whether there isn't a player on this team, or the other team, or anybody in the press box or anybody in the stands who doesn't think you've been taking too many pitches, I notice you have, and if I don't say anything, I'm not worth anything. Then I'm like a guy with two strikes just standin' there with the bat on my shoulder and my dick hanging out. That's my value, noticing."

Alcazar took his leg off the desk and stood up straight. "Yeah, but maybe you notice wrong."

"Oh yeah, sure," Howie said. "But I got a better batting average, noticing, than I ever did, batting."

Even Alcazar had to smile a little. "So why don't you tell me instead of running your mouth off to the newspapers?"

Howie hitched up his belt, getting the top of his pants as right as the bottom. "I did," he said.

"Come on."

"You don't remember because you were so pissed off. But it was three nights ago, in Kansas City, and you took a couple of good pitches and got behind in the count, and then Mullins jammed you and you popped up and took us outta the inning." Alcazar frowned, remembering. "You can eat Mullins for lunch, too. So you came into the dugout, and as you walked by me I told you you were taking too many pitches altogether, but you kept on going right by me. You had the red ass, and I didn't go after you, because then you'd've said I was showing you up. I'm not stupid. Gimme a break. I'm not lookin' for trouble with you." For emphasis, he added: "For Chrissake."

Alcazar nodded, sort of. He started to leave, then turned back. "I still wanna know why the fuck we didn't get Casagrande."

Howie had to smile. Tacitly, Alcazar was admitting that he *was* taking too many pitches. If indirectly, he was bitching that if he had an outstanding hitter, like Casagrande, batting behind him, he wouldn't have to be so choosey with the pitches they threw him. But Howie didn't call him out on it. He just said: "You have to ask Harold. All I know is Casagrande's agent asked for too much, and he wanted a fifth year, too. Maybe we'd give in on the one, not the both."

"We shoulda paid," Alcazar said. Howie could have asked him then whether he'd have sacrificed some of his own seventeen-million-plus-a-year to make it possible to afford Casagrande, but, of course, he let that thought go unsaid. He knew he should've had the guts to say it; he would've said it to anybody else, but he wouldn't say it to Jay Alcazar.

Howie did say: "All right, can I ask you a question?"

"What's that?"

"Why do you hate the name Chief so?"

"Nah, never mind that."

"Okay, just curious. I'd show you my dick, too."

Alcazar smiled, and said "Fuck you"—but in a jovial way. Then he left. Howie thought: okay, that went well at the end. He came in all pissed off, but he listened. Some. Maybe there's a chance for us. He picked up his cap and put it on, squaring the bill just so. He looked at himself in the mirror. It was important, he thought, to look as good as he could. If you just looked like a manager, that was half the damn battle. Well, maybe a quarter of the battle, maybe an eighth. Anyway, the point was if you *didn't* look like a manager, you were dogmeat. From the word go.

That night, Alcazar fell behind in the count every time. He let a couple of real lollipops go by. Howie didn't say anything. The next game, back home in Cleveland, Alcazar went after the first ball once, and lined it for a double. The night after that, Howie didn't think there was a single good pitch Alcazar didn't swing at. But Howie didn't say anything then, either. Neither did Alcazar. He would never admit that some busher had actually helped his ass at bat.

But when he came around to score on Nakamura's single up the middle, he passed by Howie and said: "All right, Willie D'Angelo."

Howie shook his head. "Willie D'Angelo what?" D'Angelo was an obscure back-up catcher with the Angels.

"How's the sonuvabitch wear his pants?"

"Bloused way up, by his knees," Howie answered right away. "Am I right?"

"How the fuck do I know?" Alcazar answered. "I was just checking to see if you knew for real." But he smiled broadly when he said that.

CHIEF

WHETHER JAY ALCAZAR WAS as gorgeous as Lindsay Traveler thought, or merely another "nice-looking guy," by her father's more grudging assessment, the world in general was taken by his appearance and by his persona. He appeared in the usual array of commercials, all the predictable stuff, plus touting his own line of casual designer clothes for JC Penney. That worked so well that Montague also got JC Penney to put his name on guy furniture—lean-back lounge chairs, den and patio sets, barbecue accessories, that sort of thing. Sometimes columnists, trying too hard, called him the Martha Stewart of the diamond, or crap like that, but it never stuck. Anyway, it never bothered Jay. He made a couple appearances in TV crime shows that used Miami or Cleveland as locales, but the rules were firm: Jay Alcazar wasn't pretending to be an actor. He played Jay Alcazar—pleasant walk-throughs, with precisely limited dialogue, in which he basically appeared as a distinguished part of the scenery.

He seldom made the columns, and, in fact, because he dressed stylishly and always shaved before games, so he didn't look grungy like most all other ballplayers, and because he seldom let himself be seen with the babes he took out, there were occasional rumors that he must be gay. It merely amused Jay; he was hard to rattle. In truth, he got laid with such facility that he'd never so much as have to leave his house in order to enjoy the finest distaff companionship. He could order in.

Almost no one was aware of it, but Jay Alcazar was also a magnificent dancer—samba, tango, all the Latin stuff, but traditional standard old-fashioned dances, as well. He was most divine at waltzing. Who knew? But he had Strauss CDs at home—*The Blue Danube, Tales from the Vienna Woods,* the works. When Alcazar found a woman who could dance nearly as well as he could, dancing became foreplay. He would guide them all around, the living room, the patio, out by the pool.

His mother, Cynthia, had made him go to dancing class as a small boy. If people had known, that would probably have only increased the fag talk. But, the fact was, if Jay Alcazar really wasn't sure who he was, neither was anybody else—and he liked it that way. When you're so well known, it's satisfying that they get you at least a little bit wrong. Also, in the whole scheme of things, it was a small matter, perhaps, but technically, in fact: no, Alcazar was not exactly the person he was supposed to be.

Howie saw the distinguished older man with Alcazar on three occasions before he understood that he was his father. Victor Alcazar was a trim fellow, with a gray pencil mustache. He seemed more Latin than his son; Jay was just too generic in his style and attire. Victor dressed better, too; he always wore a sports jacket, often even a tie, and usually a white straw fedora. He was, as well, seventy-two years old, so there had been that good reason of age why Howie hadn't automatically assumed that he was Jay's father. Besides, Mr. Alcazar was much lighter of skin than Jay, who was himself invariably described as "coffee-colored"— that caramel shade that must be the prettiest of all, because it is why white people, in the hopes of attaining it, spend so many hours lying in the sun, smeared in grease, sweating and burning and risking death by cancer.

Then, at Yankee Stadium, in July that first year Howie managed the Indians, Jay introduced him to his father. Howie took this token of familiarity as another good omen. The team was playing well, winning. The Tribe—the Indians were affectionately called the Tribe whenever they were going good— were only a couple games behind Detroit in their division, and ahead of all the other runners-ups in the league, in position to make the playoffs as the wild card even if they couldn't finish ahead of the Tigers. Most everybody on the team seemed happy enough, and most everybody was having a good year. Wyn'amo, in particular, was hitting better than he had in three seasons. Batting ahead of Alcazar obviously agreed with him. Everybody praised Howie for that wise lineup alignment and, even more, for supplying the kind of discipline that the team needed.

Then, one night, after the Tribe won their fourth in

a row at home, beating Toronto, Alcazar came into Howie's office after all the newspaper guys had left. This was the first time he'd approached the manager alone since that colloquy in Minnesota. "You got a minute?" he asked in a noticeably more solicitous tone than when he had previously stormed in.

Howie said sure and asked him if he wanted a beer. Alcazar said no thank you, he just had a favor to ask. "Try me."

"When we go to New York next week, I'd like permission to stay at another hotel." Howie took a sip of his beer. Quickly, Jay added: "Teddy used to let me do that. In New York. There's just so much crap that goes on there."

"I don't know."

"I know you don't wanna do what Teddy did, but—"

That pissed off Howie a little bit, and he let him know. "Hey, come on, Jay, there's altogether a lotta stuff Teddy did I didn't change."

"Yeah. I know. But, it's just everybody lookin' for me. You know New York."

"You think the team will get its nose outta joint?"

"Because I stay at a different hotel?" Howie nodded. "You been the manager five, six months. You oughtta know. It's your team."

"Well, it's your team too."

"All right, you ask me, I don't think they'd mind. They didn't last year. They know what kinda bullshit I gotta put up with in New York."

Howie took that under advisement, sipping from his beer can, then staring at it awhile as if it was a crystal ball. He was positive this was some kind of a bad idea. He could just see it in the newspaper: one rule for twenty-four guys, another for The Chief. You see, fans: already, Traveler is losing control. Still, Howie knew that it was a reasonable request; he *did* know what Jay had to put up with everywhere—and in New York the crap rose to another power. Almost instinctively he said: "All right, let's try it this one trip."

"Thanks, Howie. I appreciate that."

"Just don't say anything to anybody. I'll tell Zeke." He was the traveling secretary. "Then just do it." Alcazar waved to him. Almost as an afterthought, Howie said: "Just tell *me* so I know: whereya gonna stay?"

"The Waldorf."

"Oh yeah, why?"

"My father's gonna be there."

All Howie said was "Oh." He barely even said that, since he was occupied taking another swig of his beer.

But Alcazar turned back and snapped: "Whatza-matter, you don't think spics can stay at the Waldorf?"

Howie's mind raced. Had he said something he didn't think he'd said? No. Had he looked funny? Snotty? No. He knew damn well he was in the clear. He slapped his beer can on his desk. There wasn't much left in it, but it sprayed out some. Anyway, it was the noise that surprised Alcazar. Howie stared at him then, stone cold. "That was a goddamn rotten thing to say to me."

Right away, Alcazar ducked his head. Howie rolled on: "Is there anything I ever said, anything I ever did that—?"

Alcazar looked up. "No. Never."

Still, Howie kept breathing hard. It was very possible that, even after all these months, this was the first time he had ever looked at Jay Alcazar strictly as just another person and not only as the great Jay Alcazar, The Chief, star of the national pastime. He said: "Where I grew up, we had an expression: common as cat shit. That was common as cat shit."

Alcazar shuffled his feet, head back down. "You're right. I got no excuse, Howie. I'm sorry." And it was, indeed, very apparent that he was sorry.

"But why?" Howie asked.

Alcazar looked back up, crossed his arms, shook his head. "Because, well I guess I always expect people to think something like that—"

"But you know, goddammit, Jay, I'm not *people*."

"I know. It just came out. I didn't mean it." Sullenly, Howie nodded and turned away. Alcazar started to leave, but then he turned back. "Chief," he said.

"What about Chief?"

"You wanted to know."

"You wanna tell me?"

"Sometimes—sometimes I guess it's just good to tell somebody the bad stuff."

Howie was delighted to be the one taken into his inner sanctum. "Yeah, I know."

Jay said: "I'll take that beer."

Howie nodded to the little refrigerator across the way. "Get me another one too."

Alcazar grabbed two and chucked one to his manager. That was a very friendly gesture. Men don't toss a beer to another guy except in the right spirit. He sat down, then, across from his manager, and flicked the tab open. "When I was a kid," he began, "we moved to a new neighborhood, and I went out for the Little League. I'm ten years old. The manager of the team—you know, the coach." Howie nodded. "His kid was the best player on the team."

"The coach is always the father who thinks his kid is the best," Howie interjected.

Alcazar shook his head in agreement, sipping his beer. "From the first day, it's obvious I'm much better than this kid. Much better. And I'm only just ten, and he's twelve. We win the league, even some regionals or some shit like that, but I could tell that coach couldn't stand me. See, he's got it figured his boy must be a natural. He's gonna get a college scholarship, and then he's gonna make millions of dollars as a superstar and keep his old man on Easy Street forever. And here I come along, this little brown-ass shrimp, and already I can hit better, throw better, the works—and so now he's gotta know his kid can't be all that good. Right away, he hated my guts. And all the more that I'm a spic."

Howie just drank his beer; he let Alcazar talk.

"Listen, Howie, this is a nice area we're livin' in back then. Anglo. My old man was a businessman."

"I seen your father."

"Right, then you know. It's not like I'm coming in from some fuckin' barrio. I mean, my house—our house—is every bit as nice as anybody else's on the team. Better. I talk English. I don't even have an accent. My father's not some gardener. But to him, to this fuckin' guy, this coach, I'm just another beaner. You ever hear about the Mariel boat lift?"

"Sure, I remember."

"Well, that was a few years before. So now it's like every Cuban is a thief or he's a scumbag fag with AIDS. So, it's not another week, this coach sees my full name, and he looks at my initials—J.F.—and he thinks he knows a little Spanish, and somehow he connects J and F: *jefe.*"

"Chief," Howie said.

"*Ah, habla espanol?*"

"*Muy poco.* Very *muy poco.* Remember, I managed in Puerto Rico two winters."

"Yeah? Well, the funny thing is, this asshole doesn't even know how to pronounce it. He says 'jeffie,' like it's spelled in English."

"Hay-fay," Howie said, pronouncing it correctly.

"Yeah. But mostly he just says the English—Chief. And the sonuvabitch stuck. Actually, I don't really mind the name."

"Call me anything but late for dinner," Howie said.

Alcazar chuckled. It was obvious he'd never heard that old gag before. That made Howie feel older. "Naw, it's just that every time I hear Chief or *El Jefe* or any of that crap, I think of that asshole who gave me the name."

"You tell many people this?"

"No, not many. That'd just make it worse. I'd have every cocksucker in Yankee Stadium screaming 'Chief, Chief, Chief ' whenever I came to bat."

"Yeah," said Howie, chuckling. "You got that." He drew his thumb and forefinger across his mouth, zipping it up. "Don't worry, your secret's safe with me."

Alcazar stood up. "When I was at Florida State," he said, "there was this Jewish guy on the team. Not a bad guy. Couldn't play worth a damn, but he was a southpaw, and he had a pretty fair college yakker, so they used him in relief and he could get a lefty out every now and then. One day we were in this coffee shop together, and somebody at the next table is bitching about Jews. And this Jewish guy can see me tightening up. I mean, I'm hurting for him. I'm about to go tell the sonuvabitch to shut up. And my friend is signaling me across the table: just let it go, let it go, Jay. Now his name is Platt or Pratt or something, not –stein or –berg or any of that. And he's red-headed. So no one in a million years ever thinks he's Jewish, and afterwards he tells me how it's happened before. He'll be somewhere and right in his face somebody will say something anti-Semitic. He says to me: 'It's worse this way, isn't it, Jay? At least you get to hear what people are really thinking.' Only I look at it the other way, that all these people are thinking bad stuff about us, but they don't say anything because this is right in their face." He touched his cheek. "So I don't really know. I only imagine. I imagine the worse."

Howie said: "I don't know which is worse, hearing it or not."

"What are you, Howie?'

"Whatdya mean, what—oh, hell, I'm just an old Anglo-Saxon, Christian white guy. I'm the majority, Jay. You're looking at the majority on the hoof."

"You're lucky."

"No, I'd rather be a minority who could hit left-handed with power."

Alcazar laughed and slapped him sweetly on the shoulder. "You know, maybe the newspapers are right about you, Howie."

"I didn't think you read the papers."

Jay snickered. "You know, guys read it to me."

"The sports page *Cliff Notes*."

"Yeah."

"And what do they say?"

"They say you're doing a pretty good job of managing this team."

Alcazar winked. Howie thought: on top of everything else, he has a helluva wink. As he walked away, Howie called after him: "Only as long as we win."

Alcazar didn't look back, just raised his hand and waggled it in salute of that sentiment.

Then Howie couldn't help but say, out loud, but softly: "And only as long as you're happy, Chief."

Alcazar waggled his hand again, only this time he left up the middle finger. But it was a fond gesture among friends, like a slap on the ass, and Howie felt good that they could carry on like this, just a couple of guys, buddy-buddy, for a moment or two in the middle of the long season.

MARGO

MARGO HAD COME TO NEW YORK the day before
Howie and the Indians came to town. It was the perfect arrangement for Howie and her to have some time
together. Thursday was an off-day and Saturday was a
day game. Howie got tickets for a musical on Thursday
and an off-Broadway play on Saturday. The light stuff
first. Better for setting the tone, romantically, you
understand.

Years before, Margo had been a flight attendant for
United. She dreamed of traveling to faraway, glamorous places like New York, but the older flight attendants had priority on all the choice trips, so poor Margo
hardly ever got out of the SFO/LAX/PDX/DEN/PHX
rut. So, soon enough, she got out of flying and took out
her real estate license.

It was funny, going out with a baseball manager.
Honest to God, sometimes she thought she'd still be
married to Ed if it wasn't for sports. If she'd ever
gotten Ed to take her to New York, the one place he'd

have wanted to go to would be Yankee Stadium. Or Madison Square Garden. They'd have had a drink (at least) at the ESPN Zone in Times Square. It was all well and good for cartoonists to draw the same dopey panels about benumbed husbands watching too much sports on television, but after awhile, if you were living it, it really wasn't a laughing matter. Still, until Ed took up golf, it was tolerable.

Howie played golf too, of course. Everybody in baseball played golf. Everybody he knew played golf. And he liked to watch golf and other sports on television, but it was only a perfectly reasonable curiosity that he evidenced. The busman's-holiday business applied here. Howie's level of interest in sports was, Margo thought, equivalent to how she would buy *People* magazine if she saw it at the supermarket, and then she would read carefully all about the shattered marriages of movie stars and what they were wearing, but if she missed the latest reports, she really didn't miss those celebrities. That same way, Howie could forget about sports other than baseball if they didn't intrude on him. He was unusually healthy in that regard.

So she had a wonderful time in New York with Howie. She'd been shopping before he came in, but he let her make up a list of things for them to do during the days when he didn't have to go up to the Stadium. Of course, he wouldn't go back to Lincoln Center, where they might just have another goddamn tribute to left-handed pianists. But they did go to the Museum of Modern Art and then just ambled around down in Greenwich Village, and as corny as it was, they took a

Circle Line Cruise. They held hands walking through Central Park and rented a rowboat on the lake there. A few people recognized Howie, and if they were Yankee fans they razzed him—but all in good nature. Margo got a big kick out of that. Howie was the first famous person she had ever known personally, except for flying, when she served one or two movie stars and then, another time, a nasty little Olympic figure skater when she was working the Colorado Springs turnaround.

Howie thought she was beautiful and told her so. He didn't mind her short legs nearly as much as he hated his own, and if Margo had gone a wee bit plump, there was a sweetness to her face, and as befit his age and circumstances that counted more for him than over-the-counter beauty. Not that Margo wasn't pretty, you understand. In fact, it had been a long time since he had woken up with a woman and just enjoyed a few moments looking at her, a fine woman, sleeping there.

Friday night, when Howie had a game, Margo went to the ballet. She'd never been to a proper ballet before, except when her mother had taken her to the Nutcracker, one Christmas long ago. When Howie came back to the hotel it was after midnight, but as always after a night game, he was too keyed up just to go to bed, whether or not anyone else was in bed with him. And tonight it had been an especially good game—and not just because Cleveland won.

"There's games like this all my life," Howie told her. "Sure, this one's the big leagues, this was Yankee Stadium, but games like this, wherever, I just feel so lucky. I don't mean because I'm there, in the game, managing the game. I mean, I'd be happy enough paying just to see the game. It's just so...well, it's lovely."

She could tell he felt a little foolish using a girly word like that, but she was touched by it. She liked his passion. She wasn't sure she'd ever heard another man talk with such affection about a thing he did, a thing he loved. Howie talking about baseball was considerably different from other men talking about golf or wine or even how much they liked her big tits when they got to them. "Tell me about it," she said.

"What?"

"Tell me why you love baseball so."

"Oh come on, Margo, you don't wanna hear about that."

"Yes, I do. I like hearing anybody being enthusiastic. Tell me: why is it so special?" She was sitting on the sofa, with her legs curled up under her, and that made her look younger. "Go on," she said, holding her hands out, "tell me."

Howie was slouched in an easy chair there. He thought for a moment, sat up straighter. "Oh, I don't know. I guess some guy who coaches basketball thinks it's just as good as baseball. Or football, whatever. It's just a game, for Chrissake. Who's to say one's any better than the other?"

"But you do say that. You feel that."

"Yeah, I do. I loved it all my life. The first time I ever played. It still breaks my heart that I couldn't play it as good as I loved it." He shook his head and said that again. "It altogether broke my heart."

"But now you're a manager."

"Yeah, in some ways that's even better. I'm still around baseball, age fifty-seven. And I get to run the game. It's deep, Margo. It's very deep. That's why it's such a good game, because half the stuff is about what's *not* happening." He jumped up. "If this guy, does this—"

"Does what?"

"Doesn't matter. He does this, then you gotta maybe expect this. Or this. That kinda thing. You gotta always think ahead. You've got to consider the possibilities. Like tonight. Dinky Furlong is pitching for me, and he's getting them out, but Connie and me, we know he hasn't really got his best stuff. They're gonna get to him, for sure, but when do I start warming somebody up? Too early, maybe I altogether waste a guy I might need tomorrow. And Furlong is very insecure. He's like some pitchers: he sees a guy warming up, he takes it personally. But if I wait, maybe then it's too late, and the Yankees are into a big inning."

Margo understood most of what he explained, for Howie was making an effort to keep it simple. "And?" she asked.

"Well, he gave me five innings. Just digging it out. All guts. I mean, his curve is his best pitch, and it's useless tonight. He's wasting with his best pitch and still handling the Yankees pretty good at home. See, that's what I mean by pretty. In many respects, that's prettier than some kid with ninety-mile-an-hour heat just blowing them away when he's on. That's what I mean by what you can't see makes it even better."

He was pacing now, animated.

"Then what happened?"

"Well, Connie and I figure, let's see if we can steal one more inning with Dinky, but we asked too much. He gives up a two-run homer to Velasquez, then he walks Crawford, so I bring in this Japanese guy we just got, Ohura, and the first pitch, a screamer, into the hole. Ycaza—I mean you can't believe it. He snares that thing, backhanded." Howie snared an imaginary ball, over by the coffee table. "Whirls, fires to second—one out." He whirled, pretended to throw toward Margo on the sofa, and then became the second baseman himself, just in time to catch his own make-believe toss, then pivot and throw to first, over by the bedroom door. "Tricarico grabs it, makes the perfect pivot—double play! We're outta the inning!"

He slapped his hands together. It was just like when he was a kid back in his bedroom in Nebraska, listening to the Cardinals games on the radio, pretending to make plays like that, pantomiming the action that Harry Caray, the announcer, described.

Margo cried out: "Yea, Indians."

He came over to her and leaned down and kissed her. She thought maybe he was going to forget baseball then and concentrate on her, but, although she didn't realize it, he was still that little boy back in Nebraska. So, instead, Howie just plopped down on the sofa next to her and shook his head. "You know what I don't get?"

"No, what?"

"The foreigners. They all go crazy about soccer. They call it the 'beautiful game.' Did you know that?" Margo shook her head. "And they're just using their feet. I mean, sure, it's amazing what some of those

guys can do with their feet, but still, hey, it's just feet."
He pointed to his own, to make sure there was no confusion. "Lemme tell you, there's kids in Little League
can turn a double-play prettier than any soccer player
can kick a ball. And something like Ycaza did tonight
on that play, in the hole, I mean, anybody could see
how beautiful that is. I just altogether love it so."

"Altogether," she said.

"Yeah, somebody else told me once I say that too
much. I don't know why. I just do."

"It's a perfectly good word," Margo let him know.

"Thanks. I try to stop, but I can't."

Margo didn't say anything else. She just looked at
him, even with a certain amount of jealousy that anybody could love something so much as Howie loved
baseball. She never had. As for Howie, he just nodded
his head.

Then, his reverie finished, he picked up the game
where he left off. "The whole night, we're behind all
the way. Two-nothing. Two-one, four-one, four-three,
five-three, five-four coming into the ninth. And they
bring in Wes Lauterbach. Their stopper. Their closer.
And he's throwing his very best. Ping-ping, with the
fastball. A splitter that falls off the table."

"I didn't think they could use spit anymore."

"No, no. *Split*ter, not spitter. It means a split-seam
fastball. I could show you if I had a ball. Splitter."
Margo nodded. She was just as glad he didn't have a
baseball. Hearing about it was quite sufficient. "But
Lauterbach has got everything tonight. He even gets
Ycaza out on a change. Two outs. Wyn'amo is up.
Wyn'amo Willis. Big black guy. The Dyn'amo."

Howie stood back up then and took his stance in the middle of the room. Margo said: "I've heard the name." Howie pretended to knock his imaginary bat on the coffee table, which he had as home plate. He'd do that as a boy, too, say when Stan Musial or Ken Boyer were up on the radio. Then he hitched up his pants and resumed his conversation.

"Nicest guy you'd ever want to meet, Wyn'amo. Having a good season after a couple not-so-good seasons. I couldn't be happier for him." Howie dropped the imaginary bat for a second. "'Course, I couldn't be happier for *anybody* having a good season for me." He grinned and took up his stance again. "Lauterbach blows the first two past him. I figure we're altogether finished." She smiled, but he was so involved in the story, he didn't even realize he'd said *altogether* again. "Two out, two strikes, no one on, we're down a run. Then Amo starts fighting him off." He stopped. "You know what I mean?"

"Not really."

"Staying alive. Just hangin' in there. He's fouling off pitches that are unhittable. And he gets one ball, and another. Fights off another splitter. Now he gets a full count, and Lauterbach sure as hell doesn't want to put Amo on and have to face Alcazar. So he's gotta be just a little bit more careful. You see? See how it changes?"

Margo smiled; she didn't really get that, but she was enjoying the show Howie was putting on.

"Still, Lauterbach comes in with a wicked fastball. It was probably a ball, just inside, but Amo can't take a chance. He can't let the game end with his bat on his shoulder. How he gets any of it I'll never know, but he just wrists it, and the ball goes humpback, just over the second baseman's glove." He pointed toward the television set, where, apparently, second base was located. Then suddenly, he paused, reflecting. "When I started they always called those Texas Leaguers."

"Called what?"

"Balls hit like that. Little pop-fly hits. I don't know why they called them Texas Leaguers. Like if you hit a high-hopper right in front of the plate, they called that a Baltimore Chop. They don't say that so much anymore, either."

"Oh," said Margo.

Howie concluded his brief detour on baseball lingo and got animated again. He stood back up at the plate and waited for the pitch from Lauterbach. "Then Alcazar comes up and boom, just like that—first pitch." He swung from the heels. "I don't even know how he gets around on it, but a shot—four hundred, four-twenty maybe, to right center. Perfectly incredible. Conacher gets them one-two-three. We win. And you know afterwards, Alcazar is just as altogether calm as can be. Another day in the office."

"He's that good?"

"The more I see him, the more I think he can be the best there ever was. I promise you, he can do everything. If I started him tomorrow, I swear, he'd pitch a no-hitter."

"He's a pitcher, too?"

"No, no, no. I just mean *if*. I mean he can do anything with a baseball, so he probably could throw a no-hitter. What the hell. He's what we call a five-tool player."

"A what-all?"

"A five-*tool* player. That means"—he ticked these off on the fingers of his left hand— "he can hit, hit with power, run, field, and throw. See? Five tools." Margo said she got it. Howie shook his head in wonder. "His father was at the game. Distinguished older guy. He's Cuban, but he's not like what you think when you think Cuban."

"You mean like Castro with the scruffy beard?"

"Exactly. He's not like that at all. He's like a..." Howie searched for the right word: "A...uh, diplomat," he finally decided. "Yeah, a diplomat. He's in town from Miami on business or something. He didn't seem fazed by any of it either. I guess that's where Jay gets it from."

"Gets what?"

"Gets not being fazed."

"Oh."

"Yeah, so Mr. Alcazar just asked me if maybe I wouldn't like to join him and Jay for cocktails at the Waldorf after the game tomorrow. I never had that, Margo. All the time I managed, I never had anybody's father ask me for *cocktails*."

"Are you going?"

"Hey, I've got a date." He came back over and sat down next to her on the sofa. He took her hands then. "I'm sorry, I didn't mean to go on like that."

"I asked you to."

"Yeah, but then I get altogether worked up."

"That's wonderful, to care so much about what you do."

Howie looked away. "I don't know. Maybe you can love a *thing* too much. I mean, it *is* just a game." He paused for a second more, and then he told her: "I loved baseball more than her."

"More than your wife?"

"Yeah. That's not right."

"Howie, come on. You can't compare loving a thing and loving a person. That's not fair to yourself."

"I don't know. If you love, you give. I gave more to baseball than I did to Sooz. I didn't mean to, but I did."

Margo looked at him, with care and consolation. They both knew it was a perfect place for him to say that he loved her, but Howie wasn't up to that. Not yet, anyway. He'd finally gotten his chance to be a manager in the big leagues, and he wasn't going to let anything intrude on that. That proved it, didn't it? He still loved baseball more than any mere woman.

Nonetheless, he did start to hug and kiss Margo then, and she responded, enthusiastically and in kind.

VICTOR

THERE WAS A STUDIED FORMALITY to Victor Alcazar that was seldom evident any longer in American men. But then, he had been born well above the salt in a society where class was distinct and observed. One could call it a snobbishness that he affected, and perhaps that had, in a way, been passed along to his son, for Jay acted as if he were nobility in baseball as sure as his father had been raised as a Cuban aristocrat.

Ironically, Victor had been Fidel Alcazar then, growing up in a family that owned a great sugar plantation, as well as holdings in various other enterprises. He was the oldest of three. There was another brother, Emilio, and a sister, Olga, between the two boys. Fidel and Emilio were not close; too many years separated them, and they were of different temperaments. Fidel was more like his father, Omar. Even as a young child, he was interested in the family businesses, and he was sent off to Princeton to round off his education, and, as well, to learn better the ways of the American giant that always pressed on Cuba's brow. Had there still been primogeniture, Fidel would have been the perfect eldest son to inherit all the great Alcazar lands. On the other hand, Emilio, the kid brother, was more of a romantic, which, unfortunately, made him susceptible to the siren call of Fidel Castro, in those years late in the 1950s when he plotted to overthrow Batista.

Emilio never joined Castro in the mountains as a *guerrillero*, but he was one of the young university students who spoke of revolution and a new Cuba, whispering subversively in the bars, rallying foolishly in the Havana streets. Naturally, this created much disaffection and concern in the family. The Alcazars had never been an especially political family, going back all the generations since they had come over from Spain. They were simply a commercial family, with profit as their ideology. The father and eldest son would argue with young Emilio, worried, first, that he was putting himself in danger, and next, trying to make him understand that he better look out for *numero uno:* however inept and corrupt Batista might be, any change of regime might very well threaten the considerable Alcazar family wealth.

But their pleadings fell on deaf ears, for Emilio was a young romantic.

Also, by the by, he was a fine baseball player, something of an anomaly in the family that had never cared much for—or displayed any—athletic prowess. Since Castro himself had been, as well we all know, a fairly good schoolboy pitcher, this created even more of a personal bond in the mind of the young man between himself and the brave rebel leader.

Emilio's attraction to Castro served a good purpose, though. It alerted his father. Long before others in Omar's oligarchy, the *gallejos* from old Spain, could fathom the genuine threat that Castro posed to their dominion, Omar took note. If his own son, a bright boy of privilege, could find such allure in Castro, then there surely must be something real to fear from this wild and woolly man hidden up in the mountains with his grubby, gun-toting desperados. Quietly, working with his eldest, sensible son, Fidel, Omar began to sell off his liquid positions, shifting the money into American banks, American securities. As it was, he was more than prescient; the only mistake he made was not also trying to sell the great plantation before it was too late for that, too. But by the time Omar Alcazar and some of his family deserted Cuba, he had moved a substantial part of his fortune to the United States, and was able to live out his life there in peace and comfort.

It was a matter of great pride, too, that his eldest son adapted so quickly to American ways and American commerce. Victor—for he expunged the name Fidel from his being and his identity as soon as he arrived in Miami—became a very successful executive and made a very successful marriage with, *nee,* Cynthia Carey of Lake Forest, Illinois, whom he had met on a business trip. Yet even as Victor melded so well into the new society, even as he married into an old-line Midwestern (heartland U.S.A!) family, even as he sired two beautiful all-American daughters, even as almost every Latin syllable and every trilling entilde faded from his speech, he retained some of the distinguishing characteristics of his patrician rearing. As

Howie had noticed, he dressed, always, as an old-fashioned gentleman; his demeanor was ever correct, and although he was too smart to exhibit it, he could not completely suppress a certain arrogance that had been born into him.

There was this, too—one other thing that Victor Alcazar brought with him from Cuba and remained within every fiber of his body and every particle of his soul: he despised Fidel Castro and all that he had done to the land of his birth. If Victor had one wish, it was that he would outlive Castro, so that he could return to his homeland, go back to the places where he had grown up, back to the haunts he loved, back just to stroll the Malecon and watch the waves crash beneath him again on free rocks, free soil, free land. But never would he go back so long as Fidel Castro ruled. He even hated any American who consorted in any way with Cuba. As he had been growing up in Cuba, Victor was politically all but nihilistic. His votes in the United States were almost strictly driven by a candidate's views toward Cuba. And it was simply unfathomable to him that anyone whose blood bespoke a Cuban heritage would seek to visit there for so long as the benighted regime ruled.

And so it was now, as Victor ate breakfast in his son's suite at the Waldorf, that he pleaded with him again not to return to Cuba, not to visit there—to honor this, his father's one outstanding request that he still extended to an adult son. "At least put it off another year, think about it some more," he said to Jay, knowing that his tone was too beseeching, lacking the dignity he so prized in himself.

"You forget, Dad, that's what you said last year when I brought up this the first time—and I did put it off. For you. But now—"

"Not just one more year to think about it?"

"No, this winter will be the time. Next year I'm a free agent, and there may be all sorts of things I have to deal with then. Besides, Dad, I'm sorry, but nothing is going to change my mind."

Victor picked up his coffee cup and walked away from the table, staring out the window, down at Park Avenue. "I fear it will hurt your mother."

"No, sir, it won't," Jay said firmly, and, then, before his father could protest: "Because I've talked to her."

Victor's shoulders sagged. He did not like to be trumped. Jay got up from the table and walked over to his father. "I told Mom what I had in mind. I told her she was my mother, the only mother I would ever have, but that I wanted to meet this woman who, you know…carried me."

"And your mother was not upset?"

"No sir, she understood. The only thing that bothered her was that she knew how furious you'd be."

"Yes, that's so," Victor said, softly. He sipped from his coffee. "So, when will you go?"

"Middle of November, something like that. Dad, I think we've got a real chance to win it all this year. I'm hoping we'll be playing all October."

"Really? I've never heard such confidence from you for your team."

"Well, we're just better this year, and Howie's a helluva lot better manager than Teddy ever was."

"You like Mr. Traveler, do you?"

Jay only shrugged, but clearly in the affirmative.

"So, how will you go? There are, thank God, proscriptions about Americans traveling to Cuba, you know? You might have been born there, but—"

"Come on, Dad, anybody with a few bucks can get in. They don't even stamp your passport."

"But you're famous. They know baseball."

"I'll keep a low profile. Don't worry. Trust me. It'll be easier for me in Cuba than at Yankee Stadium today."

"And you think you can locate, uh, this woman?"

"I know how to make contacts. There's agents I know who helped some of the Cuban ballplayers come over. They're smart guys, and they can put me in touch with the right people."

"You really think you can find her?"

"Yes sir." Jay flipped his hands open before him. "If she's still alive. And she should be. She wouldn't be that old."

"And what will you say to her?"

"I don't really know, Dad. We'll just see how it goes. Maybe it'll be very quick."

"Yes," Victor said. He turned, then, and looked back out the window. He understood now that his son absolutely was going to go back, and he knew what he must tell him, that Rita Garcia—for that was the woman's name—had not given Jay up. She had not willingly agreed to let him go to the United States. But Jay had never known that, and Victor, if he could help it, had never planned to tell him.

But now, if Jay were going (and he surely was), then he must provide him with that information, tell him what really happened when he was taken away to freedom. He thought on it, watching the traffic move below, knowing that he was honor-bound to own up to the truth. But no, Victor decided, it is best not to tell his son now. He is happy and doing well. That news might upset him and affect his play. It would wait till the season were done, and perhaps...perhaps then, when Jay learned the truth, perhaps then he would not go.

So Victor only turned back and, rather formally, said: "You have made me so proud, always, *mi hijo.*" My son.

It was so odd for Jay to hear his father use any Spanish that it took him back for a moment. But quickly then: *"Gracias, padre."*

They both smiled at this unusual diversion into the family's old tongue. Then Victor went on, comfortably back in English: "And so this is your decision, and it is considered, and I promise you that I will never again protest it. We'll only talk again before you go—after the World Series."

"Yes, sir," Jay said, and he wrapped an arm around his father's far shoulder and kissed him on the cheek. It had been some time since he had kissed his father, and it made him remember all the times past and think again how odd it was to kiss a man's face, even one just shaved, and feel the rough whiskers there.

HOWIE'S LIE

In just the short time it took Howie and Flint to get back to the team's hotel, the word had gotten out. There were cameras set up, and the lobby was aswarm with reporters and still photographers. As soon as they spotted Howie, it was bedlam, as they bunched up, all banging into each other, shoving microphones forward, trying to get close to him. Howie even had to smile. It was the sort of mess an old minor-league manager of his used to characterize as "a bunch of monkeys fucking footballs." Howie held up his hands like a traffic cop.

"I can't say anything," he said. "I'm sorry. Look, I'm not trying to be evasive, but this is under orders. A lawyer. And, you know, that's the way it's gotta be. Doug'll have the statement in, what—?"

Doug shouted: "If you guys'll just let me go. Ten, fifteen minutes." After all, he only had to type up what the lawyer, Mundy, had written.

The mob parted, if only momentarily, to allow Flint

passage, so he could get the statement prepared for them.

Quickly then, they regrouped as a mass, shouting more questions at Howie. What exactly happened? Where is he now? Who's the woman? Has he been charged? Howie sighed and said he was sorry, but didn't he say he couldn't say anything? So, of course, they screamed more questions at him. So he just gave up and began to fight his way out.

O'Reilly pulled at his sleeve and whispered "Howie, Howie." O'Reilly had a habit of whispering questions, even if there was a crowd around, because it somehow made it seem more personal, seem that he had an *intime* relationship with the manager.

"Bobby," Howie said, not whispering back, "Jesus, how many times can I say I can't say anything?"

"Just tell me," O'Reilly whispered, "have you seen him?"

Howie pondered that for a moment. There was no sense being ridiculous. "Yeah, I can tell you that. I just left him." And louder now: "And he's not in the hotel, so there's no sense looking for him."

"Well, is he gonna play tonight?" O'Reilly asked, louder now, to get over the murmurs.

Howie stopped pushing long enough to stand there and say: "You bet your ass Jay Alcazar's gonna play tonight."

Well, that was enough of a crumb to give everybody pause, so Howie took advantage as they scribbled down his words, barging through the rest of the crowd and past a cop who had been stationed at the elevators. The officer recognized him and passed him through, and Howie went up to his floor.

He turned down the hall toward his room. The cops must have finished their inspection of Jay's room. Anyway, the door—that damn door—was closed. There was no more commotion in the hall, so that it stretched out the way hotel corridors do, with the sense of horizontal endlessness. How many hotel corridors had Howie Traveler traversed? He thought once that when he died, whether he went to heaven or hell, or wherever, if he went anywhere, he would only get there down a hotel corridor. In their long, linear, empty extension, they were the closest vision Howie had of eternity. That sounds silly, only not if you had turned down as many hotel corridors in as many hotels in as many baseball towns as he had.

Now, as he neared his own room at the end of the corridor, another door opened and a man came out, thanking someone in that room. Howie nodded. The man nodded back, sized him up for a minute, and then said, half in declaration, half in interrogation: "Mr. Traveler…?"

Howie was used to this sort of recognition—especially in a hotel where the team was staying—so he responded with a put-on smile and a perfunctory hello. But the man didn't turn away then and go back toward the elevators. Instead, he hurried after Howie, calling his name again. Howie stopped by his door and prepared to give an autograph.

Instead, the man held out his shield and identified himself as Detective So-and-So, with the Baltimore City Police Department. He explained that he had just a couple questions, so Howie ushered him into his room, and they sat down.

"I imagine you know what this is about," the detective said.

"Jay Alcazar."

"Correct. But understand, sir, I'm not talking with you because you're his manager, but because we're talking to everybody this end of the floor."

Howie nodded as casually as he could. But he knew that his whole self had tensed, and he only hoped that somehow his anxiety didn't show as much as he felt it did.

The detective took out a notepad. This was life follows art, because although Howie had never been questioned by a cop before, he was momentarily distracted, interested to see that a real cop did it the same as ones on TV shows. "Did you leave your room at all last evening, Mr. Traveler?"

"Yeah. I went out for dinner. My daughter and I went over to Little Italy. Cipparelli's."

"That's a nice place." On TV, the cop would also then have asked what he'd ordered and made some comment about what he himself preferred to order at Cipparelli's, but the real-life cop was more direct. He only asked: "About what time did you get back to the hotel?"

Howie thought for a moment. He figured around ten. "About nine-thirty," he said, straightaway. He was surprised at how easily he had, well, fibbed. Understand, he really didn't know. He just thought ten o'clock, which is why he said nine-thirty, placing himself safely in his room before the door down the hall had opened onto this other world.

"Are you sure of that?"

"No, not really. I don't remember checking the time.

My daughter lives in Washington and had to drive back. So it wasn't late."

"But you'd say around nine-thirty?"

Howie shrugged. "Best guess," he said.

"Did you come directly up to your room?"

Howie took advantage of this question to get a little chummy. "You follow baseball, detective?"

"I've been for the Birds all my life."

"Well, this isn't about the Orioles. But maybe you know: there's been rumors I was gonna be fired, so believe me, I didn't hang around the lobby to get grilled some more. I came right up."

"About nine-thirty?"

"Yeah. About."

"And as you came down to your room, did you see anything?"

"See like what?"

"Like unusual."

"You mean in the hall?"

"Well, in particular, did you see any door open? Mr. Traveler, did you see Jay Alcazar's door open?"

Howie shook his head and said "No," as casually as he could. He made sure not to make a big thing of it. "Nothing," he added in the same everyday tone, shrugging to try and show lack of emphasis.

The detective got up then, and, apologetically, tapping his notebook with his pen, volunteered a bit more than he had to. "I didn't imagine it was you. I'm sorry, we just have to talk to everyone down this end."

Howie nodded. Then he stood up himself and sighed, shaking his head. "I'm sorry myself. I'm kinda rattled by all this."

"I can understan'," the detective said. Then, of course, he asked for an autograph for his son and left. When grown-ups ask for an autograph, they always say they're getting it for a child. Howie thought that if they were so embarrassed about asking for an autograph, then they wouldn't. But they do; they just lie and say it's for their child. It's something like how you don't want to let other people see you looking at pictures of naked women in a skin magazine.

Howie watched the door close. He was surprised that he wasn't frightened that he had lied to a cop, a detective, an officer of the law, city of Baltimore, state of Maryland. In fact, he was rather amazed at how easily he had done it, and, to boot, how well he thought he had done it.

All he could think about then was to wonder when was the last time he had lied. He could remember only one time and that was in the family, that was with Suzie, and he absolutely had to then. But just that one time. Oh, sure, a little social fib here or there, a bit of prevarication when it was the easy way out of nothing. But lied? Flat out? Just that one other time.

Worse, Howie really didn't know why he had lied. Had he lied to protect Jay Alcazar or had he lied because Jay Alcazar was the best player on the team and he still was the manager of the team because Jay Alcazar had momentarily saved his ass by getting arrested?

MUNDY

IT WASN'T UNTIL JAY WAS ALONE with Walter Mundy, the lawyer, at the Cross Keys Inn that he began to fully appreciate what had really happened to him. He was still angry, but not so befuddled now, and being safely tucked away in a hotel room gave Alcazar a little breathing space. Besides, he understood that this man he was with, who'd he never met until a few hours ago, was crucially important to his future. Well, also his present. And luckily, what he'd seen of Mundy, he liked. Still, Alcazar was smart enough to be curious.

"How the hell did you get involved in this?" he asked.

"Who's Fred Montague?"

"My agent."

"Well, you called him, right?"

Jay said, "Uh-huh."

"And he called a lawyer he knew in Miami, and he called me."

"This is what you do? This kinda case?"

"This is what I do," Mundy said. "And just to give you some assurance, I think I'm as good at what I do as you are at what you do."

Alcazar couldn't help but chuckle. "I'm havin' a bad year."

"Well, we all have rough patches. What counts is cumulatively, Jay, cumulatively. But..." And here Mundy, who had been sitting on the desk, rose to his feet and approached Alcazar. "But it's not my ass that's on the line. If you find yourself in any way uncomfortable with me, any way doubting of my abilities, you tell me, and I will not only bow out gracefully, I will make sure that everything I have been privy to is passed on, fully and expeditiously, to whoever succeeds me. I'm no dog in the manger, and I'm no good to you, Jay, unless you have faith in me. Savvy?"

Alcazar looked up sharply: "Do you have faith in *me*?"

Mundy thought: well, he isn't just another dumb-ass ballplayer. That was exactly the right question. "Yes, I do, as a matter of fact. Because I have reason to. First of all, you absolutely act like a man who has been wronged—that is, an innocent man. And more important, everything you've done so far has been exactly right. You've kept your poise, and you didn't let the cops get one word outta you. Who was that scumbag basketball player they caught in Colorado a few years ago?"

"Kobe Bryant."

"Right. He ran off at the mouth the minute they picked him up."

"Of course now, maybe *he* was guilty," Alcazar said.

"All the more reason to put a cork in it." And they shared a little laugh.

But Mundy was pretty sure the message got across: I think you're innocent, pal, but, whatever, keep that particular relevant information to yourself. He paused, then, and pulled up a chair across from where Alcazar sprawled back across the bed, leaning on his elbows. "And that's the main thing here, Jay. You don't say nuttin' to nobody." Alcazar nodded, but it seemed too perfunctory to Mundy. He patted him on his leg. "Sit up."

Alcazar followed orders. Mundy looked him in the face. "I mean *nobody*." Then, softer: "I didn't ask you—you're not married are you?"

"Christ, no."

"Okay, that's good. Any woman you're really going with?"

"No."

"Good. That's a twofer. There isn't anybody you're gonna feel like talking to, to explain yourself, and it also means you weren't cheating on anybody. There's nothing wrong with an unattached young man having a roll in the hay with an unattached—and willing—young woman."

"Goddamn road beef," Alcazar muttered then, almost reflexively.

"What's that? Road what?"

"Beef. Road beef. Just an easy piece of ass on the, you know, the road."

"Well, she isn't any more. And she's not a cunt or a bitch or anything else derogatory. She is Ms. Tricia, uh,

Smith. That's all. Without the pejoratives. The negatives," Mundy added quickly in case Alcazar didn't know what "pejoratives" are.

In fact, he did. "I follow you. This is just a little misunderstanding between a gentleman and a lady."

Mundy leaned forward again. "Exactly, but lookee here, Jay, there's a lotta people glad to see this come down on you. Savvy? You're rich and handsome and young and everyone is sure that ballplayers think they're entitled to take whatever they can, so they're going to be very happy that this is happening to a rat-fuck ballplayer. Excuse me."

"I know," Alcazar said, softly. "And some of 'em aren't going to like it that I'm a Latin fucking a white girl."

Given Alcazar's celebrity, that hadn't even occurred to Mundy, and he let it pass. "So you don't wanna give anybody any chance to build on that. You let me be the bad guy." Alcazar nodded. "But remember, too, there's another side of the coin. Our friend Tricia is a grown woman, she has drinks with you, she accepts your invitation, at night, to come up to your room for another drink, and so she's gonna have a hard time convincing anyone that she's little Miss Prissy." Alcazar smiled broadly at that. Mundy went on: "So right now, it's strictly a he-said/she-said deal."

"What d'ya mean 'right now?'"

"If the medical tests show any vaginal wounds, any cuts, bruises, then that could complicate things. Or if somebody in another room claimed they heard her scream."

"Aw, come on. She didn't."

"I'm just telling you what's possible, Jay. But as long as there's no incriminating physical evidence and as long as nobody comes out of the woodwork as some kind of a witness, we've got a mature woman willingly going to a man's hotel room in the evening. No matter what she says, the Baltimore City police can't make anything out of it if that's all they got. But don't kid yourself—they'll be doing their homework, because they don't want anybody to say that you got off easy just because you're Jay Alcazar. And that's good."

"Why is that good?"

"Because you *are* innocent, and when the police find out that there's no case against you whatsoever, that is going to make it that much more difficult for this woman to file any civil suit against you."

"The cunt."

Mundy waggled a finger at him. "Jay, what did I say?"

"The lady."

"Exactly. My best guess: I do not think the lady wants you in jail. I think she just wants a piece of your bankroll. So, while we have to direct our attention to the possible criminal charges now, we'll keep the civil in the back of our mind."

"Don't worry. She's already taken me." Quizzically, Mundy cocked his head. Alcazar explained: "You don't think this hurts my endorsements—or any new ones?"

"All the more reason to clear you one hundred per-cent...or, one hundred and ten percent, as you guys always have it in sports—clear you a hundred and ten percent so this, uh, cunt...bitch...road beef"—Mundy grinned—" is completely discredited."

Jay chuckled. He liked this Mundy guy a great deal.

"Now, Jay, you sit tight here. The room is registered under the name of Louise Mason—an associate of mine. Nobody knows you're here. Order some room service, and call me for anything." He handed him his card. "My assistant is Shelley. Wherever I am, she'll get me, pronto. And you're sure you want to play tonight?"

"You bet your ass. I kept playing that time in Boston I almost got killed, didn't I? If I don't, they'll just say it proves I'm guilty."

"Good. I've never rooted against the Orioles in my life. I will tonight." He slapped Jay on his shoulder, then shook his hand, taking advantage to look into his eyes for any truths he might find there.

As soon as Mundy was gone, Jay began to retch. He hadn't eaten since the night before, so there was nothing for him to throw up, but he gagged, over and over again.

Then he sat down, composed himself, and called his parents. His mother answered, and he chatted as casually as he could pretend to do so with her for a moment or two. Then he asked to speak to his father. "Dad," Jay said, "I'm in some trouble, but it's going to be okay." Then he told his father the story, much as he had told it to Mundy. He left out one thing, but then, maybe by now Jay didn't even remember that the lady had scrambled to the door and opened it. It had happened so fast, he'd closed it so fast, maybe he really wasn't holding anything back; maybe in all the excitement, it had simply slipped his mind.

It was difficult speaking to his father. All Jay's life, he had never seen or heard his father cry. Now, it had happened twice in just the last few months. First: when he had gone to Cuba against his wishes, and now: when he told him about last night in the hotel room, because Victor understood right away that the good family name would be besmirched for the first time since his brother, Emilio, had turned his back on all those he loved and signed on to the cause of Fidel Castro.

CELEBRITY

UNLIKE, PARTICULARLY, FOOTBALL AND basketball players, baseball players do not grow up in the spotlight. Those players, like Alcazar, who succeed and become famous are more like actors or singers who plug along for years, then suddenly have a bombshell movie, a hit song. Basketball players, however, might as well be Prince William or Prince Harry. The best of them become "names" when they're barely into puberty. They're fawned over, cheated for, given advantages and material things (much of it illegal swag). Football players do not enjoy quite so much national adolescent attention as their basketball brethren, but they too are heroes early on. The stands are packed for them in high school, and in college the huge stadiums, those American collegiate cathedrals, are filled. And, of course, the games are on television. Football and basketball players adapt easily to adoration, as they grow naturally into their celebrity and take it on as a matter of course.

It was different with Jay. Even though he was considered the prime prospect in the country from the time he was a junior in high school, he was barely known beyond close baseball circles. For whatever reasons of history, baseball was never a spectator attraction in school, the way that first football and then basketball became. More, perhaps, than a star in one of those sports—or in other games like tennis or golf, even hockey or swimming—Jay grew up like some musical prodigy, someone known only in that small world as a potentially fabulous violinist or tenor. He perfected his art in relative seclusion—all the more so inasmuch as his father and mother took no special interest in baseball. Oh, young Jay's name would be in the hometown paper, and the college recruiters and major league scouts started coming round, but there really wasn't a lot of public fuss about it.

Even at Florida State, where he was recognized within the baseball universe as a player of brilliant potential, he was not as well known on campus as any of the regulars on the basketball team or most all of the hordes of football players who suited up every week before eighty thousand fans and the networks. There were some professors who did not even know that the good-looking Hispanic in their classroom was actually what was classified as a "student-athlete." So Jay was able to enjoy college much as any regular student would. Because he was a good enough scholar when he felt like it, he got little special attention from the athletic department tutors, and although he did get laid a great deal, that wasn't because he was a star; it was because he was handsome and beguiling. There are no cheerleaders in baseball, no pom-pom girls with their big, bursting breasts jiggling before the crowds, eager to service the players afterwards. In fact, during the World Series, it is the players' wives the networks seek out to show America. Baseball is not sexy at its roots.

Alcazar became no better known after he turned pro. The best basketball and football and hockey players his age are immediately raised up as prizes to the major leagues. But Jay? Even as the first player drafted in all the country, he was started out in Class A, down in Kinston, North Carolina, playing before crowds of so much as four or five thousand only on those nights when there were special country music promotions or keychain giveaways. That was the distinct way of baseball. Howie understood it well. You could be the greatest natural athlete in the world, as fast as a cheetah, as powerful as a rhino, but that wasn't enough in his sport. There was the craft to learn, too. You must apprentice in baseball. Jay knew how good he intrinsically was, but what the hell— starting at home, nobody had ever paid him that much attention. He had had no connection with glamour; he could only imagine. He had to be patient.

Alcazar would get a little taste of recognition in Winter Haven, Florida, each spring training, when he was assigned there for a couple weeks, a protected species, on the Indians' expanded roster. But then he would be farmed out again—after Kinston, a year at Akron, Double A, and then Buffalo, Triple A. He surely could have jumped all the way to the majors that season, but the Indians were a dreary team at that time and there was no sense taking a chance and rushing their most exquisite prospect up a bit too soon just so he might possibly ease them out of the cellar. Let him marinate another season in the minors.

But the next year the Tribe front office knew they couldn't hold him back. In the shopworn parlance of the game, Jay Alcazar had *arrived*. Suddenly, after all these years, all his short life of playing games before drop-in assemblages, he was on stage before twenty, thirty, forty thousand—every night. It was fabulous; he drank in the panoply and the sudden hugeness of it.

At first, it was downright fun to be a male starlet. There were newspaper guys wherever he turned, radio people shoving microphones in his face, television cameras with famous television faces interviewing him, playing up to him. Just like that: ta-daa! But it wasn't even as if he'd been some leggy dancer taken out of the chorus and made a leading lady overnight. That chorus girl, after all, was already on Broadway, a part of the best of it, while the baseball player shot out of nowhere into the national glare, with nothing in between.

But here was the funny thing. It was all so easy for Jay. Not just the playing, not just that he hit .331 and smacked thirty-six home runs and batted in one twenty-two his first year in the majors; Rookie of the Year, unanimous. The rest of it was just as easy. It was amazing, for instance, how effortlessly he dealt with the media, how naturally it came to him. Why, even as a rookie, Jay could speak platitudes with aplomb, respond to the most pointed questions with inconsequential babble that satisfied the quote takers as sure as if he were speaking with the rhythm and eloquence of Bishop Tutu. Of course, there was good reason that his responses came with such facility. Hadn't he seen athletes doing that on TV ever since he was a child? Hadn't he read their banal responses enough himself? Hardly without knowing it, he was as schooled in being a modern luminary as he was at hitting the cut-off man or taking the good outside pitch with two strikes left.

Ty Baggio, the maestro himself at this sort of thing, watched in admiration as the rookie pleasured the writers with humble chestnuts after he'd saved a victory for Baggio by whirling, then throwing a perfect strike from foul territory to catch the tying run at the plate. Baggio gave him a thumbs up after the press platoon moved off to record these gems of Alcazar's. "The rain gives away to bright sunshine," he declared.

Alcazar moved over to him. "It's all horseshit, isn't it?"

"Oh no," Baggio said with a straight face. "It's not horseshit. It is, however, bullshit." Alcazar looked puzzled. "Look, Jay, if you're going to be a big-league star, you've got to know the difference between horseshit and bullshit."

"What's that?"

"Horseshit is only an adjective. It's a horseshit game. I threw a horseshit pitch. But bullshit is a noun."

"Yeah?"

"Sure. Don't they teach you anything in the minors? It's bullshit having to talk to the writers. Our horseshit manager knows bullshit about pitchers."

Alcazar nodded, solemnly acknowledging that he had learned the God's truth. From the horse's mouth. "I never knew that. Why?"

"Beats me, Jay. I'm not a country boy myself, so I've never examined horseshit or bullshit, but there must be a distinct difference. It's as much an accepted part of the game as resin bags."

"Gosh, I'll try to remember," Alcazar said, keeping a serious mien as befits such a serious issue.

"Well, you're in the bigs now, buster, so you better fucking get...it...straight." Alcazar smiled. "And that's no bullshit."

Anyway, the newspaper boys quickly celebrated Alcazar as "mature" because he played their game so well, too, always giving them something obvious. *I was just looking for a good pitch to hit. Perez is just one great pitcher. We're not out of it yet. We just need to hit better with men on base. No, this wasn't my biggest thrill, but it sure meant a lot to me. I wasn't trying to hit a home run, just make contact.* And so forth and so on. "Focus," Baggio told him one day. "Just tell the cocksuckers you're focusing better or you need to focus better. You can dine out on focus all season." So, Alcazar added focus to his regular repertoire. But, of course, despite all the rhetoric, day after day, no matter how much he appeared before America, never did anybody ever really learn anything about who Jay Alcazar was or what he might actually have been thinking. He remained invisible in plain sight, silent in the midst of his own din. And that was just fine with him, because that's the way he preferred it.

Midway through his rookie season, Moncrief wanted to move Alcazar's locker to a corner of the clubhouse, where he would be better able to entertain the media multitudes. Sam Hooks, who was the manager that year, wouldn't do it, though. Hooks was hard-knock, old school. Rookies didn't get corner lockers. Never had, never should. There were discrete social rules to obey—and after all, baseball was the only sport where a team was a club and the locker room was a clubhouse.

After the season, of course, Hooks got fired and was replaced by Teddy Phillips because, it was said, the venerable Hooks *didn't understand the modern athlete.* Moncrief was particularly afraid that his manager was too doctrinaire and might upset his star rookie, but truth be told, Alcazar himself didn't think about Hooks one way or the other. After all, Hooks just wrote in Jay's name in the three-hole for every game, and that was that. Alcazar hadn't really ever paid much mind to coaches or managers. Why bother?

The media eventually did get to be a pain in the ass, of course. They were just so ubiquitous and so repetitive. But Jay understood that he must put up with them. After all, they were just always there. Before the game, on the field, even as he waited to take his licks in batting practice. After the game, surrounding his locker as he made some effort to get off his sweaty togs. Even naked, as he padded to the shower, with just a towel round his loins in deference to the brassy female reporters who were allowed in locker rooms now. Why would anyone want to talk to a naked man? Jay wondered. Who wants to talk to anybody naked unless they're also naked? Or the writers would snare him in his transit through the hotel lobby. *Just a couple questions, Jay.* Their presence was so constant that Alcazar soon simply accepted it as a necessary part of the life, like buses and airplanes and autographs and *per diem.*

Alcazar looked at it this way: most of the retinue that surrounded him was there to serve him. His agent, Montague, first of all, and Brenda, Montague's secretary, who answered all his mail and dutifully reminded him of obligations and birthdays. The team's public relations people. Dougie Flint was especially good at making sure different girlfriends were well separated from each other at the home games (not to mention Flint's even trickier task of separating the seats for the girlfriends and the wives of the married players).

Then there were Alcazar's reps at Louisville Slugger and Nike. The Indians' coaches and doctors and trainers. Your every medical whim immediately attended to. Plus massages. The equipment guys. The clubhouse guys. Everything your heart desires: food and drink, batteries for your appliances, charging for your cell phones. The best attendants even had Mother's and Father's Day cards—stamped, you understand—available in May and June, because who could expect big-leaguers to remember such a thing themselves, let alone actually purchase Hallmarks? And: *Don't worry, Jay, I'll mail it for you.*

They were all especially attentive to him, not only because he was a monster star, but because he learned early on to tip excessively. Jesus, after all, he just had so much money, it was easy enough to pass some of it around. *Hey, thanks a lot. Buy yourself something, honey. Come on, take it.* They did. They all did and loved him all the more for it.

But withal, Alcazar understood, that despite all this, notwithstanding the twittering attentions heretofore only paid to medieval royalty, nobody gets it all. In every life a little rain must fall. In his case, the drizzle was the media and the torrents were the fans.

Now, it's important to understand that Alcazar, like most good athletes, really wasn't much of a sports devotee himself. He just liked *playing* the games. So, in Alcazar's mind, fans were simply such inexplicable assholes. How could anybody get that worked up over a game you weren't playing yourself? The worst were the ones who would scoot all around him or the other players, adoring, kiss-asses. The players called them "green flies," from what buzzed around manure. Then there were the pathetic top-heavy, silicon-laden groupies, and the nasty little grasping children. Baggio lumped those two groups together as the "cunts and runts."

Actually, Jay came to despise the children most of all. Of course, he would not dare reveal this dreadful fact to anyone. Hate children? Who could not suffer the wee ones, the hope of the future? But the little bastards he encountered were such rapacious creatures. *Hey, gimme an autograph, Jay. Jay, Jay, sign this ball.* They came to the park with their moms and dads, and they knew it was a special treat because games were so expensive now that they weren't just games anymore. They were events. And once there, the tykes had to have everything: drinks and eats and souvenirs and, best of all, an autograph from a real player. It was amazing to Jay how few of the little moppet cocksuckers ever said thank you. Children at ballgames were, if he'd stopped to think about it, like ballplayers in much of their own lives.

Well, Jay didn't stop to think about it, but one time Montague called him up and said a rich real estate guy on Fisher Island would pay $100,000 just to have Alcazar show up for two hours at his son's bar mitzvah. Jay told Montague: "I wouldn't do it for a million. What'd I be, a fuckin' Cuban toy for some snotty rich kids? Stick it, Freddy." Montague was surprised at the vehemence of the response.

But Alcazar would do this. Whenever the Make-A-Wish people would ask him to spend time with some dying kid who longed to meet him, he would go out of his way for that. Montague got him associated with a fatal children's disease, and he would go to the hospital and talk with the sick kids and autograph anything they wanted, give them balls and bats and a few bucks of his walking-around money to go buy whatever they wanted. He didn't mind visiting those poor children at all. It was just the normal kids at games who screeched and hollered and demanded and never said thank you when they cornered him for autographs. Them, he came to hate.

The media he tolerated—well, abided. The press were, after all, professionals. Or, anyway, if not quite that in his mind, they were paid to ask all their asinine questions. See, unlike the dopey fans, they had an excuse. Alcazar tended to like the older writers better.

The most balanced of them were jaded, who, after years of watching thousands of games, had learned not to take it too seriously. On the other hand, too many of the young writers wanted to find out what rock groups and TV shows he liked, stuff like that. They wanted to *share* with him. Alcazar didn't want to be their friends. He just wanted a nice, symbiotic relationship, where he gave them the quotes they wanted (and sometimes a harmless little skinny) and they gave him a reputation as a nice guy, good man, generous aristocrat, team player, boy next door. That was the idea. Focus. See? That was what he focused on.

HUEY

ALMOST ALL OF THE PLAYERS hated Huey, the old columnist for the *Plain Dealer*. Nobody could much understand it, but Alcazar got along with him. But then, he had liked Huey from the beginning, when he had met him at his first spring training with the Indians in Winter Haven before he got shipped out to Akron, Double A.

"So," Huey had abruptly began his introduction in the clubhouse, "you're the *wunderkind* who's going to make us all forget Babe Ruth?"

Alcazar was taken aback. Even back then, still a minor leaguer, after only one season down in Class A, he was already used to journalists kissing his ass. Well, he was used to everybody kissing his ass. So who was this grouchy old fart in cloudy sunglasses? And what the fuck was a wonder-whatchamacallit? But Jay recovered quickly. "You're so old you remember Babe Ruth?" he asked.

Huey admired the riposte. "Actually, kid, I was

prominent in attendance when Abner Doubleday invented baseball. I was that very poet laureate who christened it 'The National Pastime.'" Huey then simply appropriated the empty chair from the next locker and plunked himself down. Alcazar immediately noticed that, for a sportswriter, he affected a more formal, if threadbare, appearance. Apparently, he didn't own any sport shirts, for Alcazar never saw him wearing any. Instead, Huey was wearing a cheap, button-down dress shirt, with the sleeves rolled up to his forearms, a tattersall vest—who in the world wore vests anymore? and, Jesus: tattersall?—and golf slacks the color of wine. All of this somehow gave off the sense of a man who was not so much deficient in style, but simply a-stylish. Now, settled, he stuck out his hand. "Mickey Huey from the *Plain Dealer.* Can you spare an old scribe a column?"

Alcazar did. He told him about leaving Cuba as a small child and growing up in Miami. Most of it was true, some exaggerated, some fabricated. For example, he told Huey his mother had died in Cuba, and he neglected to mention that his father in Miami wasn't really his father. Then, Huey himself botched some of the facts (and some of the fibs) himself and added some hyperbole of his own, some studied anti-Castro hysterics—he practically had Fidel himself murdering Jay's mother in cold blood. But, altogether, it made for a very nice column. Best of all, it became the quasi-official biography of young Jay Alcazar, the one every other writer would refer to and repeat over the years, so that after awhile the tale, with all its errors and elaborations, was set in stone (or anyway, on the

Internet). This saved Alcazar the need to keep discussing his upbringing or to repeat the little white lies.

A couple of days after the column appeared, Alcazar came back to the team hotel after dinner. Huey was sitting at the lobby bar, his sleeves rolled up per usual, in his dress vest, bitching about something to the bartender. He spotted Alcazar and called to him: "Hey, Babe Junior. [For the rest of his life, he would always call him Babe Junior, or just Junior.] Join me. I'll buy you a proper libation."

Alcazar stopped dead and feigned a fainting spell: "A writer is gonna buy me a drink?"

"Don't look a gift horse in the mouth."

So, what the hey, Alcazar went over to the bar and slid onto the seat next to him. "Nice column, Mr. Huey."

"You read it?" He seemed genuinely surprised.

"Of course I did."

The bartender came over. Alcazar ordered a Dos Equis, but the bartender wanted to see his ID. Huey roared. "You featherbrained dolt, this noble specimen before us is the second coming of Babe Ruth. He's already got more money in the bank than either of us will ever accumulate in a lifetime of honest toil, and he possesses a future of untold promise. And you dare seek to card him?"

"I'm sorry, sir, I have to ask."

"Well, show him the goods, Jay."

"I'm sorry, all's I got is a credit card." He started to get back off his seat.

"Belay that," Huey snapped, motioning him to sit back down. He reached into his briefcase and hauled out the Indians' press guide. "Look," he snapped at the bartender, pointing to Alcazar's picture. "That's this young gentleman, right?" The bartender nodded. Then he pointed at his birthdate—which made him six months past his twenty-first birthday. "His majority is verified here, is it not?"

The bartender was obviously a worry-wart. "Well, this isn't really an official picture ID," he said.

Alcazar started to get up again. This time Huey put a hand on his shoulder and physically pushed him back down. "For Christ's sweet sake, man, here's his photo, here's when he was born. It looks like a picture ID, it walks like a picture ID, *it's* a picture ID. Would the sainted Tribe of Cleveland lie?"

"Well, you know," the bartender said, looking only at Huey, "these guys, where they're from—nobody really knows how old."

This time Alcazar raised up, but it wasn't to leave. It was to look the bartender in the eye. "Excuse me, but I'm an American from Miami, Florida, mister."

"You give young Galahad a beer," Huey said, growling.

The bartender backed down. "Yeah, okay," he said (if without graciousness), then scooted down the bar to retrieve a beer bottle.

Alcazar took his seat again. "Mr. Huey," he said, "don't ever write that."

Huey said: "Don't worry. It'll be sufficient unto itself just to tell the tale 'mongst friends a few years hence. If you're anywhere near as accomplished as they say, that'll be the last time anybody on the face of the earth won't recognize you." He raised his glass;

even to Alcazar's untrained bar eyes it appeared brown enough to be a double Scotch. "And I was the witness to that signal encounter. The last time the esteemed Juan Francisco Alcazar ever went incognito." Alcazar smiled. He'd never heard anybody speak quite like this; it was intriguing.

"Of course, you understand, I don't have a clue how good you are. It's just what they tell me. We're all supposed to be experts, but, in fact, we don't know our asses from our elbows. We're only bloody chroniclers. Forty years, I still can't tell a slider from a curveball, and I don't have the foggiest what a *cutter* even is."

Alcazar laughed. Helpfully, he made a darting motion with his hand down by his belt. "What's that?" Huey asked.

Alcazar did it again. "A cutter: down and in. A good cutter goes down and in. Think of this, sir. A hand job."

Huey pondered that for a moment. "Ah, yes. I am forever in your debt, Junior, for now the movement of a cutter is emblazoned in my fading memory. Down and in. Down and in." He raised his glass to Alcazar just as the bartender brought the beer and (very politely now) poured it into a pilsner glass. Jay thereupon returned Huey's gesture and hefted it to him. "Thanks for the beer, Mr. Huey."

"And you can tell your grandchildren that a gentleman of the fourth estate actually bought you a drink. Precedents abound." He clinked their glasses. "Come on now: you actually did read the column?"

"I told you: of course."

"Well, you've got to understand, Junior, that is not necessarily a guarantee among our incumbent athletic heroes. Most of them nowadays have eschewed the written word so that they might spend their valuable *down* time playing video games and watching those wretched highlights on ESPN where screeching passes for narration. You must excuse me if I'm naturally dubious about anyone I write about actually reading my priceless prose." He sighed, twirling his finger in his glass. "It does make it difficult doing this job as a writer, when so many of the people you write about don't know what the Sam Hill writing is."

"Hey, I done went to college two years," Alcazar said, mock offended.

"It is precisely my experience with athletes who've allegedly gone to college that leads me to despair of our system of higher education. But" —Huey tilted his glass toward Alcazar— "present company excepted."

Alcazar waited a moment, then: "You're tired of all this, aren't you, sir?"

"All what?"

"Baseball. All sports, I guess."

"I suppose. My, how it's changed. When I first came into this enterprise we sportswriters took ourselves much too seriously. We actually thought we were important. I was a kid, not much older than you, working for the United Press, God rest its soul, in Cincinnati. It was a pennant race, and all the fabled hotshots came in from New York. Giants walked the earth in those days, Junior! Dick Young, Red Smith, Jimmy Cannon, Jim Murray! Any of those names mean anything to you?" Alcazar shook his head.

"Yeah, ashes to ashes. Well, I'm sitting in the press box next to old Jimmy Cannon, and he's bloviating about this and that, and I'm a nobody, but I'm providing him with a worshipful audience, so he's very attentive to me, and all of a sudden, he says...he says this in a very heavy voice, whispered, in strictest confidence...he intones: 'Kid, I woke up this morning with a hard-on, and I just looked around where I was, so I just tucked it back'—and Mr. Cannon did this"— Huey made the gesture of tucking his own imaginary erection back in— "Just tucked it back and said: 'Jimmy, you're just a big-league guy in a bush-league town.'" Alcazar laughed. "Yeah, we knights of the keyboard thought we were king shit back then." He made the tuck gesture again. "Yes indeed, a big-league guy in a bush-league town."

Alcazar laughed once more. "You liked games then, Mr. Huey? You liked it then?"

"Sure, Babe Junior, in my salad days I was in their thrall. I'd endured a couple wasted years in the army. We had to go into the army then. In those halcyon days, we were still a democracy, the U.S. of A. So, upon my return to civilian life, I was bright-eyed and bushy-tailed. I suppose I liked being a scribe then as much as you like playing baseball now." Huey paused then and signaled for another scotch. "Whatdya say, Babe Junior, another one? Remember: my tab."

"No thanks, sir. We gotta be out early tomorrow."

"Well, do your best."

"I will, don't worry."

"No, I mean that with all my heart. I've seen too many guys piss it away. The broads. This liquid temptation." He held up his glass. "Not to mention what are so delicately called *recreational* drugs. And now the ghastly amounts of moolah, as well, that encourage entirely too many of your caste to take the money and *not* run. Still, I never could comprehend greatness being wasted. To be that good, to have that much of a chance to really be special at one thing here on God's green earth—and as thousands cheer!—Jesus, how could you not live up to the bounty our creator has munificently presented you with and give it your all?"

"I won't piss it away, sir."

"No, I don't think you will, Junior. I see honesty behind those bright young eyes. But after awhile, you watch so many come and go. As I got older, there were two things I always told myself around players—to satisfy my existence, you understand. Or, my vanity. Number one: no matter how good you are, buddy-boy, I'm gonna be here long after you're gone. And number two: you need me. You need me to make you famous. Write about me, they used to say. Plead. *Plead:* 'Gimme some ink, Mickey. I need some ink.' And you know what?"

The bartender brought the new scotch. For the first time, Alcazar could tell Huey was a little smashed. Not a lot, but just enough to get sentimental. "What's that?"

"What's what?" Huey asked, sipping his new drink.

"What's: 'And you know what'?"

"Ah yes, thank you. Well, what's what is that neither one or two obtains anymore. First of all, I'm *not* going to be here after you're gone. I'm gonna be out of this dodge before you even reach your prime—the victim of either senility or downsizing. And second: you *don't* need me anymore. Not you, not any player."

Huey pointed to the television over the bar, down a ways, that was wordlessly showing a sing-song NBA game from some Sunbelt outpost like Charlotte or Memphis. "As long as you're displayed in living color on that contraption, you don't need me. That's the reality now. I'm not going to outlast you, and you don't need me. So, I came into this enterprise a very important appliance and shall go out a little piece of bric-a-brac."

Alcazar polished off most of the rest of his beer, and Huey could see he was preparing to leave.

"But before you rendezvous with the sandman, Junior, let me assure you that I do yet provide one specific function that well serves the game."

"What's that, sir?"

"Me and my journalistic brethren keep you heroes real. We see you every day, even when you're bare-assed naked. We watch you and talk to you and then provide to the wider world some approximation of your humanity. You probably loathe our ubiquity, our prying presence—"

"No sir, not really."

"Well, thank you, but I'm sure in time you will not be so generous with that assessment. But, curiously, we trespassers upon your privacy give you what the other public people in this world lack: the grace of the everyday. Movie stars, those dreadful rap people, politicians, tycoons, so-called—they're all so protected, so insulated, and hence they become cardboard figures. They're simply gossip on the hoof. But you players, you cannot entirely sequester yourself in gated communities. You must engage us every noon and night, home and away, and because of that intrusion, you become real. That's why people care so about you. We modest archivists of fun and games can still take a little credit."

"It helps that we're good, too, doesn't it?"

"I don't mean to diminish your competence. But it's best mixed with the authenticity we give you. There was a historian, very bright man named Daniel Boorstin. Did you, perchance, encounter his works when in the halls of academia?" Alcazar shook his head. "No, I didn't suppose so. History has lost its appeal to the multitudes—except, of course, for home-run records. But, anyway, what Daniel Boorstin said many years ago was that everything was becoming so false in this world, that eventually the only two real things that would be left would be crime and sport."

"Crime and sport?"

"Yes, and given that Dr. Boorstin said this before the depravity displayed by Mr. O.J. Simpson and Ms. Tonya Harding, he was especially prescient. So, Babe Junior, I will do my best to keep you real. You hold up your end of the bargain with that Louisville Slugger, and you'll be just fine."

Alcazar said: "Okay, Mr. Huey, it's a deal." He finished his beer and started to walk away. Huey called to him. He turned back.

"Hey, Junior." Huey reached down and feigned rearranging a hard-on again. "Big-league guy," he said, chuckling. Alcazar smiled broadly.

In the eight years Mickey Huey still wrote his column before he dropped dead in the press room at an ice hockey playoff game in Edmonton, Alberta, Canada, he was the only writer Alcazar ever gave little scoops to. Very few of those bijoux he revealed really meant anything, but still, it surprised all the other players. Most of them couldn't cotton to Huey. He was too blunt, cynical and not deferential enough. He made no effort whatsoever to learn that handshake black people favor. Alcazar, though, actually appreciated how blunt he was. You had to live a long time to be brave enough to be that honest, he thought.

One time he explained to Ollie Jorgenson: "The main thing about being really famous is, you begin to wonder what everybody you meet *really* wants from you. Once you catch on what they want, it's not so hard. But it just takes so much time to figure each guy out. I always know what Mickey wants, though, because he tells me. And you know what, best of all?" Jorgenson shook his head. "He really doesn't give a shit how good I am. He just wants me to do my best. That's all, and that's nice."

THE INTERLOPER

As SPECTACULAR AS ALCAZAR PLAYED his first two seasons with Cleveland, his third soon exceeded all expectations. He was still only twenty-five, but already it was clear that now he must be the best player in the game of baseball. The demands upon his time began to grow almost exponentially, which was why Teddy Phillips felt obliged to allow him special privileges—like staying in that different hotel in New York. Alcazar was now moving out of the realm of mere sport into crossword puzzles and David Letterman references and *People* magazine's roster of the best-looking people in the known world. He began to withdraw all the more, not so much because he wanted to, but because it was the only way he could maintain his brilliance. In some respects, hereafter, Alcazar was only of the team but not really on it.

At the All-Star Game, in Phoenix, he belted two home runs, one of them a grand slam, and as July wore on he was still hitting in the three-sixties, notwithstanding that he was also the top slugger in the game. He had a good chance to become the first player in forty years to win the Triple Crown—that meant leading the league in batting average, home runs, and runs batted in. The Indians themselves had moved up to become serious contenders, and so when the team made a swing along the eastern seaboard late in the month, the baseball networks chose to air the Cleveland games nationally virtually every night they could.

In Boston, Alcazar won the first game with a home run deep to right. The comparisons to Ted Williams were everywhere lifted to the heavens. The next night, both starting pitchers were knocked out early, but before the enthralled crowd the home team came from far behind to trail only 7-6 in the fourth inning. Boston still had runners on second and third, too, when the next Red Sox batter bounced a single to center just beyond Ycaza's reach at shortstop. The runner on third scored, of course, but the man on second improbably also tried to make it home, then found himself hung up well short of home plate.

A rundown ensued. Back and forth, back and forth. From his vantage in right field, Alcazar watched the action intently. So did everybody else in Fenway Park. A rundown is so un-baseball—more like the lateral action of basketball or hockey—that it is a bonus diversion on those rare occasions when it occurs.

When the runner was, inevitably, tagged out, the catcher quickly pivoted to throw to second base in the event that the batter had designs on moving up. Only then did Alcazar—and much of the crowd—realize that the scruffy young man in baggy shorts and a black T-shirt had used the distraction round home plate to vault over the short fence in foul territory in right field and dash toward where Alcazar was stationed. Three members of the park security, themselves diverted by the rundown, were now rushing out to capture the interloper. Alcazar crossed his arms in disgust and prepared to wait out what would be the usual run-around until the jack-off was seized and hauled away.

It was only then, when the man wasn't more than ten or fifteen feet away from him, that Alcazar realized that he was carrying a pistol. Just then, as the man slowed his pace, he carefully raised his arm, pointing the weapon directly at Alcazar. "Don't move," he shouted, all the while himself stepping closer and closer.

Then, for just an instant, the man whirled about, clearly displaying the pistol to the security guards. "No closer," he screamed. Immediately, they stopped. Nothing like this had ever happened before. Just as quickly, the man swung his arm back toward Alcazar and purposefully, menacingly came even closer to him. Reflexively then, Alcazar did something that made no sense, but which everyone could understand. He dropped his glove and held up his arms to show that he was unarmed. As if he had carried a gun to right field. But all the years of watching this sort of thing played out in the movies and on television had conditioned him to respond just so.

The man, unmoved by the gesture, only said: "You took my girl, you fuckin' sonuvabitch."

Alcazar slowly dropped his arms to his side.

There had been gasps and shouts throughout the stands as the spectators first spotted what was going on. This macabre scene was leavened, though, with a certain amount of nervous laughter, because, quite naturally, it all seemed so bizarre that many people could not believe that it was real. Now, though, with each passing moment, more and more of Fenway Park fell silent, stunned, until the whole great place was hushed.

Alcazar realized for sure then that the man must be quite mad. He thought of the girl tennis player—what was her name?—who was stabbed on court by just such a maniac. He also decided that somewhere in Boston, police sharpshooters with rifles and telescopic sights must already be scurrying on their way to Fenway Park—and he was right, although he gave too much credit to their speed. In any event, he knew that somehow he must engage the man and keep him talking.

"I'm sorry, I don't think I know your girl," he said, as conversationally as he could.

Now the man was upon him, hardly a step away. His right hand, shaking a little, held the gun out, pointing it directly at Alcazar's head.

"She knows you," the man said. "You win the game last night, you beat the Sox, all she can talk about is how *cute* you are."

"But I don't know her."

"You will. She'll fuck you. That's for sure."

"I got my own girl," Alcazar said. He didn't really, but it seemed the wisest thing he could say. "I'm not fucking anybody else."

"Don't give me that shit. You guys get all the ass you want."

"But I don't want it."

"What's the matter—you too good for my girl?"

Uh oh, Alcazar thought: damned if I do, damned if I don't. "No, no," he hurried to say, "I'm just, you know, faithful to my own."

The man laughed at that as surely as if Alcazar had said the moon was made of cheese. His eyes were vacant and yet somehow they were aglow. Was he high on drugs? Alcazar's mind was bouncing this way and that. Was it better that the guy might be on something or better that he was simply crazy? He didn't know.

But at least, as awful and as incredible as the situation was, the surprise had faded. He was beginning to accommodate himself to his predicament, and he realized that he might not have enough time for sharpshooters to arrive or for anybody else to save him. What cop in the stands would dare risk taking the man out with a pistol? Even if some marksman shot the man dead, the jolt of the bullet hitting him might be enough to twitch the finger that touched the trigger that would discharge the gun that was pointed right at his head. Here Alcazar was, surrounded by almost forty thousand people, and yet he was, simply and completely, alone in the sights of a gun that was pointed inches from his temple.

"Well, let's get outta here," Alcazar said. "You got the gun on me. I can't get away. Let's get off the field."

The man shook his head in disbelief. "No, can't you understand, asshole? I wanna fuckin' kill you right here so Liza can see it herself."

"How will that please her? I mean if she likes me, you killing me—"

"It'll show her just because you're some fuckin' superstar don't mean shit." His hand shook a little when he said that, and Alcazar knew that he couldn't risk waiting, playing the moment out much longer. He had no choice but to somehow go for that gun—even with its barrel only inches from his head, and the finger twitching on the trigger.

Meanwhile, in the television truck, the producer was faced with an excruciating decision. It was network policy that when some fool ran on the field not to show him gamboling. Don't encourage the other idiots watching out there. But then, when the true nature of the intruder's purpose became evident, the producer was left with an impossible choice. Did he show the potentially tragic scene in right field or keep the cameras on the players and fans watching? Either way, he knew he would be second-guessed and castigated. For a few seconds he pondered. Then: "Go to Camera Three."

The assistant pushed the button. The scene in right field was on national television.

In the booth, the announcer spoke to the producer: "You can't do that, Steve. Jesus Christ, we might see Jay Alcazar murdered right before us."

"I can't pretend nothing's happening," Steve said, shaking. "But I won't come in close." That was the best compromise he could figure—a two-shot. Maybe they would call him with instructions from New York and take his ass off the hook.

The TV announcer spoke into his microphone: "Ladies and gentlemen, some maniac has come out of the stands with a gun and is apparently threatening to kill Jay Alcazar. I can't say anything more. Please, just pray for Jay." Then he fell silent and prayed himself.

In the press box, high behind home plate, the silence was preternatural. Nobody so much as pushed a computer key. Mickey Huey was the one who finally spoke. He said: "Please, God, no." Then, as if freed from the shock, others began to call out in disbelief, to offer their own desperate curses or prayers. Huey thought: "Christ Almighty, now we've got a public execution."

In fact, it was more; it became a public execution for the whole nation, as quickly, one after another, the cable news networks began to pick up the game feed. All across America, people suddenly found themselves watching in horror. At their home in Miami, Victor and Cynthia Alcazar, who had the game on, but had really only been paying attention when their son came to bat, now leaned forward in their seats, grasping hands. Cynthia began to sob, so Victor let go of her hand, reached around, and held her to him.

In Fenway Park, nobody moved except for a few parents who began to usher their children away. Here and there, people ducked their heads. Many began to cry. The security guards held their positions, of no good use.

Alcazar wasn't facing straight at the man. His body was situated so that he was still pointed more in the direction between third and home, where the rundown had taken place in what seemed like hours ago. The man, to his side, was slightly in front of him, though, so Alcazar could see him well enough without having to turn his head. And he could see that the hand appeared to be less steady all the time. It isn't easy for anyone to hold one hand straight out for any period of time—even without some heavy object in it.

"I promise you, I'll never go near Liza."

"You do know her, don't you? The bitch lied."

"No, I swear, I don't know."

"Bullshit, you just called her by her name, didn't you?"

"But that's because you said it. You said Liza."

"No, I didn't."

"Yeah, you did."

It was, of course, a perfectly foolish argument, but in whatever tiny way, it distracted the man. So, it must be now. If not quite so rationally, but all in an intellectual swirl, this is what went through Alcazar's mind: I have as fast a hand-eye coordination as anyone in the world. I can react quickly enough to hit a ball solidly that is thrown toward me at almost a hundred miles an hour from only sixty feet, six inches away. Everything I have ever been given, everything I have ever learned, prepares me for this. I can't wait. I must risk my death and act at this moment, because every moment after this can only be more dangerous for me.

And so, right then, he did act. In one motion, Alcazar ducked his head and brought his right arm around, swatting at the pistol. The shot exploded. All of Fenway Park screamed. The bullet passed by Alcazar's left shoulder and buried itself, harmlessly, into the right field turf.

In the next instant, Alcazar whirled around and grabbed for the shooting arm. It was no contest. The man barely resisted. He fell to the ground, and Alcazar easily took the gun away. Once he acted, it was over that fast. The security guards rushed up and were upon the man and held him down, punching him a couple of times for good measure.

Alcazar slumped to the ground and just sat there, seated, his arms draped over his knees, his head down between them. The other players descended on him, all of the Indians on the field running out from their positions, the pitchers in both bullpens behind him vaulting over the right-field fence, dashing to him from the rear. Then came all the other players from both teams from the dugouts. They surrounded Alcazar, but no one dared approach him until Ollie Jorgenson arrived from third base. He broke through and knelt by Alcazar. "You all right, man?"

Alcazar looked up: "Yeah, Olliekins, I'm okay now. Could I get some water, though? My throat's dry." He touched it. Only then did he lean back some, so that Jorgenson embraced him and held him for a few moments.

The crowd made a noise no one at a ball park had ever heard before. What it was, was chatter, as suddenly everybody felt the need to say something. Some people—even strangers—hugged each other. Others cried, great happy tears rolling down from their eyes. Those who had drinks suddenly remembered and took big gulps.

Up in the press box, everybody cheered and some of the writers also embraced one another. It took a long while before it occurred to some of them that they were still reporters and had to find information about the would-be assassin. Others began to look up at the television sets, waiting for them to replay the denouement. O'Reilly was sitting next to Mickey Huey. He said, "Can you believe that?"

Huey said: "I thought angels only sat on Junior's bat. Now we know he is crowned with cherubim."

Then he looked back down on the field, where the cops roughly led the man away. The gun still lay where Alcazar had plunked himself down. Gingerly, one of the officers stepped in and picked it up. Alcazar stared at it, curiously, almost with a certain awe. The cry for water had gone out, and a bat boy arrived with a bottle. Alcazar drank from it robustly, not caring how much spilled onto him. It was only then that all the players began to applaud him, and that spread to the stands and soon all of the spectators in Fenway Park joined in, and the clapping continued for minutes, as Alcazar got to his feet and began to walk slowly to the dugout, surrounded by his fellows. It was as if a convoy escorted him there.

In the dugout, all his teammates began to hug him and shake his hand and pat him on the back. One by one, the Red Sox came over, too, marching by, waving to him—or, the ones who knew him well enough, themselves jumped into the Indians' dugout and embraced him.

Wyn'amo called together all the certified Christians on both teams, and they kneeled around the pitcher's mound and gave thanks to the Lord God for Jay's deliverance. The feeling in the air was so tense, so studded with fear for what almost was and with relief that Alcazar had escaped death, that even some not-so-certified Christians joined in—so many of them out there, kneeling, praying, that it looked like a football team.

Nearby, Teddy Phillips and Gassaway, the Red Sox manager, conferred with the umpires. Luckily, the crew chief for this game was Reifschneider, who was the senior umpire in the American League. He felt very confident: "Gentleman, I don't give a rat's ass what the rules are, but I say we call it a night, and finish this tomorrow before the next game."

Gassaway looked at Phillips. "It's okay with me, Teddy."

From over where he was sitting in the dugout, Alcazar got up. He had no idea what was being decided. He called over to Reifschneider: "Hey, Doug, just gimme a couple minutes to go into the clubhouse. I wanna call my Mom and Dad."

Reifschneider said: "Don't worry, Jay, we're gonna call it and finish tomorrow."

Alcazar popped up to the dugout steps. He had a funny, crooked smile on his face. "You're what? You're gonna let that crazy sonuvabitch ruin this for everybody?"

"You mean you wanna play, Jay?"

"You bet your ass."

Reifschneider looked at the two managers. They both shrugged. "What the hell," he said.

In the clubhouse, Alcazar called his parents and assured them that he was fine. Cynthia was still crying, in that sort of gasping way where relief has only dubiously overcome fright. "You're not going to stay in the game, are you, honey?" she asked.

"Yeah, Mom, I'm fine." Then he went into a toilet stall and toweled himself off and changed his jock strap. Alcazar didn't want anybody to know he'd peed in his pants. Otherwise, he didn't seem any the worse for wear.

When he went back out to right field, he got another standing ovation. As a tribute, all the Red Sox players came out of their dugout and cheered, too, and when Reifschneider, who was umpiring at first base, started clapping as well, all the other umpires joined in. Maybe people wanted Alcazar to doff his cap, but, under the circumstances, that seemed ludicrous to him. He just bowed his head. It took a long while to settle things down.

Then, in the sixth inning, Alcazar came up to bat with one out and nobody on. Bartlett, the big left-hander, was on the mound for the Red Sox. Again, all of Fenway Park was on its feet, cheering for the visiting player—although you could sense that the fervor was already diminishing some. Anyway, Bartlett was so rattled (and so afraid he might hit Alcazar) that his first pitch bounced in the dirt about two feet wide of the plate. When Bartlett got the ball back, he just waved at the catcher to stand outside and screamed for all to hear: "I can't pitch to this guy now."

He walked Alcazar intentionally on the next three pitches, but the next two Indians went out.

It was the ninth inning when Alcazar came up again, leading off. The score was still tied at seven-all. Turcotte, the right-handed closer, had just come in. He threw as fast as anybody in the majors. Alcazar was already able to put things in perspective. He thought to himself: well, he's probably going to show me some deference, too, and he'll be scared to come inside on me. So, he set up, expecting an outside pitch. Sure enough, that's what Turcotte threw, and Alcazar went with it to left, banging a double off the Green Monster, the great, high wall there. He came around to score what turned out to be the winning run when Ollie Jorgenson singled him in. Alcazar slid across neatly, just beating the tag.

In the press box, for the first time in his professional life, Mickey Huey just put his head between his hands, bowed it and cried. He had a lot of company, though.

In the dugout, Ty Baggio announced: "Just back from the dead, is The Chief—on the all-time resurrection list, number two."

In the clubhouse afterwards Jay patiently told the story of the madman as he remembered it, recreating the dialogue and his feelings to all the media. He told just about everything very lucidly and in vivid detail, except for the fact that he had been so scared that he had peed in his pants. He was embarrassed about that and never told a soul.

MONCRIEF

HAROLD MONCRIEF WAS A TALL MAN, almost six-foot-nine. He was always calling attention to his height, just in case nobody had noticed him looming over the room like a giraffe. Constantly, he would make references to the terrible impositions that tall men had to endure—as if being tall was the equivalent of having multiple sclerosis. Howie wondered: how many times to how many people could one man bitch about the legroom on airplanes? As if everybody else was flying from Cleveland to New York in king-sized beds.

Naturally, Moncrief was always mistaken for being in basketball, and, of course, he identified himself as a former player, but in fact he hadn't been much good at that. If Moncrief hadn't been six-eight and change he wouldn't even have qualified to sit on the bench in college, recipient of a free ride and a degree in sports management. But he was a very thorough fellow and one of the first of that new breed of baseball executives who used all sorts of novel, esoteric statistics to judge players. His favorite word was "fungible." Players were fungible, interchangeable. Statistics did not lie and therefore were gospel. Baggio called him "Record Temperature."

Moncrief was not, however, very good at judging people. At the time Moncrief hired him, Howie found it ironic that after all these years of banging around baseball, he would get his main chance from someone who really didn't appreciate him. Moncrief essentially picked Howie because he was the anti-Phillips, the flip side of the incumbent who had, he believed, failed. He wanted a tough guy, yes—but he didn't want one who'd already built a reputation. Sam Hooks, Phillips' predecessor, had been hardboiled, but he'd managed two other teams and had all sorts of admirers, so there was hell to pay when Moncrief had fired him before he hired Phillips. This time, Moncrief wanted someone who would not dispute him too sharply when his statistics spoke loudly. Get him away from numbers and Moncrief wasn't that sure of himself.

He chose Howie not only because Howie was the right type, but also because Howie would be grateful.

And he'd almost hit the jackpot. Howie had nearly won the pennant his first year out of the box. But now it was his second season and it didn't seem that Alcazar was happy with Howie any longer. One game in particular had absolutely stupefied Moncrief. It had been back early in June, in Chicago. The White Sox were leading the Indians 8-4 in the last inning. Willis led off with a walk, and then the Chicago pitcher, Mercer, threw two balls to Alcazar. The second one was even in the dirt.

Now, if ever there was a pitch for Alcazar to hit, here it was. Mercer absolutely had to get the ball over the plate this time. But Howie told Frosty Westerfield to give the third-base coach the take sign. Alcazar glanced down to third and, with surprise, saw that he was supposed to leave the bat on his shoulder on a two-oh pitch. If you couldn't see the disgust on his face, his body language showed it to the world. And sure enough, Mercer threw the next pitch right down the pike, as Alcazar had to watch it go by.

Westerfield said: "He coulda hit that sumbitch a country mile."

Howie answered: "Yeah, that's what I was afraid of."

Westerfield said: "What?"

Howie replied: "I'll tell you later."

Mercer couldn't steer another pitch over the plate, and Alcazar walked. Two men on, nobody out. Unfortunately, though, the White Sox brought in another reliever, Frenchie Dufour, and the fat little Canuck got Jorgenson to hit into a double play. When Alcazar dusted himself off after sliding into second and came back into the dugout, he sneered at Howie. And then, right away, the next man popped out, so the Indians lost.

After the game, Howie called Westerfield and Alcazar into his office, and this is what he said: "Look, I've seen a lotta games like that. The last inning, my team's down four, five runs, and we get a man on, and the next guy hits a home run. And then what, there's nobody on base, and we gotta start all over. It's like all the air goes out."

"Howie," Westerfield said, "if Jay hits the ball outta

here, it's 8-6. You gonna tell me 8-4 with two men on is better than 8-6?"

"Yeah," Alcazar chimed in.

"Yeah, as a matter of fact, I am," Howie said. "In the circumstances. There's nobody on base, it doesn't feel like a rally. It just feels different. You need for a rally to build. I seen it a hundred times. I've *felt* it."

Alcazar just shook his head. "You're outta your fuckin' mind, Howie," he said, and he and Westerfield gave each other a look. *Can you believe this shit?*

But the funny thing was, when Alcazar had a beer with Baggio after the game, and he repeated what nonsense Howie had told him, the old pitcher said, "You won't believe this, Jay, but I was sitting there when you were up, and I was thinking: 'I hope he doesn't hit one here.'"

"No shit," said Alcazar.

"No shit," said Baggio. "And it's so crazy, I really didn't quite know why I thought that, but now I know. Howie's right, Jay. Sometimes the *mood* makes more of a difference than the score. It's nutty, but Howie's right. He's got the instinct. It's just that nobody else would have the balls to admit a goofy thing like that."

Alcazar said: "Well, I guess I gotta play another couple thousand games to understand."

"Somethin' like that, Jay. It's osmosis. It's like global warming."

But, of course, when Westerfield told Moncrief that Howie actually didn't want Alcazar to hit a home run, Moncrief thought his manager must be certified. Where in the holy book of statistics was anything to explain that? Besides, you don't want to do anything to upset The Chief—especially since Alcazar was going to be a free agent after the season. So Howie, like a statistical player, was fungible too, all the more so as the season proceeded, unattractively.

And now Moncrief had arrived in Baltimore. "Don't sweet-talk me, Harold," Howie said as soon as Moncrief got to his room. "I was gone, right? You had Diaz all warmed up in the bullpen. This is the day I was supposed to get fired."

Moncrief was already lounging on the sofa in Howie's suite, his long legs stretching out forever. "This is no time to talk about that, Howie. We got enough to concern ourselves with. Jesus." He unstretched himself and went over to the mini bar and pulled out a Scotch miniature. "I'm sorry, I gotta have a drink. You wanna drink?"

"I got a game to manage tonight."

"I never drink in the day," Moncrief said, pouring the Johnny Walker over some ice cubes. "Either Mark Twain or Will Rogers or Ben Franklin, one of 'em, said: never accept a drink during the day or turn one down at night. Well, every now and then my watch breaks."

"Believe me, I'd like to have one with you, but then I'd like four more. You ever smoke, Harold?"

"Nah, I didn't want to stunt my growth."

They both laughed. A little. They were trying the best they could. "Well, I smoked. I haven't smoked in fifteen, twenty years, but I'd like a smoke right now, too."

Moncrief flopped back down on the couch. "So where's the lawyer?"

"Flint's in touch with him. He said he'd be by to see you when he could. He's trying to find out about the woman's medical exam."

"Christ, can you believe this?"

Howie said: "I asked, were you gonna fire me?"

"And I said, this is no time to discuss that."

Howie crossed his arms and said: "Yeah it is. Because I've been altogether embarrassed these last few days."

"Hey, Howie, you're a manager. It goes with the job."

"Fine. And I played the good soldier. But once this crap with Alcazar blows over, I don't wanna go right back on the hot seat."

Moncrief sat up. "What did I tell you on the phone this morning? What did I tell you? I told you the job was yours for the rest of the season."

"And then you're gonna fire me?"

Moncrief tossed back the rest of his Scotch. "Well, probably, Howie. You're obviously just not working with Jay, and, you know, he's a free agent after the season."

"If we make the playoffs?"

"If we make the playoffs, what?"

"Then I want another year."

"I can't promise you that."

"Then I can't promise you I'm gonna stay around and every day have to listen to how I'm gone. I'm too proud for that."

"Come on, Howie, I gave you a chance."

"And I appreciate that. I altogether do. But if I'm gonna be a good soldier, I want your word that I'll get the shot for another season." Quickly then: "Harold, if we win, Harold. Christ, what are the chances? We're eight games out of the wild card and there's only forty to play. And now we got Jay with his tit in a ringer. What's your gamble? We keep losing, you got my promise to stay around through the rest of the season and keep the lid on things. We win, everybody goes home happy. Then, hey, you can't fire a guy who holds the team together through a thing like this and comes back from eight games down."

"Well…" Moncrief said, because he didn't know what to say.

"Give me your word."

Moncrief rubbed his chin. "Oh, what the fuck," he said.

"That isn't exactly how I woulda wanted it put, but I'll take that as your word."

Moncrief nodded, grudgingly.

Finally then, Howie leaned back in his chair. "All right, now I'm gonna give you some good advice."

"What's that?"

"If we don't make the playoffs, and we probably don't, and I'm dead meat, don't hire Diaz to replace me."

Moncrief was offended. "You're not telling me who to hire to manage this team."

"Hey, Harold, this is like me talking from the grave. You'd be wise to listen to me."

"Why?"

"Why? Because I know this sounds old-fashioned, but this is my team right now, and just because I'm gonna get axed, doesn't mean I won't still care about this team. And I'm tellin' ya, the altogether worst thing you can do is hire Nino Diaz."

"He's a good baseball man."

"Don't play that song to me. You and me and the whole world know that you're hiring Nino because he managed Alcazar in the minors and they got along, and Jay's Latino, so you'll give him a Latino manager."

"Obviously, Howie, yeah, we wanna keep the best player on the team happy. For Christ's sweet sake, figure it out. It's like the goddamn stewardesses."

"What stewardesses?"

"What stewardesses? The ones on airplanes."

It was a small thing, and she was far away in the East Bay, but Howie had to stick up for Margo's former profession. "They're not stewardesses anymore. They're flight attendants."

"Well, kiss my ass." Moncrief sucked the ice cubes in the glass where the Scotch had been.

"All right," Howie said, "so, what about the flight attendants?"

"Every time. I swear, every fucking time I get on an airplane, the top of the door is like this." He took his palm, made it flat-out, level to the ground, and held it away from his upper lip. "Here. I am looking right at the top of the door, the plane."

"Yeah?"

"And you know what they say, the stewardesses? They say"—Moncrief went to falsetto: "'Watch your head.' What the fuck, Howie? The goddamn top of the door is right in front of my eyes, and I gotta be told to watch my head? Jesus."

"So?"

"So what?"

"So what's this gotta do with Jay?"

"It's like I said. As tall as I am, I don't have to be told to watch my head when the door is right in front of my head. And I don't have to be told to keep my best player happy. I don't have to be told that."

"Well, hiring Diaz is *not* how to keep him happy. That's what I'm tellin' you. You don't know how Jay thinks, because I'll bet you dollars to doughnuts that you hire Diaz, and Alcazar will stick that right up your ass." Moncrief's head flipped back like he was whiplashed. "Because you don't know how Jay thinks."

"And you do?"

"No, maybe nobody knows how Jay thinks, including maybe Jay, but you hire Diaz, you hire the Hispanic, I'll tell you: Jay will think you're patronizing him." Howie shrugged. "Which of course, you are."

"Aw, come on."

"I'm just telling you. The message you're sending is that Jay Alcazar is a prima donna who can only play his best for another *hermano,* another Latino. And that's gonna piss him off somethin' terrible, and he'll sign someplace else."

Moncrief chewed on another ice cube. "Well, this is something to think about," he said.

Howie went on: "I'll tell you something else. If I'd told you this a week ago, you'd just think I was saying it to save my ass, but I don't rub Jay all that wrong. That's just newspaper talk, because it's the simplest conclusion. Understand, he's not crazy about me. He suffers me. That's what most big stars do. They suffer the manager. Jay suffered Sam. He suffered Teddy. You put Frosty in there for me tomorrow, he'll suffer

Frosty. It's got nothing to do with personalities. It's just the nature of the beast." He pointed a finger at Moncrief. "You know what Casey Stengel said?"

The general manager shook his head. He knew numbers that seemed to add up much better than words that people tried to clarify things with.

"Old Case said that 'The secret to managing is to keep the five guys who hate you away from the five who haven't made up their minds.' Look, I gotta be some kinda complete fool to make it so's a guy like Alcazar hates me. He plays every day. I kiss his ass in the newspapers. The guys who hate me are Hernandez and Dickerson and Willard and Miranda, because I sit their asses on the bench most of the time, and they all think they're Babe Ruth. All the experts—excuse me, all the jack-offs who *think* they're experts—they think that managers spend all their time worrying about the big stars. If you got a brain in your head, you'd know it's the other way 'round. It's the guys who don't play regularly, who are upset and insecure—those are the ones I spend all my time on. Because every now and then you need them, and you want them to come through for you."

Moncrief was listening now. With all his years in baseball, that had never occurred to him before. The numbers-*cum*-players he had on all his spreadsheets didn't have normal human reactions, fears, and complexes. Now all of a sudden he was hearing about a very un-numerical, un-statistical situation, and he found himself not only listening to old Howie, but paying attention to him. Moncrief was smart enough to understand that Howie knew he didn't have anything to lose now, so he'd be wise to hear him out. Had there been a single other person in the whole Cleveland organization who'd told him that hiring Nino Diaz to manage the team to please Alcazar would really piss him off? Anybody at all?

Howie went on: "Whatever Alcazar's problems are, trust me, it has nothing to do with yours truly. And he's not in a slump. A guy doesn't hit a couple games: hey, right away we say he's in a slump. What the hell is a slump? Anybody ever say you were in a slump, Harold? Or some guy selling insurance? Or some guy working in a hardware store? Hey, Joe Schmo, you didn't sell enough hammers this month, so you're in a slump. Nobody says that. Jay Alcazar isn't in any slump. There's just something altogether happened to him."

Moncrief sat up at that. "Whatdya mean: 'Happened to him?'"

"I mean, nothing to do with baseball. He's a different guy showed up this season. Something happened to him over the winter. Jay's changed. And I don't know whether it's permanent or not. But I know something happened that changed him. Lemme tell you, what happened here to him last night—that wouldn't've happened to Jay last year."

Moncrief mulled that over. "You make it sound like you really think he did rape the woman."

Howie wished he hadn't said that, but he also knew he couldn't take it back. "No, I'm just saying, nothing like this would've happened to him last year."

THE EYEWITNESS

HOWIE'S PHONE RANG. It was Warren Mundy, downstairs in the lobby. He came right up to meet Moncrief. Howie asked him if he wanted a drink from the minibar.

Mundy said: "H.L. Mencken was our wisest Baltimorean. One thing he said was: 'Never accept a drink during the day or turn one down at night.'"

Howie smiled over at Moncrief. Will Rogers? Mark Twain? Confucius? He didn't know pundits any better than he did ballplayers. "Well, would you like a Coke?" he asked Mundy.

"Sure."

"Diet or regular?"

"Regular," said Mundy. "I watch my weight, and I notice only fat people drink Diet Coke."

Howie gave a little laugh, but Moncrief either didn't get it or thought it was inappropriate to make jokes at a time like this. Anyway, Mundy brought Moncrief up to speed on the situation and then said: "All right, I've also got some new news, and, generally,

I'd say it's pretty good. They've examined the woman. There's no vaginal damage whatsoever. Nothing torn, no bleeding."

"That is good news," Moncrief said.

"Unfortunately, there's a slight new bruise on her left wrist." Mundy held up his own right wrist and encircled it with his right thumb and middle finger. "Right here. Right where, well, where you would grab someone if you wanted to grab them. It's consistent with that. But it also could be a bruise you got for knocking your wrist against a door knob. Anything."

"Good," said Moncrief.

"Maybe. Maybe not," Mundy said. "And there's a little cut right here." He pointed to his cheek. "Just a speck, hardly see it. I'm not even sure she knew it was there. But it's exactly where"—he put one of his hands over his mouth for a moment—" exactly where your fingernail might scratch someone if you're trying to put your hand over somebody's mouth to keep her from screaming. Of course, also: a little scratch like that—a million things."

Mundy reached under his seersucker suit jacket and played with his suspenders, as if he were addressing a court. Moncrief said: "So, how's that add up?"

"Well, if you're making a case against Alcazar, that's a tough sell. Absent any other supporting evidence, a very tough sell."

Moncrief beamed. Howie's expression didn't change.

"But if I were the woman's lawyer, I would then bring a civil suit. I would say it was apparent that Mr. Alcazar grabbed her—manhandled her. She tried to scream and he muzzled her. Manhandled, your honor, muzzled. Will the court please look at these pictures that clearly show, et cetera, et cetera. Well, counselor, why did no one hear a ruckus? Because, your honor, Mr. Alcazar is six-feet-two, two-hundred, and what—"

"Two-ten, two-fifteen," Howie said.

"Two hundred-ten, two-fifteen pounds, he had been drinking, he was violent, and my petite client—"

"Is she petite?" Moncrief asked.

"She would be downright dainty if I was representing her. My petite, dainty, very fragile client was scared out of her wits in the presence of this lustful monster, she did not wish to anger Mr. Alcazar any more lest he brutalize her, and so she wisely kept quiet after he removed his hand from her mouth and reluctantly submitted her trembling self to his savage assault."

Mundy took a big gulp of the Coke, and returned to speaking in an everyday voice. "Listen, she's a mature woman who's obviously sexually active. As horrible as being raped is, at a certain point there's something to be said for accepting the lesser of two evils. She knows the guy isn't going to kill her. He's not some scumbag who's dragged her into an alley and can give her AIDS. So, if it please the court, she just gritted her teeth and let him get off. That's not unusual in a date-rape kinda case."

Moncrief nodded, pursing his lips in that way to suggest he'd already figured that out. Howie, though, shifted slightly away from Mundy, ducking his head. Mundy continued:

"And remember, she'd had wine, some drinks, so presumably she was more relaxed than she might normally be. So, you're her lawyer, you take the scratch mark on her cheek, the bruised wrist, you account for the lack of any vaginal injury with that argument, you make Mr. Alcazar into a celebrity brute who thinks he's entitled just because the lady came to his room to enjoy an adult beverage, and you seek damages in civil court."

"What would you do?" Moncrief asked.

"You mean, what would I advise your player?" Moncrief nodded. "Well, the lady seems formidable. She's no dummy. And usually, when injured parties—alleged injured parties—are no dummies, they get a good lawyer. Witness who Alcazar hired, Mr. Moncrief. It might very well be that I would advise Mr. Alcazar to pay her off, seal the records, and get on with it. Sometimes you just get a fucking when you…get a fucking. Especially when you make, what, fifteen, twenty million dollars a year.

"But," Mundy went on, "that'll be his call. Anyway, it'll take awhile before my dear friends in the Baltimore Police Department acknowledge what I think they already know, that they've got no criminal case. But they don't want every feminist and every gadfly screaming that they didn't do their job because it's a celebrity, so they'll have the rape unit go over every angle. And again, and again. Jerk-off stuff."

He paused. His cell phone was ringing. It rang with the tune to "Maryland, My Maryland," better known in other precincts as "O Tannenbaum." "Hello, Shelley, what's cookin'?"

Right away, Mundy's rather blithe expression changed. "Jesus," he said at last. "Give me that one more time." And: "Where did you get that?" And finally: "That's the horse's mouth, all right."

As soon as he flipped his phone shut, Moncrief said: "That didn't sound good."

"No, we've got a wrinkle."

"What kinda wrinkle?" Moncrief asked.

"Well, a would-be wrinkle. The woman claims that when she rejected Mr. Alcazar's advances and he rejected the rejection, she tried to get away, and he grabbed her and pulled her back. Unfortunately—so she maintains, you understand—she had managed to get to the door and pull it open. And some man was there, in the hall, and saw her before Alcazar slammed it shut."

Howie cast his eyes down and shuffled his feet.

"Who's the man?" Moncrief asked.

"Don't know. But it shouldn't take much to tell if she's bullshitting. Presumably, the only men who could come by Alcazar's room would be other guests on that end of the corridor. They've already interviewed some, but, of course, some of the others had already checked out. They've gotta catch up with them outta town."

"How'd you find this out so fast?" Moncrief asked.

"It's not that big a town, Baltimore, and I've been here all my life," Mundy said. "Besides, people just like to pass stuff along." He reached under his jacket and pulled at his suspenders again. "Okay, maybe it's a wrinkle. But I wouldn't worry too much. It sounds like she's just trying to put the pressure on. A guy walking down the hall sees a woman almost getting raped, he might not be a hero, but he's at least gonna call security. So how do you figure?"

"Yeah, right," said Moncrief.

Howie looked up then, and for just an instant he saw Mundy eyeing him. He remembered, then, that he had mentioned to the lawyer this morning that he had walked past Alcazar's room on the way out of his own. A curious man would have asked him if that wasn't what he'd said this morning, but, of course, Warren Mundy was Jay Alcazar's lawyer, and therefore he wouldn't be too curious about some things.

Their eyes fell off one another, though, and then Howie had to look away.

BEING AWAY

THE REASON SUZIE COULD NEVER make Howie feel guilty about being away so much of the time, working at baseball, was because he knew he was doing the best he could for his family. Or, from another point of view: he didn't believe he could do anything else. He had left Wichita State after his sophomore year, and while, of course, he had always planned to go back in the fall semesters until he earned his degree, that scheme, for all his best intentions, soon fell between the cracks. There was, after all, no money in minor-league baseball. In Howie's whole playing career he only once made more than a thousand dollars in any one month, and he attained that lofty plateau only that one time he made it up to the Tigers for a few games, the eleven at bats, the one glorious line-drive single off Dave McNally.

So, in the off-season, instead of school, he was forced to find what work he could—clerking in stores, helping a friend in the trades, driving a school bus, all the extra

Christmas jobs. After awhile, after he married Suzie and especially after they had Lindsay and then Davey, she would always plead with him once the season was over to give up baseball, take a real job and night classes. Their biggest fights came over money and his playing baseball, which were, essentially, one in the same, because there was no money in baseball.

Unfortunately, Howie was cursed by that worst of professional maladies, the ill fortune of almost. He was nearly good enough, so that he always was teased to try one more season. Jesus H. Christ! Howie Traveler was no idiot; he knew himself: short-legged, right-handed-hitting outfielder without power. Not even the Japanese leagues wanted to import that package. But Suzie didn't understand those prejudices, so Howie would impress her with his statistics. *I hit .312 this year. They need an extra outfielder in Detroit. They gotta take me up next spring.* But in his heart he knew they didn't and they wouldn't. Only he couldn't give it up, because he loved it so much and because it was all he knew.

The fact is, Howie was scared when he was away from baseball, and so when the chance came to manage in the Braves organization shortly after his thirty-first birthday, he took the job. There was a little more money in that, even if it was way down the chain, in A ball. More important, the dream was revived. It didn't matter if you were right-handed, lacking power, as a manager. Howie *noticed;* he could think his way to the big leagues.

"The kids trust me, honey," he told Suzie after that first season, with as much pride as surprise in his voice. "They listen to me." It even felt better than hitting .312 in Triple A. He had thought the players would take to him because he had seen how, as he got older as a player, the younger kids did look up to him. But it was the sort of thing you couldn't be sure of till you were tested. And he passed. They did trust him and they did listen to him. And most important: even when he disciplined a player, he saw that they didn't resent him for long. Tough, but fair: that was the identity Howie Traveler developed—which is the best one any coach in any sport can hope for.

He also had that instinct that only good coaches have, which is that you say that you treat everybody on the team the same and pretend to hold to that fiction, but, in fact, you actually treat everybody quite a bit different. The lesser talented a player was, the more you encouraged him; the better he was, the more you demanded of him. The guy who had a thick skin you made into a whipping boy. It wasn't fair, but that type could take it, and it put the fear of God in the others. Howie was always toughest on the number-one draft choices, who came in with big bonuses and big reputations. He rode them. The other players loved that, and when the top draft choices complained, he told them he held them to a higher standard. And they bought it, most of them. The ones that didn't were going to wash out anyhow, and you might as well find out early on that they were mushy so you could tell the organization to write off its mistake.

He moved up to Double-A; left the Braves because he got a better opportunity and more money from the Yankees. It was all so different when he had been a player who just filled in and got passed along, for now, as a manager, he was a prospect himself, no less than the big-ticket draft choices were as players. The Yankees paid him extra to go down to Florida after the season and coach in the rookie league. It meant that much time away from his own two kids when they were growing up, starting new school years, but, after all, Howie had always been an organization man, no matter what organization he was in at the time. Finally, in fact, he and Suzie had enough to buy their own little house. They bought in a tract west of St. Louis, because that's where her parents lived. He felt more comfortable about Suzie after that. She had her mom to help with the kids. She was also close to her brother's wife, Grace. When Suzie would come to visit him during the season, she seemed more relaxed. Also, she could better believe him this time when he told her he was going up someday, that he was going to make the majors as a manager.

In fact, when the Arizona Diamondbacks came into existence as an expansion team, Howie applied for the job as manager of their Triple-A team in Tucson, and he got it. He was back in Triple A. The inside baseball magazines began to mention him as a smart baseball "mind." It didn't pan out, but there were even feelers from a couple new major-league managers about bringing Howie up as one of their coaches. But he did get the job managing Santurce, in the Puerto Rican League, in the winter. It meant being away from the kids almost that whole year, even just getting home for Christmas Eve and Christmas and flying back to Puerto Rico that night, but what a plum it was, actually managing a few big-league ballplayers.

Howie began to achieve a good reputation, too, for getting along with minorities. It was different now than when he came up as a player, when it was basically just the whites and the blacks. Now, there were all these different kinds of Hispanics, as well as the whites and the blacks. He caught onto something fast. "It's interesting, Sooz," he'd told his wife when she came to stay a few days with him in Norwich, Connecticut one summer. "The white guys and the black guys are closer now than when I was playing. It's like they see themselves more the same."

"Why?"

"Because they talk the same. They're different from all the Hispanics, and the more Hispanics come in, the more the white Americans and the black Americans connect. It's culture. The inner-city blacks don't play baseball much anymore. They just play basketball. So the black guys have backgrounds more like the white guys. Suburbs, maybe some college. You gotta know this stuff."

If anything, he was just as good with the Hispanics. He caught onto the Puerto Rican-Dominican rift early. He began to pick up a little Spanish and one off-season, when he went home, he took night Spanish classes at the community college. It was the first course he'd finished since he left Wichita State. And then the two winters in Santurce made him nearly legitimately bilingual. He'd plead poor-mouth, *muy poco Espanol,* but, in fact, he could make himself clear. Also, and just as important, he could pick up what the Spanish boys were jabbering about when they might be jabbering about yours truly.

In a way, he began to see himself as a minority, for in baseball he had been put upon, discriminated against. When he was managing Tucson, a Mexican kid named Reuben Tavares, who was one of the Diamondbacks' top prospects, a big, left-handed reliever with a heavy fastball, started to piss and moan all the time about how difficult life was for him in the States, how much prejudice he faced.

Howie told the pitching coach, Nick Waxter, to stop kissing Tavares' ass, and he brought the pitcher into his office and screamed at him in his best Spanish to cut out the bitching, that he had everything going for him, that he, Howie, had been discriminated against all his playing life in baseball. "I've been the nigger, Reuben, I've been the wetback."

Tavares wanted to clock Howie, but the manager didn't back down, he stood up to his big pitcher, and told him to stop being a baby and be grateful that the organization prized him so. Tavares was in the majors by the end of the season and told everybody that not only was Howie Traveler the best manager he'd ever had, but he was the main reason he'd gotten it together and added a foot to his fast ball and made the Diamondbacks.

Suzie never really stopped loving Howie—or he her, for that matter. She began to hate baseball, though. It wasn't that he loved it more than her, which she accepted, but it was the mystique of it. Other men loved their work. Her brother, for example, was a high-school mathematics teacher who never made any money but just adored teaching children. Suzie could understand that. But baseball was

like some mysterious island, where the baseball people disappeared. Oh, she learned the game well
enough. She could keep score and understood things
like on-base percentage and passed balls and inside
clichés like "can of corn" and "on the black." But the
game swallowed her husband up.

Actually, as much as Howie felt guilty that he loved
baseball so, Suzie felt guilty that, at times, she wanted
him to fail. Because then he would be forced to do
something else, and then he'd be home. She had very
mixed emotions when he started managing and
appeared to do well. *Here we go again,* she thought.
He—the game—had led them so far down the garden
path as a player, that she naturally assumed it was
going to happen all over again. But she bit her lip and
held those thoughts to herself. Probably, the marriage
was over then and there, for she simply did not believe
in him anymore.

When they did argue, though, it would be about
Davey. Suzie would say things like: Davey needs you
around more, Davey misses you, when, of course, she
really meant that she wanted him there for herself.
But, then, Davey surely did need his father. It was
always the greatest irony that Davey Traveler, the son
of the baseball player, Howie Traveler, never really got
to play baseball with his father. The other fathers
would play catch with their boys after work, even
coach Little League, but, of course, Howie was away
with real players. The shoemaker's son had no shoes.
Soon, Davey rejected baseball. Maybe he wouldn't
have been any good anyway (Howie consoled himself
with that thought), but there was no doubt that he gave

up baseball so early on because it was a way of sticking it to his father. Actually, he was not a bad athlete.

Davey, though, liked motors, engines—things in which Howie had no interest whatsoever. The boy flew model airplanes and read drag-racing magazines, knew the names of more NASCAR drivers than big-league ballplayers. He fiddled around with the family cars, souping them up some, and pined away the days till he would be sixteen and could get his driver's license. "I've got the money for a car saved up," he told his father as that blessed day approached.

"It's the insurance that costs," Howie explained to him. Davey said he understood that, and was going to help pay for it with a job he had been promised, working with guys he had gotten to know over at the Shell station. "Grease monkeys," Howie thought. "Guys with gasoline assholes."

He and Davey didn't have anything more to talk about, because Howie didn't know anything about cars and Davey didn't care anything about baseball. Of course, Howie told Suzie: "It's a good thing Davey isn't into baseball, because then he would just be competitive with me. Boys should do what they love, and not what their father wants them to do."

"Didn't you want him to be a baseball player, though?"

"Only if he was left-handed," Howie replied, chuckling. But Suzie was sure he was lying, that he had always dreamed that his boy would play ball.

Lindsay, who was two years older, was much closer to her father. It wasn't just the Daddy's Girl stuff, either. Early on, he simply found that they got along well. She was always so grown-up—probably because Howie was away so much and she, the oldest, had to help her mother more—but Howie caught on quickly that she was much the smartest in the family. She was pretty, too, and although she took more after Howie, she got all the best of his looks. Above all, thank God, she didn't get his short legs. In fact, Lindsay had long, lithe legs; she was cut high. The only thing he didn't like about her was that she kept her hair short. He was always after her to let her hair grow, so much so that Suzie would break in, and say, "For God's sake, Howie, leave her alone, her hair looks great."

But Lindsay didn't mind. She just seemed to understand that Howie liked long hair on women. Besides, Lindsay could give it right back to her father. Even when she was just a kid, she would tease him about what dopes most ballplayers were. "Come on, some of 'em are very bright," Howie would say, taking the bait. "I had a guy from Yale at Norwich."

"But they're all still children, Daddy."

"Well, that's true, sweetie. That's another thing altogether."

"Your father's still a child, too," Suzie put in.

Howie just shrugged. Perhaps he knew that when he was away and Suzie would complain about him and baseball, Lindsay would stick up for her old man. Curiously, even about girl things, like boyfriends, Lindsay would confide in her father.

The lines at the Travelers were never drawn—nothing dramatic like that—but the fact was that Suzie and Davey were pretty much aligned on one side, and Howie and Lindsay on the other. Certainly, though, nobody ever talked about it. It was not a troubled family, surely not, to use the preferred word, *dysfunctional*. There was no hate, no real anger. It was just that Howie kept chasing after what he loved, but he failed, and then when he was finished as a player he set up another chase with the same target. The major leagues. The bigs. The show.

Life revolved around excuses. Why Howie wasn't good enough. Why he couldn't quit. Why he had to be away. And deep inside everyone, even Lindsay, had doubts that he would ever win the chase. And the better Howie got at managing a baseball team, the more he shied away from trying to manage his family, because that was harder and because that wasn't fun or satisfying the way baseball could be.

REACHING HOWIE

THE PHONE RANG JUST AS Howie was getting back into his apartment. He didn't know that the phone had been ringing off and on for hours. He hadn't bothered to get a phone machine. "Howie, it's Sam. We've been trying to reach you." Sam was Suzie's brother, the high-school teacher.

"We've been in Mayaquez and just got back," Howie said.

"The schedule said you were off."

Quickly, Howie said: "It was a makeup game." This was pure bullshit. The schedule was right. It was an off-day. It was just that after the game the night before, he had gone out with a tourist he had met three days ago from Providence named Harmony, and they had spent the night in her hotel room at the El San Juan.

Jesus, Howie thought, *the one time I get a strange piece of ass, they're trying to reach me from home.* He was, in fact, so intent on getting his story straight that he did not stop to think: well, why would they be trying to reach me? He did not hear the clutch in Sam's throat.

Sam said: "I'll put Suzie on."

Only then did Howie think: why is Sam at our house when it's Tuesday morning and he should be at school, teaching?

Suzie came on, but she was hardly cogent, she was crying so. Howie could make out: "Where the hell have you been?" but after that, and after he tried to explain about the makeup game being in Mayaquez, he couldn't comprehend anything she was saying except for Davey's name. And so he understood that something had happened to Davey even before Lindsay took the phone and in a clear, controlled voice, said: "Daddy, Davey's had a bad accident."

Howie sat down on the couch there. "What kind of accident?"

"A motorcycle accident."

"Davey doesn't have a motorcycle."

"He took it from the Shell station, where—"

"Who would let him take a motorcycle?"

"Daddy," Lindsay said, raising her voice. "Daddy, it doesn't matter why. Davey is hurt, bad."

"How bad?" He was starting to comprehend now.

"Very bad, Daddy. He's in a coma, and—" And then even Lindsay, strong, stable, grown-up Lindsay, began to cry, and Sam got back on the phone and explained the full situation, which was that Howie's only son and heir was brain dead.

They didn't pull the plug till Howie was able to get back to St. Louis, late that night. Really, too, it was no consolation to see Davey one more time, because his face was all scratched and blown up, and there was a bandage over one eye and most of that whole side of the boy's face. He was still only sixteen; he'd only had his driver's license for three months, when he snuck the cycle out. He spun out and crashed only four blocks from the Shell station, a half-mile from home.

But after Howie had sat with the boy for awhile and kissed him, Suzie and Lindsay came in, and they all hugged one another, and then they went out and told the doctor that they should end his life support and pass on his organs to somebody else. Howie said: "I just don't wanna hear anybody say: 'Davey woulda wanted it that way.'"

"Well, he woulda, Daddy."

He pulled Lindsay to him and hugged her, while he kept hold of Suzie's hand. "I mean, I know he woulda, sweetie, but he wanted to live. That's what he really wanted."

Mercifully, nobody asked him anymore why they weren't able to get hold of him in Puerto Rico. Probably nobody had believed him, and Howie understood that, and what did it even matter? There was just too much sadness. Suzie filed it away, but, of course, all anybody wanted to talk about was Davey. Howie knew it would be best for him if he could go back to Puerto Rico after a few days to try and put his mind back to baseball, but he stayed with Suzie, to help her. Lindsay went back to college. She was a freshman. "Do the best you can," Howie said.

He and Suzie did their best, too, but one time Howie began to express guilt, that maybe if he hadn't been away, if he'd been home like most fathers, then—.

Suzie interrupted. "Please, Howie. It doesn't make any difference. If you had been sitting at home every day, Davey still woulda been at the station, and he woulda taken that damn thing out, and nothing would have been any different."

But Howie didn't want to be convinced. He wanted to blame himself. "Maybe if I hadda been here, he wouldn't've taken the bike out because he would've been scared if I found out." Suzie just walked away. But, Howie thought, maybe if he'd gotten out of baseball when he couldn't get past Triple A, then he and Davey could've played baseball together, done more father-son stuff, and Davey would've never even gotten into engines and cars and motorcycles and hung out with the guys with gasoline assholes. Howie needed to find some guilt, because the fact of the matter was that he was shacked up with a woman who wasn't Davey's mother in a room at the El San Juan Hotel when Davey spun out and landed on the pavement, brain dead.

Even after he and Susie divorced, a few years later, Howie would always make it a point to get back to St. Louis, just to visit Davey's grave. Religiously, he always made it at least once a year. It would've been more if he'd ever gotten a job in the National League, so that he'd've come in to play the Cardinals, but that never happened. So, he would find a day to fly in, rent a car and go to the cemetery, or, once, when he got the bench job with Seattle, he drove all the way down from Chicago on a day off.

Flying or driving, it was a long way to go, just to stand at a grave. But he certainly wasn't going to see

Suzie and her new husband, or her folks, or Sam and Grace, the old in-laws. There wasn't anybody in St. Louis for him to visit with anymore except for his boy, dead in the ground. What Howie started to do then is he would at least take the time to police the cemetery. It wasn't a terribly large one. So, he would walk all about, picking up any trash or any dead flowers, or, at the veterans' graves, sticking back American flags that had fallen over. He also took it upon himself to make sure the place didn't get junky.

Howie was perfectly amazed with some of the crap people would put on graves. Not just flags or flowers. They were okay. But all sorts of tacky mementoes. People would, for example, leave little teddy bears. For Chrissake, teddy bears are not to be left outside. Some people put up little Christmas trees and never took them down. Once, late in July, he found a big, fat Easter bunny and a whole bunch of plastic eggs scattered about the grave of a grown man. People would sometimes leave notes weighted down with a rock, but then in the rain, the ink would run and then it would end up just so much litter. He never told anybody, but Howie would just pick up the stuff he didn't like and put it in his rented car and throw it away when he got back to Avis. He thought that was the least he could do for Davey. He thought that was something that Davey would have wanted. Anyway, he wanted Davey's graveyard to be as clean and well-kept as a baseball diamond. That was what he thought somewhere in the back of his mind.

THE SUNDAY NIGHT GAME

Perhaps because the seasons of his baseball life had been fraught with so little strife, Alcazar was not a player used to dealing with personal anxiety upon the field. But when he reached Camden Yards this evening, his heart was racing. He did not want to deal with people. He did not want to look at people or have people look at him. Gratefully, he sequestered himself in the manager's office that Howie had handed over to him, and when Ollie Jorgenson came to fetch him for batting practice, Jay stayed in Jorgenson's wake, proceeded directly to the bat rack, picked up his lumber, stepped into the cage, took his licks, ran some by himself in the most distant reaches of the outfield, and then retreated again to his new sanctuary.

Wyn'amo came by and said he was praying for him. Jay thanked him. Moncrief felt he should drop in on Alcazar, too, show him personally that he and the whole Cleveland organization were fully in support. Alcazar appreciated that gesture, too, but then Moncrief took all the grace out of the atmosphere when he spotted a mirror on the wall, and went over to comb his hair and then spent the next five minutes boring Jay with tales of all the mirrors, in men's rooms all over the world, that were placed too low for him to effectively view his noggin. Another minute of Moncrief whining and Alcazar would have declared for free agency on the spot. Then, a few minutes later, after Moncrief had departed, Howie knocked on the door and stuck his head in. All he said was: "Jay, you still wanna play, Jay? No one would blame you if you didn't."

"Fuckin' A I wanna play," Alcazar said, but with such evident false bravado that Howie paused for a moment, thinking maybe he should try and talk him out of it. But he didn't. Better than Alcazar right now, Howie could separate his mind, put the events of last night—what he saw as the door opened and closed— aside from his thoughts of baseball. And now Howie thought only of the game. Jay Alcazar was his best player, and much of what success Howie had enjoyed with the Indians was due to him. He would not desert him now—not on the field of play.

On the other hand, as he closed the door, he could not help thinking how rattled Alcazar was. The man—the player—had always seemed so impenetrable, so oblivious to outside influence, that it could not help but surprise Howie how downright human Alcazar seemed now. He thought for a moment and then knocked on the door again and entered. Alcazar looked up. "You wanna hear a good joke, Jay?"

"You're humoring me?"

"Well, distracting you."

"Okay."

Howie came over to him. "There's this guy," he began, "that the Indians catch—"

"Us?"

"No, no, no, not us Indians, the real Indians, the ones they call Native Americans—Cherokees, Apaches, what-have-you."

"Oh, okay."

"So these Indians, they're gonna, you know, scalp him. But the chief says: 'White man can have one wish.' And the guy says, "Well, okay, I'd like to talk to my horse." This seems kinda strange to the Indians, but, you know, it's the guy's last wish, so they let him, and as soon as he talks to his horse, the horse turns around and gallops off like a sonuvabitch. Now the Indians are curious, and so they wait, and pretty soon, here comes the horse back with a beautiful blonde on its back. She's stark naked. So the Indians are impressed, and they let the guy go into a whatdyacallit, a teepee, with the blonde, and you know..."

"Yeah, okay."

"So now the chief says, 'White man can have one more wish.' And the guy says okay, he wants to talk to his horse again. So he does. Horse gallops off, comes back this time with a beautiful redhead."

"Naked?"

"As a jaybird." Alcazar actually smiled a little. Howie went on: "So the Indians let him go back into the teepee with the redhead—"

"Where's the blonde?"

"Uh, that's not important. She's gone or she's with the squaws or what-have-you. Now, the guy's, you know, screwing the redhead. And when he's finished he comes out, and the Indians—they're really impressed now—they say, okay, you get one more wish, and he says—"

"He wants to talk to his horse again."

"Exactly. And he goes over, but this time, he turns that horse's head so he's looking right at him, and very slowly, very clearly, he says to the horse: 'Now listen carefully to me. Bring me a *poss*-ee.'"

It took a few seconds, but then Jay began to chuckle. "Posse. Yeah, that's a good one, Howie."

Howie just said: "Have a good game, Jay," and left him alone again.

But he did not have a good game at all. Howie had known all sorts of players who, in the face of some personal trauma, seemed to actually play the game better. The field became a refuge. In Triple A one year at Syracuse, a first baseman named Willie Michaels was in the newspaper a week in a row, front page, out on bail on charges of throwing his girlfriend down the stairs and generally attempting to mutilate her. Michaels never had a better week in his whole career. If he'd only played like that all the time, he'd have been a star in the majors. There were players in trouble who could find the zone.

But Alcazar was the opposite. It had seemed to Howie that he had somehow been distracted all season, but tonight he was a disaster. It was clear that he could not put his personal situation out of his mind. In a way, it was odd. Howie thought (well, many people did) that Jay Alcazar was not only the best player in the game, but the best player under pressure. The numbers geeks, like Moncrief, even had a variety of inscrutable statistics that absolutely supported this conclusion.

But then, Howie knew, that should not be surprising. In baseball, as in most any sport, at the most excruciating moments, pressure is never faced in isolation. There is somebody else, the opponent, who is also under the same pressure. The pitcher who faces Alcazar in that crunch situation is subjected to just as much strain. And even as a kid, Alcazar had fathomed, almost instinctively, that if nothing was really changed, that if things were only heightened, then what difference did it really make whether it was two outs in the ninth with men on base and down a run, or no outs in the fourth in a 6-1 game? It was still just me versus the pitcher. And I can hit pitchers. So what the fuck is pressure?

If anything, because most pitchers could not think this through, they were inclined to tense up when facing Jay Alcazar when the pressure was on, so, if you thought about it—and Jay did—the deck was stacked even more in his favor when the pressure was on. He even loved those moments.

But tonight was different. Tonight all he could think about was the mess he was in and how all the twenty-eight thousand, seven hundred and forty-six people in attendance at Camden Yards were staring at him, convinced he was a rapist. He could not put that out of his mind. He was even sure they were all staring at his crotch. The first time up, with Wyn'amo on second, after he'd doubled off the wall, Alcazar checked his swing and bounced a little dribbler down to the third baseman. Howie wondered: did I ever see Jay check his swing before? He saw the pitch, and if he liked it, he took his cut. There was never any indecision, never ever—it seemed—a time when Jay changed his mind in mid-stroke.

The next time up (mercifully, with nobody on base), he struck out, looking. The kind of fastball, low and outside, he could crunch. Howie had figured out a long time ago how a lot of guys have a tendency to swing at a bad inside pitch, but let those kind of good down-and-away pitches go by, because there's a sort of optical illusion that makes it seem that outside pitches are further away than they seem. Alcazar, though, could somehow divine exactly where outside began. He would swing—hit—the ones that caught the black, the edge of the plate, but look at the ones that missed, as Howie would say, "by the proverbial cunt hair," as if they were a foot wide. This time, though, Jay just stood there, bat on his shoulder, when Buster Phelan caught the corner.

Of course, just before that pitch, somebody from the box seats had thrown a big old-fashioned hotel key out onto the field. Most people couldn't tell what it was, but Alcazar saw, and it rattled him all the more. Howie thought: well, thank God it's Baltimore. If it was New York, a hundred wise guys would've thrown out keys (or maybe rubbers), and the whole Yankee Stadium would be making kissing noises every time Jay came up. Or Philadelphia. Christ Almighty, if it was Philadelphia, who can even imagine how bad it would be? One time in Philadelphia, when they had an Easter Egg hunt for the kids between games of a doubleheader, the fans booed the little children who couldn't find eggs. All things considered, Baltimore was pretty well behaved.

On the bench, Ty Baggio, who was pitching, came over and sat down next to Howie. "You oughtta take him out," he said.

"He wants to play."

"Jesus, he's overcast skies. He's embarrassing himself."

Howie turned and looked straight at Baggio: "Ty, you tell 'im that, Ty."

"You're the manager, Howie."

"All right. I'm the manager, and I haven't got the balls. Sue me."

Baggio left and sat down at the other end of the dugout. Out loud, if only to himself he said: "Unable to think straight tonight, is the one-and-only." Baggio was pitching a very good game, too. The Indians had scratched out two runs, and he'd held the Orioles to one. It stayed that way for another three innings.

Then, in the top of the sixth, Alcazar somehow got his bat on the ball—late, but he hit it anyway—and while it was a fairly easy grounder, the Oriole shortstop booted it, and Alcazar was on first. The first pitch—the very first—the pitcher picked him off. He didn't even hear the first-base coach screaming "Get back! Get back!" The fans hooted riotously. Somebody else chucked another hotel key onto the field—only this one was attached to a pair of panties. Camden Yards roared.

Alcazar dusted himself off, and, head ducked down, hurried back to the dugout. He passed Howie there and stopped. "Don't fuckin' take me out."

"You know I won't."

"You did once, Howie."

"That was different, and you know it. You wanna stay in, I'm not takin' you out." This was another one of those times Howie wished he still chewed tobacco and could spit for emphasis. But those days were gone, so he just kept looking at Alcazar.

"I know I'm horseshit," was all Jay said, and then he moved on.

In the bottom of the next inning, the seventh, Baggio got the first two batters, but then Bayer doubled, and Connie Rogers, sitting next to Howie, just said "Yeah," and Howie went out to the mound and took him out for a right-hander, Conaher.

The Oriole batter was, of course, also a right-hander, the second baseman, Musimanno. Spray hitter, not much power. Alcazar should have come in more, played Musimanno shallow. But he didn't. Still, he should have caught the fly Musimanno hit. Instead, he got a late jump on the ball and misjudged it all the more, and it dropped in for a single. The runner scored easily from second, but Alcazar screwed up the rest of the play too, throwing to the plate way late, missing the cut-off man, so that Musimanno scampered to second. He came in with the winning run when the next batter singled: 3-2, Orioles. It should have stayed 2-1, Indians.

His fourth time up, in the eighth, Alcazar popped out, weakly, foul, to third.

Jorgenson and Baggio came to see him in the manager's room afterwards. Could they do anything for him? Go out to dinner together? A drink? "That's where I fucked up last night," Alcazar said. He flung his shirt aside. "I'm sorry, Ty. I cost you a W."

"Hey, Jay, how many Ws have you gotten me?"

Alcazar tried to smile. Jorgenson and Baggio left, but then Wyn'amo came in with a plate of food from the post-game buffet. Jay stayed for a long time, messing with the food, brooding by himself, before he finally dressed and left. A number of newspaper guys remained, still anxious to talk to him, but he strode through their midst without a word. Then he spotted Mickey Huey, just standing there by himself some distance from the horde, and turned to him.

"What'd that guy say?"

"What guy?"

"You know, the old fart in Cincinnati when you were a kid."

"Oh him," Huey said. "He told me: 'I'm a big-league guy in a bush-league town.'"

"Yeah, that's me tonight."

Huey replied: "Well, Junior, you know what Winston Churchill said when the lady told him he was drunk?"

Alcazar shook his head. But he stopped to hear. Thanks to old Huey for saying something different. All the other writers moved closer. Huey leaned closer so no one else could hear. He wanted all the others to think he was really getting the skinny. "Sir Winston said: 'Yes, madam, but tomorrow I'll be sober, but you'll still be ugly.'"

Alcazar smiled, even rapped Huey a little on the shoulder. "Yeah," Huey went on, "tomorrow you'll be Babe Ruth again, and the rest of us will still be bush."

Alcazar actually managed a smile, and resumed his stride, fast and determined, out to the limo where Walter Mundy was waiting for him. The lawyer commiserated with his defeat, but, nodding up toward the driver, said they would talk alone, back at the hotel room, out at Cross Keys.

"There's one wrinkle," he said, when they were in Alcazar's room.

"A wrinkle?" Jay sat down in the chair by the bed.

"Our lady friend has told the cops that when she tried to get away from you—"

"Which she never did."

"Which she never did, yes, but she says she did, and she says when she tried to get away from you, she managed to open the door."

"Bullshit," Alcazar said, slapping his hand down on the table.

"She never opened the door?"

"Not till she left…with a big smile on her face."

"Okay, but what she's told the cops is, she tried to get away from you, she opened the door, and you grabbed her from behind and pulled her back. But here's the kicker: just before you…just before she said you shut the door again, she saw a man in the hall."

Alcazar's mind was racing. Maybe he shouldn't have lied just now to Mundy. Maybe he should apologize and tell him the truth. But why? There wasn't anybody in the hall. Yeah, it had all happened very fast, and yeah, he was concentrating on grabbing her and pulling her back, but surely he would have seen some guy if he was out there. So: to hell with it. "Look," Jay said, "if she says she saw this guy, where the hell is he?"

Mundy shook his head and smiled. "That's the un-wrinkle. As I understand it, the cops have now reached every man registered on that floor down that end of the hallway, and no one saw a thing. Some of them had checked out, but they got hold of them all, and…nothing."

Alcazar just shook his head in perfect disgust: the nerve of this woman.

"Actually," Mundy went on, "this is good. It's the part of her story that could be verified, third-party, and no one backs her up. You're the police, you catch someone in a lie, it naturally makes you suspect the rest of the story. Savvy?"

Alcazar smiled smugly and held out his hands: I told you so.

"So, she made a big mistake, Jay. If she's going to say I struggled like a tiger, I even got away from this monster at one point and opened the door, but he pulled me back, the brute—fine, that spices up her account. But she went too far, throwing in the mystery man. So"—he slapped his hands together, in a washing motion— "sleep tight, my friend."

Jay rose from the chair. "Thanks, Walter. And get me out of here tomorrow and back in the hotel with the team."

"Will do."

For the first time, a scintilla of confidence began to creep back into Alcazar's mind. Okay, his image had taken a hit, but once the charges were dropped, even if he had to pay her off a little to make sure she didn't sell her story to some scumbag tabloid, it would soon all be forgotten.

As Jay lay in bed he even began thinking about the game tomorrow night. Cooper was starting for the Orioles, and he always hit that fat sonuvabitch.

HOWIE, ALONE AGAIN

How many times had Howie Traveler come down an endless corridor and into a hotel room late at night? For most years it had meant lodging with a roommate. Probably you came back together right after the game. Maybe you'd bring a couple cans of beer with you. You'd talk the game over, talk baseball, talk women, movies, maybe watch Johnny Carson. Of course, it wasn't always easy with a roommate. Some guys were night owls, or some made enough noise when they got up early that it woke you up. Every now and then you'd get some lowlife who thought it was funny to fart. There were even a couple of guys who would bring a woman into the room and screw her right there in the next bed if they thought you were asleep. Common as cat shit, Howie would say. Then, as Howie got to be a veteran, twenty-seven or -eight, and viewed as a wise old head, the team would room him with a prize kid. He felt like a baby-sitter.

When he became a manager, though, it meant his own room. Every night, coming back after a game, after maybe a bourbon or two down in the bar, he would turn the key and enter the room and hope that that little red light on the telephone would be blinking. Oh, sometimes it meant a problem. Davey had brought home a bad report. Or it was midnight and he hadn't called in like he'd promised. Or maybe the worst time of all, when Suzie left the message that Lindsay had just quit college—just like that, more than halfway through the spring semester. *Call me right away, Howie. No matter what time you get in.*

But most times, the red light simply felt warm. He would never turn on the room light until he'd first looked for that little light, blinking, blinking, blinking. It must have been like a campfire suddenly appearing round the bend if you were some cowboy or soldier out in the middle of nowhere. Sometimes he could even call back. His friends or his children or his wife knew his schedule, and so they would usually say: well, don't call me till tomorrow. But every now and then: I'll be up late, so call me whenever you get in. That was the nicest. Someone who wanted to hear from him when he was nowhere, and it was lonely in the black of night.

It was funny. Even in the last years of the marriage, when it was unraveling, when he would talk to Suzie late at night from the road, they seemed happier and closer than when they were actually together. Especially if Howie's team had won. But, whenever they would share the minutiae of the day, talk about all the meaningless little things, how curious that when he was with her at home the little things didn't seem to be anything but meaningless. On the road, though, they all seemed so much more interesting. Suzie seemed more interesting. He recognized, then, that he must seem more interesting too, to her, when he was away from her. And, of course, eventually it occurred to him that that must mean that he was not very interesting to her when he was actually with Suzie, flesh and blood. After so many years away, on the road, Howie knew: it isn't absence makes the heart grow fonder, absence itself just becomes fonder.

But, oh, it was so lonely, every day waiting for the hours to pass so he could get out to the park. He learned to read more and not just watch television, but, however the time passed, it was only a matter of passing time—*killing* time: how apt—until he could get to the park. Baseball was the sanctuary. But Howie also needed that little red light on the telephone in a dark room at night almost as much, for without that there was no other beacon in his life. And no future. Just road games stretching year after year, all the way to his dotage. When cell phones became de rigueur, he didn't tell many people his mobile number. He had come so much to look forward to the little red blinking light.

In Baltimore now, of course, there would be no little red light, for he had told the hotel to take no calls. Howie Traveler didn't exist, telephone-wise. Or, anyway, land-line-wise—. People who *mattered* had his cell phone number. After he poured himself a bourbon from the mini-bar, he pulled out his mobile and checked for messages. Bonanza! They were exactly the two he wanted—the two women in his life, Lindsay and Margo.

He looked at his watch. It was almost midnight, which was too late to call Lindsay, but it was not even nine in California, so he called his sweetheart. He had to see her. He had to, as he told her, because he hadn't been fired, and they could celebrate. But also he had to see her because now Howie was ready to tell her about what he had seen, the door opening and Alcazar closing it, and him lying to the cops, and keeping it quiet and all the rest. He had to tell someone, and now at last he had decided that Margo had earned that assignment.

Naturally, she had heard all about Alcazar and the charges against him. It had even made the network news, and it was all they talked about on cable. They could beat a story like this to death on cable. And Alcazar wasn't even a white person. But Howie only gave her a brief rundown and told her he would tell her the rest when he was with her.

"Look," Howie said, "we're in Chicago Wednesday and Thursday. You ever been to Chicago?"

"Only at O'Hare, when I was flying. What's in Chicago?"

"It's a pretty city. There's the Loop."

"The what?"

"The Loop. You know, it's downtown."

That was not much of an endorsement. Margo said: "I don't know, Howie. I've got two or three houses that just might sell. I can't just pick up. The kids, you know."

"All right. We'll be back in Cleveland Friday. Please, come there, honey. Even if it's just a weekend, even just a day."

"Just a day, all the way to Cleveland?"

"I gotta see you, honey." Margo had never heard Howie direct such urgency to her. So of course she would come. But even before she had a chance to accept, Howie added: "I gotta hold you, Margo."

It was an odd, even old-fashioned term, but it was exactly how Howie felt right now. Yes, of course, he wanted to make love to her, but even more than that, what he needed right now was to hold someone close to him. Or even better: have someone hold him.

"I'll see if I can't get there Friday," Margo said. "Saturday for sure."

Howie took a deep breath, and, for the first time, he said, flat out: "Margo, I love you, Margo."

Surprised as she was, very easily, she replied: "I love you, too, Howie." She had grown sure that he was going to say that sometime, and so she was prepared how to respond, in kind. Besides, from the moment he got on the phone, she had appreciated that he was more emotional than ever. It seemed like that admission must finally be coming.

Then Howie said: "I need you, Margo."

She wasn't prepared for that. "I want to hold you too, darling," is what she said. They blew kisses to one another over the phone, and he did feel a little better.

TAMPA BAY

HOWIE NEVER FELT COMFORTABLE in bright colors. Perhaps it had something to do with baseball, with him always wearing the uniforms that were simply home white or away gray. Perhaps if he'd been in football or basketball, where flashy colors were the order of dress, he would have grown up feeling more comfortable with greens and reds, your pastels in the summer, maybe even purples and golds.

But he shied from such plumage and attired himself almost exclusively in earth tones. Suzie first, then Lindsay as she got older, Margo now: they all would pick out some bright shirts and ties for him, and while he'd wear them once or twice to be polite, soon enough these vivid garments would move to the back of the closet, to the bottom of the pile, and, in time, they would be completely forgotten, lost under the weight of his standard drab wardrobe.

So there was Howie, always in earth tones. Like taking Margo all around New York that bright summer's day in brown shoes, tan slacks and olive green shirt. Like even his bathing suits were grays and dark greens. Nobody in baseball ever noticed this, though. None of the players ever said, Jesus, Howie, it's Puerto Rico, it's the tropics, for Chrissake, why don't you get out of those dreary old maroons and at least get one shirt with flowers or parrots on it?

But while Suzie could generally overlook Howie's wardrobe when life together was going well for them, his clothes were exactly the sort of thing that began to nettle her as she became more and more disenchanted with his desultory career. First, she would see other men in clothes she liked and think how they would look good on Howie. Then she would see other men in clothes she liked and think how good the men looked in them. Drab wears on a woman.

But all that aside, nothing was ever the same after Davey was killed. Both Howie and Suzie knew, in their hearts, how hurt the other one was, but it was easier to assuage their grief by pretending otherwise. "You don't even think about him anymore," Suzie said.

"Of course I do. I think about him all the time."

"You don't even want to go put flowers on his grave."

"It's today I don't feel like doing that, Sooz. It's just I can't do that today. Maybe tomorrow."

But when tomorrow came, it would be Suzie who wanted to run away from thoughts of Davey. She wanted to have a happy day and do happy things.

The trouble was, of course, that grief in a marriage is not something that can be scheduled together, like breakfast and the cocktail hour and bedtime. Shared grief is more like finding the mutual best time for sex. Anyway, even when they were emotionally attuned, how do you lean on someone when they want to lean on you? So, since they couldn't hold each other up, the marriage began to collapse around them. And they could divert their grief for Davey by blaming each other for their failings, for one not grieving as much as the other.

And then one night, when they couldn't lean on each other anymore at all but didn't have the energy to run away either, Suzie suddenly broke the compact, reached back and snapped: "You were with a woman that night, weren't you?"

And Howie said: "For God's sake, how can you say that?"

"Well, you were, I know."

"No, I wasn't, Sooz. I swear to you I wasn't."

So in addition to the detective in Baltimore, this was that one other time he had lied, flat out. He had to. Because if Howie had not, if he had admitted that he was in bed with another woman when his only son lay smashed and broken and dying, it would have somehow diminished his love for Davey. Howie had to lie for himself, even if Suzie surely knew he was lying to her. "Do you think I wanted to be away?" he screamed at her. "For God's sake, I had to make a living."

At least that way he'd turned the subject back to baseball, where the arguments usually were located. It didn't even bother him so much, then, when Suzie snapped: "Yeah, and why can't you make a real living instead of staying in a stupid game?"

She always said something along that line when she was really mad.

Howie and Suzie did finally begin to crawl out of the depths of their grief—even if, like their grieving itself, they didn't do that mutually—but Lindsay was off again to college, and Suzie was left alone when Howie had to go off to Spring Training again. He knew how much more lonely she had grown because now there would be more of those blinking little red lights whenever he came back to his hotel rooms.

And then, not long afterwards, over and over: "Why do you think Lindsay *really* left college, Howie. Really?" She had told her mother she was just stressed out, and told her father that, too, but that didn't make any sense. There had been no evidence of that before. She had, in fact, been doing beautifully in her grades and her phone calls home were filled with nothing but enthusiasm and joy for the college experience.

"What difference does it make?" Howie would ask. "She's back now. She's fine." In fact, it did seem that Lindsay was pretty much back to being herself. She had switched schools, left the University of Missouri and gone to Coe, in Iowa.

"But don't you want to know what happened to her?"

"A lot of kids hit a wall in college. I've seen the same thing with players. Big, strong kids who are doing great, and they're making money and all, but all of a sudden they can't handle the experience. And these are boys."

"It just wasn't right with Lindsay. Don't you want to even know?"

"It's over, Sooz. What difference does it make?"

In fact, by now, though, Howie had learned what had happened, and that made it all the more conflicting, because Lindsay had finally chosen to tell him, even though she didn't want her mother to know the truth. And it gnawed at Howie. In a way, it was worse than what he and Suzie went through after Davey died. At least they were going through that together. Now, he not only had to endure the anguish he knew Lindsay had suffered, but he couldn't even talk about it with Suzie.

Maybe, though, they would have muddled through and somehow come out some other side if it hadn't been for the Tampa Bay offer. It was the culmination of the dream, the faith their marriage had been founded on, that Howie Traveler would finally make it to the top, to the big leagues—if not as a player, then as a manager. The Devil Rays wanted to interview him to be their skipper, to be one of the thirty managers in the major leagues of baseball.

"Oh my God, Howie, that's wonderful." Suzie flew into his arms and let out some kind of little noise he hadn't heard for years.

"Now sit down, Sooz."

He pushed his hands down, quieting her, directing her to the sofa. He sat in the big chair, facing her, inches away. She couldn't contain herself, though, bouncing up and down on her seat. She barely exhaled the question: "How many are they interviewing?"

"Well, three, and one of them is Mitch Porter, and just between us chickens, I'm pretty sure they're only interviewing him because they have to, 'cause he's a minority."

"Who else?"

"Roger Neville."

"Who's he?"

"He's in their organization. He's their Triple A manager at Durham."

"What do you think?"

"I…I think they want me, Sooz. In fact, I'm pretty sure they do. Bailey Magnuson—we were together in the Yankees' organization; he's Tampa's assistant farm director now—and he told me, you know on the Q-T, that it's my job to lose."

"Oh my God, Howie." Suzie grabbed his hands in hers and tapped them on her knees.

Howie knew immediately that this was one other time he should have lied. He was so proud that the Devil Rays wanted him, though, that he'd felt that he had to tell her that. He had to let his wife know how men in his profession valued him. He needed to say that for his self-esteem. And he needed to tell her so that she would hold him in more of her own esteem, that at last he wasn't just another busted busher. He was desired as a manager of men at the highest level of the national pastime.

"Oh, Howie, how much?"

"Well, they're cheap, but probably five hundred thousand."

"A year?"

"A year."

"Cheap? Oh my God." There had never been any doubt that they would pay to send Lindsay to Coe, expensive as that was. There had been a little money they'd saved up for Davey's college, and that had helped. Still, it was a struggle now. But half a million a year! They could get a new house in Tampa. Bradenton maybe. Or Clearwater. Dunedin. Suzie knew the area from Spring Trainings past. She could even see a house on the water. Or, at the very least, on a golf course by a water hole. "How long will the contract be for?"

"They'll probably only go two years. But probably put in an option for three."

"Oh my God, Howie." Suzie clapped her hands together like a little girl.

But Howie grabbed them and brought them down to her lap. He took a deep breath. "Suzie," he said, "now listen to me: I'm not going to interview for the job."

Suzie didn't hear at first. Then she just stared at him, unable to comprehend what she thought she must have heard. She looked so puzzled. Finally, she said: "But you said they want you for the job."

"I probably shouldn't have told you that, but yeah, I've pretty much got it."

"But not interview?" She shook her head, more in confusion than despair.

"Listen to me, honey. It's a dead end. It's a cheap team, a rotten stadium. Nobody can succeed there. Nobody. Not Bobby Cox, not LaRussa, not even Casey Stengel, if he came back from the grave. Two years there, we'll finish in the cellar, they'll get rid of me, and then I'm toast."

"But you'll get another job then, Howie."

He shook his head. "Not manager, honey. Guys like me, the best we can hope for is one shot." He held up his forefinger. "One shot." He waggled the finger. "And if we don't score with that, there'll never be another."

"But maybe *this* is your only shot."

"Maybe."

"This is what you've worked for all your life, to be a manager—a big-league manager."

"No, Suzie."

"No?"

"What I've wanted is to be a *successful* big-league manager. That's what I've worked for all my life."

"But even if you fail here, everybody will know it's not your fault. They'll see you can manage, and you'll get another chance. You've always told me they just recycle the same old guys."

"They recycle the same old guys who were in the majors, honey. Or the ones who get a chance and succeed the first time. Nobody'll ever gimme a chance again. I'm fifty-one years old, and I'll be finished." He reached over to her, to take her hands. "No, Sooz, I can't go there, Sooz."

"But this is everything we've ever worked for." She pulled away from him, hiding her hands from him. "Goddammit, *I've* worked for this. This is what you told me, Howie. You can't do this."

"I'm sorry, honey, I have to."

She got up straightaway, and left, making a shooing motion toward him, crying, and later that evening, dry-eyed, speaking very directly and without a great deal of emotion, she simply told him that, under the circumstances, she didn't want to stay married to him anymore.

Howie told Suzie that he realized she was upset, but not to be hasty about things, to think this over, which she did. A week later, she asked him to leave the house because her mind was made up. What she said, at last, was: "You broke your promise to me, Howie."

Since he was still the third-base coach for Milwaukee, he decided he would move up there, permanently. He rented a U-Haul and packed up all his stuff. When he thought he had just about everything, he came inside to say good-bye. They had really acted in a most civil manner toward one another. He had slept in the guest room, and they had even had a couple meals together, if in front of the TV.

Now Suzie was standing at the top of the stairs, holding out the fabulous houndstooth jacket she had given him two years before when he had gotten the third-base coaching job at Milwaukee. "Don't you want this?" she asked.

"No, really," Howie said. "It's not me. Give it to the Goodwill."

Those were the last words they exchanged in their own house after twenty-six years of marriage, because then Suzie just turned around with the jacket and walked away.

GREAT

BY THE TIME ROGER NEVILLE got fired by the Devil
Rays after two years, leading them to horrendous suc-
cessive last-place finishes, ninety-nine losses one season and a hundred and two the next, Suzie and Howie
were so far removed from one another that it didn't
even occur to him to think: "I told you so."

He had moved on in baseball, too. After a couple
more seasons in Milwaukee, he had gone to the Seattle
organization. He managed the Seattle Triple A team at
Tacoma for a season and then became bench coach for
the Mariners. The people who knew he could've had
the Tampa Bay job came to admire him for his sagacity in not accepting it. The reputation in baseball for
Howie Traveler was, in fact, quite a good one, although
it too often tended to be on the order of respect for an
aged family retainer. More and more, he was thought
of, foremost, as old, as in "old Howie Traveler." "Veteran coach" almost became a title. Occasionally, even
the adjective "grizzled" was applied to him—and that's

always a positive thing in these manly environs. And sometimes: "rumpled." He had been everywhere, punched all his tickets—minor-league manager, major-league coach on the lines, bench coach, manager in winter ball. Everybody knew that Howie knew everything there was to know about the game of baseball and that he didn't take crap from anybody, but now, it seemed, he was too long in the tooth to be eligible for the top prize.

In fact, two years after he got to Seattle, he happened to meet the athletic director of the University of New Mexico in spring training, and he nearly took the job as varsity coach there the next year when the AD offered it to him. He thought that then he could just drift out his years as an affectionate old baseball professor. However, Howie needed a few more years to qualify for a full major-league pension, so he turned the offer down and stayed on at Seattle, sitting on the bench in the dugout there alongside Abe Henderson, the manager.

For the first time, Howie began to feel silly dressed in a uniform. No other coaches in any other sport dressed like players—just baseball managers. "Well, Abe," he said one time, "it's a good thing we don't coach swimming." Henderson didn't get it right away. "You know," Howie explained, "and have to wear bathing suits." But still, Howie put on his knickers and jammed his hands into his back pockets and went back to work at the ballyard.

It occurred to Howie at some point that a man who kept his hands in his back pockets, palms facing out, looked learned. Thereafter, he worked at that.

He got along with Abe well. They cogitated together in the dugout and drank together in the hotel bar. And although Howie was his strong right arm, a loyal lieutenant, he was also perpetually envious of Abe, longing for his job but learning to accept, with each passing season, that his own chance ever to be a major-league manager was passing him by. After awhile it didn't even bother him that, following a loss, on the team bus back to the hotel or the airport, all the players got out their cell phones and jabbered away to girlfriends. "These guys," Howie said to Abe, "losing a game doesn't bother them near as much as when their battery runs out." With cell phones everywhere now, nobody much skylarked on team buses anymore. That used to be the hallmark of a team, farting around on buses.

His world was changing under his feet. Bats were made of better wood, balls packed tighter. Pitchers hardly ever brushed anybody back anymore. Hitters could crowd the plate. Christ, he could've hit .400 in any league the way it was now. It also occurred to Howie that there were no more fat guys left in baseball. Everybody was buff.

He sent Suzie a sweet letter, and some flowers, wishing her well, when she got married again. Lindsay suggested the flowers. By now, frankly, Suzie had faded into the past. His whole life had been two things: baseball and the family he had shared with her. It was surprising to him how quickly she and all their years together tumbled from his memory once she was gone and only baseball remained. Indeed, when he did think about Suzie, it was often as much about Davey, and that just made him sad again.

In a way, too, Lindsay no longer seemed to connect him to Suzie. When they'd been married, Lindsay had been a girl. Now, she'd been through college and law school and had taken a job in a city far away. She was a grown woman, apart from that girl she had been once, apart from the mother she had had. Especially before he took up with Margo, Howie called Lindsay often, but in some respects it felt more as if he was talking to a friend, not his child. He would bounce things off her, and ask for her advice even when the decision was obvious, because he needed her to stay involved with him.

But, no, as for the past: that was all baseball now. In the home movies of his mind there weren't any children opening presents at Christmas or having their birthday party or losing a tooth. Instead, it was just hotel corridors and bars and games and teams and teammates. He still remembered the best hits he got, the best plays he made. He could still see that one solid single up the middle off Dave McNally.

Ironically, after all the years of dreaming about it, when the Indians called, it was completely unexpected. He had heard all sorts of other names that were supposed to be considered for that job—especially Nino Diaz. All the organizations he'd been with, all the friends he'd made through the years who were now in positions of power, and still Howie'd never really had any connection with Cleveland. He'd never even met Moncrief.

But as sure as Moncrief liked his players to fit into the right statistical template, so did Howie conform to all the characteristics Moncrief assigned to the manager he needed at this fortuitous moment. Old, not

young, Tough, not easy. Congenial—good at schmooz-
ing with the newspaper and television boys. Knows
the league. A loyal organization man, *i.e.* will be grateful and not contest me. Comes pretty cheap. Gets
along with the Spanish boys. Especially: never had
any issues with Jay Alcazar. Tick, tick, tick, tick 'em
off. At the end of the day, old veteran coach Howie
Traveler, rumpled and grizzled, was the one guy who
didn't have any blank spots on his resume. He wasn't
necessarily the best choice; he was just Mister All-
Around, the only one who still had all his minutes left
on his baseball cell phone.

Of course, it also helped that he commiserated
mightily with Moncrief when he moaned how awful it
was that people were always asking him how's the
weather up there? "That must be a sonuvabitch to
deal with," Howie allowed. Moncrief liked that sort of
compassion in a manager.

But Howie was nobody's fool. He had to appreciate
the whimsy of it, how, after all these years of making
a place in baseball, he finally got to be a major-league
manager because he simply filled a figure-filbert's for-
mula. He wasn't even a person, just the right blend,
like coffee. Oh well, beggars can't...

Suzie sent him a magnum of champagne.

Howie saw that Lindsay's fine hand was wrapped
around the bottle. But that's okay. Dad: why not send
Mom flowers on her marriage? Mom: why not send
Dad champagne on his ascension? And for just a
moment—only that—he wondered if Suzie had
second-guessed herself when she heard the news that
he had finally reached the mountaintop.

At first, too, Howie was indeed all Moncrief had hoped he might be. Well, the Indians did lose the first four games of the season, and that was enough to prompt Peterson, the new young columnist from the Akron *Beacon Journal*, whose mission in life it was to throw gasoline on fires, to immediately second-guess Howie's appointment. But Howie kept his cool. "This isn't football, gentlemen," he philosophized in the dugout the next evening before the assembled media multitude. "There's a different pitcher every game, and there's a hundred and sixty-two of those. The last time I was taking geometry, four out of a hundred sixty-two is only two-point-four percent."

"You do that in your head, Howie?" Sinister Bill Williams of the Canton *Repository* asked. He was called "Sinister Bill" because he saw the dark side in all fun and games.

"Of course," Howie said with a wink, and everybody around him laughed.

Charley Grabowski of the Kansas City *Star*—the Tribe were playing in K.C.—said: "Hey, Howie, it's algebra, not geometry."

Howie shot back: "Look, I was on an athletic scholarship. They passed me anyway."

All the writers roared at that. Most of them knew Howie from all his years coaching, but coaches were not quoted. He had just been on deep background as a coach. Coaches only became quote-eligible when they became managers. And now when Howie was described as "grizzled" or "rumpled," the words had even more of a sage connotation to them. Sometimes, too, he was even identified as "wisecracking" or "blue-collar" or "street-smart," all prize sports-page encomia.

Anyway, that night after the Tribe lost its first four games, Baggio gave Howie six shutout innings, the Indians beat the Royals 6-1, to get off the schneid, and then they swept the next two games as well. So, when they opened at home in Cleveland, they were three-and-four, and after a day off Baggio won the opener, too, to even them up. The Indians were never under .500 again and always in contention for the playoffs. Even if they might not be able to catch Detroit to win the division, they were definitely in the hunt for the wild card.

But then, not long after that series in New York late in July when Margo was visiting Howie, Wyn'amo Willis pulled his hamstring. The condition lingered. He couldn't even come back as a designated hitter. The reporters were beside themselves. When will Amo be back, Howie? How soon? Howie just said: "Gentlemen, I don't deal with the dead," and shook up the batting order. He moved Alcazar back into the three hole and bumped Jorgenson up to cleanup. Wyn'amo's replacement at first base was Sticks Farley, who was a much better fielder, but far less of a threat at the plate.

It didn't matter. Alcazar absolutely took command. He had been having one of his typically superb years, but now, somehow, he raised his game to even greater heights. At the plate, coiled in his closed stance, he stepped into the pitch and his front leg hit the ground, Howie swore it was as if he took an electric charge, and the current would run up his body, charging his hips to rotate, his body to turn, his arms to come round, his wrists to turn over, until at last the jolt ran down the handle of the bat to the sweet spot and ripped hell outta that poor old horsehide. Shazam! Like whatshisname, that minor-league Superman with a lightning bolt on his chest, from Howie's old funny books.

"I never seen you with such an edge on the pitchers," Jorgenson told him.

Alcazar replied: "Ollie, I don't want an edge. Edges can get in the way."

Jorgenson said: "I never thought about edges like that." Himself, he was just an ordinary talent, and he'd always had to look for an edge.

Alcazar hit his fortieth home run on August 10— and the most he'd ever had before for a whole season was fifty-six. He led the league in RBIs, too, and at .361 was second only to Pepe Davila, the little spray hitter from Texas. Good grief—he could win the Triple Crown a second time! Alcazar was even running the bases and fielding his position better than he ever had. Perkins of *Sports Illustrated* had written an overwrought panegyric comparing Jay to a magician and calling him "The Great Alcazar." It stuck. At least for awhile, The Chief took a backseat.

Facetiously at first, perhaps, but with unfettered admiration, opposing players started calling him simply: "Great." As a name. As in: "Hey, Great" or "Yo, Great" or "Great somehow got around on that pitch." Nobody ever remembered that before, not with Ruth, not with Williams, not with Mantle or Mays or anybody in recorded diamond history. Just: Great.

BETWEEN
FRIENDS

LATE IN AUGUST, after Alcazar single-handedly beat the Angels, going three-for-four, with a home run, driving in all five runs in a 5-4 game, he and Jorgenson went out to dinner at a little Mexican place in Newport Beach where the owner always put them outside where nobody would bother them. Alcazar knocked back two margaritas. He was feeling good. Ollie Jorgenson was a good old buddy, the one guy on the team he could relax with.

The trouble was, as Alcazar had learned soon enough, that once he became a superstar, many people he'd known began to act differently around him. It was as if he'd had a sex change operation and even old pals couldn't remember him the way he was born and grew up. Jorgenson, though, perfectly sensed how to treat Alcazar. The two of them had met in the minor leagues, before Alcazar was a celebrity. Somehow, Jorgenson had learned to assign Alcazar just enough deference to justify his new exalted state, but otherwise he acted in the same manner as when they'd met in Class A, a couple of new pros, trying to both hit home runs and get laid every night. Alcazar even liked it that Jorgenson could kid him, take him down a peg—but never, ever did he mess with him that way when anyone else was around.

Likewise, Jay called Jorgenson "Olliekins," but only when it was just the two of them. That was because, in Spring Training one year, Alcazar heard a really desperate little homely girl call him that in a moment of high ardor in the backseat of a car Alcazar was driving.

Now, the two of them alone at the Mexican joint, Jorgenson said: "You know, Great, you're fucking up the whole team."

"Ollie, I told you: cut that Great shit out."

"No, the way you're playing, we're all just sitting on our asses waiting for you to bail us out."

"I don't know what. I'm not just in the zone now. I'm not just seeing every pitch like it's a grapefruit. I *expect* it, Olliekins. I swear, when I grounded out that one time tonight, I'm thinking: how the hell did I do that?"

"Wait'll I tell ESPN that." The burritos and salads came.

"Yeah, and I'll have Moncrief trade your fat ass to Kansas City."

"Naw, don't worry, Great. I'm saving all the good stuff for my book, *My Amigo, Great.* That'll be in the first chapter, along with the time you got the blow job in Akron between halves of a doubleheader and then went oh-fer."

"Cocksucker," was all Alcazar said, with his mouth

full. To be whole, a man needs to be kidded, to be told off in the right light way by other men he likes. Otherwise, no matter how much of a hot shot he is, he doesn't feel like a man. In this fashion, Jorgenson gave Alcazar his manhood.

Jorgenson raised his Dos Equis to Alcazar. "Jay," he said—you see: he knew just how far to take their familiarity; no more "Great"— "No, I'm serious, I've never seen even you like this before."

"Well some of it is, I just taste it. I really think we can win it all. And when Amo went down, I just told myself: hey, spic, see if you can't kick it into another gear. See, I'm not sure that him getting hurt isn't a blessing in disguise. The last couple seasons, he's been runnin' out of gas down the stretch. Now he's like getting a month off. He comes back, when —?"

"Week, ten days, they say. To DH, anyhow."

"Yeah. The big guy should be fresh as a daisy." He laid off another margarita and ordered a Dos Equis for himself instead. After awhile, Alcazar said: "And I feel good in here, too, Ollie." He tapped his heart.

"Jesus, are you in love?"

"You'll be the first to know, darling. No, I had a little family issue, and I solved it."

Ollie looked up. "What's that?"

"This is really between us, but I'm going to Cuba this winter."

"No shit."

"My father still has this hard-on for Castro, and it's been, you know, somethin' between us, but now I'm going."

"He's cool?"

"Not really. But it's settled." Alcazar sipped his beer and thought what he'd say for a moment. Then he volunteered this: "I've got family down there I've never met."

"Oh," Ollie said. "Like what?"

"You know, family." Ollie was cagey enough just to let it go. But for once, Alcazar went ahead and opened up. "My mother—you know, not my real mother in Florida, but the lady who carried me. Well, after she meets my father, and she's pregnant, that sonuvabitch Castro put him back in jail."

"He'd already been?"

"Oh yeah, long time. Ten, twelve years. My real father was named Emilio. He's the kid brother of my father here, Victor. And he bought into Castro at first, but then he saw what was happening, so he turned on him, and that's when they put him in jail. He comes out, they got him working in the sugarcane fields. I mean, that must be the worst goddamn job in the world. Anyway, that's when he meets my mother, and then she's pregnant with me, but he's still working against Castro, so they put him back in jail. He died there a little bit later."

"Jesus, I'm sorry, Jay."

"Yeah, I never knew my father—Emilio. Anyway, back then, I also still had an aunt in Cuba. Olga. My father...well, she's both my fathers' sister."

"When is this?"

"Nineteen-seventy-nine. I'm a year old."

"Okay."

"So my aunt—Olga—she and her husband are going to try to get out on one of those makeshift boats.

So they ask my mother—her name is Rita—they say, we haven't got enough room for you, but we can take the baby."

"This is a helluva story."

"You ever tell anyone, Ollie, I'll break your fuckin' neck."

"Don't worry."

"So my mother, Rita, says yeah, it's my baby, but I don't want him growing up on this rat-fuck island. She says she'll try and get out herself as soon as she can. So she gives the baby to Olga, and they set off for Florida in this old piece of shit, which breaks down and drifts, and some of the people even die, including my aunt."

"No."

"Yeah. Olga. You see, my father lost both his brother and sister to Castro. Don't get him started."

"Whatever happened to your mother?"

"That's it," Alcazar said, taking a swig of his beer. "She never made it over. And then my real father dies in jail, and we lose all contact with her. That's what I want, Ollie. I wanna see if I can find her and get her over here."

"You ever try before?"

Alcazar shook his head. "You know, I always thought, well someday. Someday I'll try and go get her. Then, uh—" He paused for a moment, and Jorgenson knew he was trying to decide whether to go on. Finally, Jay did. He said: "Then, that crazy thing in Boston last year."

"Oh yeah."

"You almost get killed, it makes you think. Some. And after awhile, I figured, if you wanna get your mother—you know, that lady—then you better not put it off, because, you know, you never can tell."

"Yeah," Jorgenson said.

"But my father hates that sonuvabitch Castro so much, he never wanted me to go. So I didn't go last off-season."

"But now you're goin'?"

"That's what I'm sayin'. That's what I settled out with Dad. So that's given me, you know, some peace of mind."

"I never knew you let stuff like that get to you on the field."

"That's what I want people to think, Olliekins. That's what I want 'em to think."

They munched for awhile then, Jorgenson appreciating that Alcazar had given away about as much of himself as he could ever expect. There would be no more revelations. So Jorgenson returned to the more prosaic, to baseball: "Well, I'm glad to hear you think we can win it, because I think so, too. If Howie doesn't fuck it up."

"You think he could?" Alcazar asked, leading him on.

"Well, you know, he's a rookie manager. You get in the playoffs, the Series, for Chrissake, he might all of a sudden feel the pressure and screw the pooch."

Alcazar just shook his head. "Nah. Howie won't feel a thing."

"Come on, Jay, he's from the bushes. He's never even made the playoffs as a coach. He gets into those games, all the bullshit coming down, national TV, all that, anybody could crack."

"No, that's the beauty of Howie. And listen, I was dubious at first. But, Ollie, the sonuvabitch has been in a million games. It's almost like it's all the same to him. The bushes, Triple A, the majors. He's even managed Puerto Rico. All just games. Believe it or not, in a way, Howie's a lot like me."

"C'mon, Jay."

"No, I'm serious. No matter who I'm facing, I figure, what's the difference: I've seen 'em all, I can hit 'em all. Howie's seen everything. It's all the same shit to him. Ballgames. There's a lot of managers, guys supposed to be good managers—all they're really doin' is managing for the next job. Do everything so you can explain it real good. Then, if it doesn't work, you got explanations. They fire you here, somebody else'll hire you for even more money because they're thinking: hey, he did his best. He knows all the right buttons to push."

Ollie leaned a little closer. Jay didn't realize it, but he didn't talk as loud as most people. Often, he would get softer as he went along. But nobody ever said, hey, a little louder, or speak up, Jay. They didn't say those sort of things to a man like him. Instead, the listeners just took it upon themselves to lean in closer. Even Ollie. People were always leaning in when Jay talked. He sipped his beer and went on: "Most managers, shit, they don't do what's necessarily right. They just do what they can justify. You follow me?"

"Yeah, I know."

"Well, Howie's not like that. He's been kickin' around the ass-end of this game all his life, and he gets this chance, and he's not figuring there'll ever be another one. So he's not worrying what anybody says. In a way, the old sonuvabitch is fearless. It's almost better he wasn't any good as a player. It's the guys who were *pretty* good players in the majors make *pretty* good decisions. That's what they are. *Pretty* good. No more than that." He pointed at Jorgenson. "You remember that game in Fenway he pinch-hit for you?"

"Kiss my ass," Jorgenson snarled, throwing the finger at Alcazar in the bargain.

Alcazar chuckled; he didn't have to recapitulate that infamous occasion. It happened in Boston, back in June; Howie only had a couple months on the job. There were two out in the ninth, Willis on third, Alcazar on second, Cleveland down 6-5. Jorgenson, a right-handed hitter, is the batter. He's having a nice season so far, hitting around .300. A little rookie left-hander named Shawn Wojcek is pitching for Boston. Clearly, the Red Sox manager is going to yank Wojcek and put in a right-hander, the better to face Jorgenson. But even in those circumstances, Cleveland is better off, because Boston hasn't got a top right-handed reliever left in the bullpen. Besides, with that inviting short wall in left field, you want a right-handed power hitter like Jorgenson up. On deck, Jorgenson is acting out the role, taking huge practice swings.

Before Boston could take Wojcek out, though, Howie sends up Frankie Willard, a little left-handed-hitting reserve infielder, to pinch hit. Willard is hitting about .200 on the season, down by the Mendoza Line, which ballplayers had named for a stiff who could never even hit in the two-hundreds. So what's the point? Now Boston can leave the left-hander on the mound in the game. Jorgenson is furious. Everybody else, Frankie Willard included, is simply puzzled. Watching on television back in Cleveland, Moncrief goes berserk. There isn't a statistic in the world that can justify this madness. Willard steps in, takes two pitches, a ball and a strike, from Wojcek, and then hits the next pitch, a fastball, right on the button. A laser shot. Unfortunately, it goes directly at the Red Sox second baseman who, reflexively, throws up his glove and snares it. End of game.

Afterwards, when Howie was asked about the decision, he retreated into some generalities that satisfied no one. Moncrief was on the phone later that night, beside himself, screaming at Howie that Jorgenson hit both the Red Sox right-handers warming up well. Didn't you look at the numbers? Didn't Frosty show you the percentages? Howie just played dumb and took the guff.

"But I kept wondering about it," Alcazar said, "and a few weeks ago, when we were in Toronto, I saw Howie sitting alone in the bar in the hotel there. And I went over, and I asked him about it. And he got this funny little smile on his face, and you know what he told me?"

"Don't ask me," Jorgenson said. He was still pissed off, two months later.

"He said, 'Jay, when that new little left-hander came in, I thought to myself, he reminds me of somebody. The way he came in over the top, throws the good, deceptive change. And it's driving me crazy. And suddenly I remember.'" Alcazar turned to Jorgenson. "Manny Velasquez," he said.

Jorgenson nodded his understanding. Velasquez, like Wojcek, was a little left-hander who threw over the top, fair fastball, good change. He was in the National League now, but he'd pitched well enough for the Mariners for two seasons when Howie was the bench coach at Seattle.

Alcazar went on: "So this is what he tells me, Ollie. He says: 'When Velasquez pitched against the Mariners, Willard wore him out. He couldn't hit a lick against most any other lefty, but put him up against Manny Velasquez, and he was dynamite. So, I'm sitting there thinking of Velasquez and how this new kid pitches just like him, and I start thinking, damn, I got Willard on *my* team now. If he can hit Velasquez, he can sure hit the Velasquez clone.' That's what he called Wojcek: the Velasquez clone. And he goes on: 'And I was right, wasn't I, Jay? Willard clobbered that damn ball. A foot either way, two runs score, and I'm a certified genius.' He told me, 'Just wait'll the next time we face Wojcek, I'll pitch-hit Willard so fast it'll make your head spin. I'll even pinch-hit him for your Hall-of-Fame ass.'"

Alcazar sat back, sipping the last of his beer out of the bottle, laughing. Even Jorgenson had to shake his head. "Well, at least that explains it," he said.

"But you see," Alcazar went on, "Howie knew he couldn't tell anybody. Who the hell is going to buy that he takes *you* out at Fenway and puts in Frankie Willard, who can't buy a base hit, because a pitcher reminds him of someone *else* a few years ago? They'll think he's nuts. But you hear what I'm saying, Ollie? Howie Traveler will play the seventh game of the

World Series like it's some horseshit game in Class A in the middle of July. He figures he got here on his own and he's gonna play it out his way. I never thought I'd say this, but I've seen enough: yeah, I'll take my chances with the old fart."

MONDAY MORNING

THE TORRENTS HAD HIT BALTIMORE late Sunday, not long after the game ended, and they continued, unabated, into the morning. It was the northern remnants of Hurricane Hermione, and with no letup expected until late in the day, the Orioles had no choice but to postpone that night's game. It could only be rescheduled for the next afternoon, Tuesday.

Both Jay and Howie had the same reaction. They wanted to get the hell out of Baltimore as quickly as possible, and now they had a whole other day, trapped by the storm, in their hotel—in this particular *cursed* hotel. Howie thought about renting a car and going over to see Lindsay in Washington, but as the rain pounded down on his windows, obscuring even any view of the harbor front that was just across the street, he quickly gave up any thoughts of venturing out. He ordered breakfast and settled in with his courtesy copy of *USA Today*.

He was still in his pajamas, topping that with his

complimentary white hotel robe—that obligatory loaner garment that is, by now, an amenity necessary to certify that a hotel isn't a fleabag—when the doorbell rang. He assumed it was the maid, so he opened it immediately. But, there, before him, stood a woman, young and attractive enough, with a yellow umbrella, still dripping, by her side. As Howie looked at her, quizzically, she stared back at him, but only when she said, "It *is* you," did he truly comprehend who she was. She waited for him to respond, but standing there more with assurance than impatience—rather like Conacher, the Indians' closer, after he got to the mound and was ready to take the ball from Howie and go to work. Finally, she simply said: "I have to talk to you."

Howie was still lost, having no idea how to respond. His mind kept turning over. "Do I know you?" he asked—but hardly with the firm expression of doubt that he sought to portray.

It emboldened the woman that he was obviously unhinged. So: "You *know* you saw me," she declared, and with that, she assumed full command, and brushed past him, into his suite. She turned back and faced him, directly. "I saw your picture in the paper, Mr. Traveler. That's how I knew who you were."

Howie still stood there, holding the door—rather foolishly ("holding the bag" comes to mind). "Who are you?" he asked, still pretending the best he could—but, really, being no more convincing.

To his surprise, of all things, as if she was on some sales call, she simply handed him a business card. "I know you told the police you didn't see me open that door. But please, don't play games with me now."

Howie glanced at the card. It contained the name of a local bank that he didn't recognize. Her name read: Patricia Richmond. Her title: Assistant Vice President, Branch Manager. Whatever this woman was about, there was some substance to her. It piqued his interest enough, so although he still tried his best to play dumb, he ventured: "You're the woman who accused Alcazar?"

"Oh, please. You know you saw me." When Howie didn't immediately dispute that again, it gave her the confidence to move even further into the room. She was very territorial. And now definitive: "I know he's a big star, and I know you're his coach, so you feel you gotta protect him. But dammit, no man should get away with what he did to me."

Howie lowered his head. She didn't know it, but what she had said had hit close to home. Now he told himself: acknowledge nothing...but, all right, listen. He was, after all, damn curious. He looked up at her.

Patricia Richmond was, as he remembered, a brunette, but perhaps not as tall as he held her in his mind. She was trim, rather good looking, and, all in all, well-shaped. She reminded him of an anchorwoman on one of the Cleveland TV stations—and that type is always just this side of real pretty. Howie recalled, too, what Mundy had said, that her lawyer would make her out to be as small as he could. She had on flats now; she must have been in high heels when he had seen her before. She wore beige slacks that were still stained some at the bottoms, from the rain, and a long-sleeved sky-blue blouse that buttoned high. Altogether, she was decorous—as obviously she quite intended to present herself.

He beckoned to a chair, but he remained standing himself, finally remembering his own attire. "I'm sorry I'm not dressed," he said. "Do you mind?"

She shook her head, almost dismissively; Patricia Richmond wanted to get down to business. "This won't take long. Mr. Traveler. I just want to tell you what happened, so that maybe when you know, you'll tell the cops you saw me open that door and him grab me and close it. That's all I want."

"Go on," was all Howie said.

He noticed how calm and controlled she was, and perhaps because she sensed this reaction, she began in that manner, without airs. "I'm a grown woman, Mr. Traveler. I'm not a silly little girl. I've been married. I understood the implications of coming up to a man's hotel room."

"Where did you meet him?"

"An old friend of mine—a girlfriend—who'd left Baltimore awhile ago, was back, visiting. She was staying here, at the hotel. We went out to dinner Saturday night, and decided to have a nightcap at the hotel. There was this player having a beer at the bar."

"Alcazar?"

"No. No, his name was Ollie."

"Jorgenson."

"I guess." She stopped then and gestured at a chair. "Look, will you please sit down? I don't like talkin' up to you like this."

Howie acceded, sitting down kitty-corner to where she was on the couch. He had to admit: Patricia Richmond was a very self-assured woman, almost too comfortable, given the circumstances. He thought maybe she must handle loans at the bank.

When he was settled, she went on: "Thanks. Okay, my friend had happened to ride on the elevator with him earlier in the day. So now, you know, he sees us and comes over from the bar, and my friend—her name is Terri—says, you know, you wanna join us? So he does, and I can tell he and Terri, you know—"

"Yeah."

"And in a couple minutes this other guy looks into the bar, and Ollie sees him, and waves him over, and he sits down with us."

"This is Jay."

"Yeah, but I didn't know."

"Come on. You didn't know who Jay Alcazar was?"

"Oh, I've heard the name, I saw all the stuff in Boston that time the crazy guy came after him, but I'm not a sports fan. No, as a matter of fact: I didn't know. Not everybody in the world knows exactly who baseball players are—you know?"

There was an ease to her demeanor that enhanced her credibility. She turned slightly on the sofa, the better to face him, and went on: "All right, both my friend and I had had something to drink. I'm not blowin' you any smoke."

"No," said Howie.

"We'd both had a cosmopolitan before, and wine with dinner. And I could tell that Terri was taken with this Ollie. I really didn't want to stay at first, I wanted to go on home, but she was talking to Ollie, and so I started talking to Jay, and, to tell you the truth, he was very nice. He wasn't like what I expected a big hot-shot star to be. He didn't talk about himself at all. I liked him, and then when Terri kinda made a head motion to me"—she tossed her own head—" I knew that meant she wanted to go up to Ollie's room."

She paused, and Howie heard the hard rain again, shooting almost sideways onto the windows. "And she did?"

"Yes. Jay said he'd get the bill. Me, I should have said goodnight, and when Jay said he had a suite, and would I like to just come up for one more drink, I said no."

"You said no?"

"Well, what I said was, I'd had enough to drink, and I had to drive home, so I better not. But then he said, well there was a coffeemaker in his suite—he always said 'suite,' I remember that. It doesn't sound quite as naughty as 'room.' Does it?" Howie nodded, thinking how it had been a long time since he'd heard anyone say "naughty."

Patricia went on: "So, he says, so why didn't I have a cuppa coffee up in his suite?" She paused and even smiled a little. "That's a new line, isn't it? Come up to my suite for a cuppa coffee."

"I'll remember that," Howie said, but then he decided that was too familiar and light, and so he promptly leaned back, resumed his more serious aspect and asked what happened next.

All of a sudden, she said: "He's awfully good-looking, isn't he?"

Howie hadn't expected that, but he nodded. "You see," she went on, "I gotta admit, from the time we left the bar till the time we got to his room—his suite—I had pretty much decided, well, you know, a guy like

this...let's see, but why not? I don't know if you'd
believe me, Mr. Traveler, but I'm not into one-night
stands. But...well, I had a long relationship that broke
up just a little while ago, and now it's this cute guy,
this very cute guy, and I mean I don't care that he's
famous, he's just cute and he's awfully nice, and
maybe I'm a little high, and so by the time we got to
his room, I've pretty much made up my mind. And I
let him kiss me as soon as we got into the room. You
know, standing up, and that was enough, and I figured, okay. You know, I'm with a hunk in a beautiful
suite—what the hey, let's make a thing out of it."

Patricia Richmond couldn't even help but smile at
the memory when she said that.

PATRICIA'S STORY

SHE DROPPED THE SMILE and shifted a little in her chair. Still, Howie couldn't help but notice that there was no catch in her voice. No histrionics. Patricia Richmond, Assistant Vice President, Branch Manager, did not seem to be putting on any kind of show for him. It impressed him. Well, she was very believable. And he was growing even more curious now. By her own admission, she's there in the hotel room expressly to get laid. Rape?

She went on: "So I asked him for a drink. I mean, I want him to woo me just a little, you know. And he said, 'Not a coffee?' And I said, 'Not if I'm gonna stay awhile.' He knew damn well what I meant by that. I mean, I'd already let him kiss me. So all he did was wink and get me a vodka outta the minibar." She shook her head a little, bemused for the moment. "I haven't had anybody wink at me like that in a long time. Guys only wink if they're creeps, real jerks, or..."

"Or what?"

"Or they gotcha, and you know it, and they know you don't mind knowing it. Kinda like a sweet conspiracy, you know? Not many guys can pull that off. So, all right, I winked back at him—holy smokes, I haven't winked since I don't know when—and then he went over and got me the vodka."

Howie had to interrupt here and make sure he had this straight. "So, you go to his room at night, you've both had some drinks, you kiss, you ask for another drink, and you let him know you're going to, uh, go to bed with him?"

"Can I trouble you for a water?" Patricia asked. "I told you this wouldn't take long, but I'd love just a water."

Howie got up and took some ice from the bucket. She went on. "I know what you're saying. A girl goes to a guy's room and tells him it's okay—it's really leading him on."

"I'd say it's kinda more than that," Howie concluded, handing her the icewater, then going back to make one for himself, too.

"Yeah, well, I agree. Mr. Traveler, I told you, I'm no innocent. I know I was, uh, you know, arousing him. And after he got me the vodka, we were right there together on the couch. This room—you know, the suite—is just like his." She waved an arm around. Howie came back with his water glass and settled back down in the chair. "We were right here, right where I am now, and after a little while, we started kissing again and fooling around." She stopped. "That was when he said something." She stopped again.

"What?" Howie asked.

"Something I found inappropriate."

"You don't wanna say what?"

"If I ever have to, in a trial or whatnot. But take my word, it was extremely rude. I got the picture real fast. I knew then what the situation really and truly was, that he was some big fucking—pardon my French—ballplayer, and he thought I was just some street tramp. Yeah, I was just there to *service* him, and never mind me. Like—wink, wink—he was entitled to do whatever he pleased, and I should just be so happy because he's this great all-star, so just like that"—she snapped her fingers—"I told myself, if you got any pride at all, girl, get the hell outta here."

Patricia drew a breath and sipped her water. "So I got up. And you know what?"

Howie shook his head.

"He thought I was going to the bedroom. That's what he actually thought—like I could hardly wait to get in there and go d—" She stopped. "Oh, what the hell, you know what I'm talking about: go down on him. That's how I got away from him at first, 'cause then I snatched up my purse, and I said something like, 'I'm sorry, I changed my mind.' I mean, I didn't curse him or anything, I just politely said, you know: no. And I headed for the door. I probably would've got away, too, but I kinda paused to straighten myself out a little, because my blouse—you know."

"I know."

"And that's when I opened the door, and then he grabbed me, and that's when I saw you, and just then he pulled me back and slammed the door with his foot."

Howie said: "Why—" He was starting to say, why didn't you scream, but he caught himself. He asked: "Did you scream?"

Patricia wasn't buying Howie's dumb act. She shook her head. "You know very well I didn't." She spoke that in a very flat but very direct way. Uncomfortable, Howie folded his arms. "All right, of course, I shoulda screamed. Then I'm sure you woulda done something. In the hall there. But it all happened so fast. I'm pretty sure he didn't even see you in the hall. And me—nobody'd ever done anything like that to me before." She paused then. "Nobody'd ever raped me before. *Yet.*" This time Howie nodded. She shrugged. "Well he did. But first he just hauled me back. He called me a 'prick-teaser.' God I hate that. *Prick-teaser.* I've always hated that. He called me that, and then he kinda half-carried, half-dragged me into the bedroom and threw me on the bed."

"Did you scream then?"

"I made the mistake. You see, I told him: 'I'm *going* to scream.' I mean, I was still trying to be reasonable. So he put his big hand over my mouth. Cripes, he was strong, and I swear to God, I thought, he could smother me with one hand if he wanted to. Also, I thought, the guy in the hall—" She paused for the moment and looked dead into Howie's eyes. "The guy in the hall, he saw him grab me. He's gonna call security for sure. Someone's gonna be here any sec. And so I struggled for awhile, you know, hitting at him a little, trying to turn away, crossing my legs tight and everything, but I couldn't do anything, he was so strong, and then I just thought well, nobody's comin' to help, and he's too strong for me, and if I don't wanna get hurt I better just stop tryin'. I mean, I'm on the pill. I'm not gonna get pregnant or anything. So...I just...let him...rape me." She said it again: "Rape me."

Howie ducked his head. He'd always wondered exactly how it was, rape. Couldn't a woman somehow...?

"And you know what?" Patricia asked. He shook his head. "When he was finished, when he rolled off me and he was just lying there next to me, kinda laughing, I asked him: 'Nobody ever said no to you?' And he actually said: 'Not yet.' I mean, what is it with these guys? Don't they live in the real world? I been with guys they didn't want to hear no, they didn't want to *believe* no, but they damn well understood when I said n-o, no. But not the big superstar. No. Not Mr. Entitled." She shrugged. "So that was it. I didn't even clean myself off. Not till I got to the ladies' room down in the lobby. I just got up and said if you don't mind, thank you very much, I'd like to go now."

Patricia took a sip of water. She was still very composed.

"Did he try to stop you?"

She shook her head. "No, not then. But you know what he said? 'Hey, come on. stick around. The next time'll be even better.' Can you believe that? I mean, he's so full of himself, I think he already believed I wanted it."

Howie said: "So, you just left?"

"Well, yeah, I started to, but all of a sudden he jumps up and runs over to me. All's he got on is his undershirt. He never got that off. I froze. I thought,

'Ohmygosh, he's gonna grab me again.'"

"Did he?"

"No, but you know what he did?" Howie shook his head. "He's picked up a bunch of bills off his dresser. I work in a bank, and I don't think I've ever seen so much. I mean, it looks like it's all hundreds, the whole wad, and he says, 'Hey, is there a Tiffany's in Baltimore?'

"I said: 'What?'"

"And he jams a bunch of hundreds into my hand, and says, 'Go on, get yourself something nice.'"

Howie said, "Well, you know, Jay's got a lot of money. He picks up checks."

"Please. This is not exactly like takin' a girl out to dinner, Mr. Traveler. This is like—"

"I can see how it would seem."

"Yeah, well now I'm really pissed. Big time. First he wants me to give him a blow job, then he rapes me, then he treats me like a whore. Who is this guy?"

Howie said: "I can see your point. It was a misunderstanding."

"Oh, yeah. Well, I just told him to take his money and shove it. That's exactly what I said: 'Shove it.'" Then she took a long drink of water.

Howie said: "So, that's what happened?"

"That's it. Look, maybe I can't make you believe diddly because he's your big star. But you did see what you saw. You saw me trying to get away from him. You *saw* that." She leaned forward now, and for the first time, she was more a petitioner than a narrator. "So will you help me, please, Mr. Traveler? Will you just please tell the police you saw me open that door and him pull me back? Will you just tell 'em that? What you saw."

Howie thought for a bit. He was still so unsure of everything. All he answered was: "I said I would listen to you. I did."

Patricia Richmond nodded. She'd gotten her hopes up because Howie had heard her out so intently, but now she seemed to understand that she couldn't sway him, couldn't get him to testify against his ballplayer. So, she simply finished her icewater, and got up without making any further entreaties. "You have my card," was all she said. "If you need to know anything else." Once again, she was all businesslike, the sales rep who'd made her best pitch.

Howie rose too. Before she turned to the door, he asked her: "Tell me one thing."

"All right."

"Do you want money from him?"

"So that's all you can think?"

"Hey, I'm just asking. You gotta know there could be a lotta money in this for you. So: do you want money from Jay or for him to go to jail? What?"

Apparently, she hadn't expected such a direct question, for now Patricia paused, and crossed her arms before her. "Look," she said, "if they think he should go to jail, okay. If they say he should pay me some money, okay too. But listen, don't you think it's gonna cost me either way? If this goes on, my name's gonna come out, and whatever happens a lotta people are gonna say: there's Patricia Richmond, she fucked Jay Alcazar, and then the tramp tried to get his money. Who's she kiddin'? Go to a hotel room with a ballplayer and then cry rape? Slut, huh? Right? So, yeah maybe I do deserve some money. He wanted to give me some money. Well, hey, maybe I should get a whole lot more. I mean, this is America, isn't it?"

Howie shifted uncomfortably from one leg to another. For the first time, a little doubt about Patricia had crept into his mind. Maybe she sensed that, too, for now she laid it on a little thicker.

"So you know what?" she went on. "Maybe all the money in the world isn't worth it. I thought about that. But then I decided, no, everybody should know that this great ballplayer raped me. He may be a big hero and all for what he did with that maniac in Boston. He may be greater than sliced bread on the, you know, the ball field. Okay, but he's a rapist. Believe it or not, he should pay for that." She paused. "Somehow," she added. "Jail or money."

Patricia walked over and picked up her yellow umbrella by the door. "But, you know, Mr. Traveler, it's really up to you. Unless you tell the truth and tell the cops you saw him grab me and shut that door, nobody'll ever believe me, will they, because it'll just be he said, she said, and who's gonna believe the slut who went to the ballplayer's room and then said no? Who'll believe that?" And she kind of stabbed the air with her umbrella for punctuation, and then the door closed behind Patricia Richmond.

Howie sat by himself for a long time, listening to the rain that still pounded down. Even if it stopped soon, would they even be able to play the makeup game tomorrow? The outfield would still be a swamp, wouldn't it? But finally, he stopped pretending to himself that he was thinking about baseball and got up and went to the phone and called Lindsay.

She'd been planning to drive to Bethany Beach in Delaware, where she'd rented a house with some friends, but she told him it was still pouring torrents in Washington, too, that she'd put off leaving for a day. What good's a beach in the rain?

Howie said: "Listen to me, honey. I've got something to tell you."

And he explained how he'd seen the door to Jay Alcazar's room open and close and how he'd lied to the police, but then how the woman had come to his room, and how she was very authentic, very persuasive, and even if he wasn't completely convinced that maybe she wasn't setting Jay up for a payoff, he had to disclose what he'd seen. He had to. He said: "Lindsay, I just gotta go back to the cops. I gotta altogether tell the truth."

"Are you sure, Daddy?" She didn't have to tell him that that would surely be the end of his time with the Indians, probably even in baseball.

"If nothing else, I gotta do it for you," he said.

Lindsay said: "Well, then, don't do anything till I get there and we can talk about it." So she got in her car and through the wind and the rain she began to drive the forty miles up to Baltimore.

THE SEVENTH GAME

WYN'AMO WILLIS DID FINALLY come back from his injury, and, just as Alcazar had suspected, the unintentional time off served him well. He finished the season with a flourish. God is great. Alcazar himself was tops in the majors with fifty-six home runs, and led in RBIs as well, and only Pepe Davila, drag bunting and slapping choked-up singles, kept him from another Triple Crown.

Alcazar pulled a groin muscle in some freakish way in the last week of the season, but it was not a serious injury, only nettlesome. Still, rest was the only satisfactory cure, and, of course, that was the one thing Alcazar couldn't be treated with, for the Indians didn't take the wild card berth until the next-to-last day of the regular season. But then they walloped the Angels in the first round of the playoffs, and although next, against the Yankees, they lost the first two games, they fought back gallantly. When Ty Baggio pitched a three-hit shutout, Cleveland went to a seventh game in Yankee Stadium—the winner to make the World Series.

For his inspired choice of grizzled old Howie Traveler to manage the Indians, Moncrief was sure he'd be voted Executive of the Year.

The seventh game, at Yankee Stadium, was a dilly. First the Yankees, then the Indians, would go on top, and just when the Yankees finally seemed to have it clinched, 9-6, Cleveland scored four in the top of the eighth. Alcazar drove in the first run that inning with a single, but when he took the cursory arc around first, Howie saw him twinge just a little. "That groin's bothering him more than he's lettin' on," Howie said to Frosty Westerfield.

Frosty replied: "Wild horses couldn't drag Chief outta a game like this."

Howie just said: "Hmm."

The Yankees tied it at ten in their half of the inning, though, but after Willis popped out to lead off the ninth, Alcazar pounded the first pitch into the gap in right center. He rambled into second, rounding the bag, all out, then prudently turned back—an easy, stand-up double. The Indian players stampeded to the front of the dugout, cheering madly. He was the winning run—halfway round. Howie sat back and watched. He didn't say anything, but he thought: *That should've been a triple. A healthy Jay Alcazar gets to third easily and all we need is a sac fly to bring him in.*

The Yankee pitching coach hurried out to the mound to confer with his pitcher, Serikawa. New York still had its relief ace, Wes Lauterbach, in the bullpen, but Jorgenson was up, and he hit Lauterbach better than most. Howie knew that, too. Plus, of course, Moncrief had the numbers to prove it. Howie almost wanted the Yankees to bring Lauterbach in: I was born and bred in this briar patch. But the Yankees had the same numbers, so they stayed with Serikawa. And as the Yankee pitching coach trotted back to the dugout, Howie looked back out to second, and in that instant, instinctively, he called out: "Miranda!"

Despite the din, the whole Cleveland dugout seemed to hear that one word. Half of the players looked to Howie, the other half to Humberto Miranda, the utility outfielder. At first he glanced about, unbelieving. So did everyone else. "Partly Cloudy," Baggio mumbled. Certainly, Howie wasn't sending in Miranda to hit for Jorgenson. He couldn't hit worth a damn. But he did have a good arm and very good legs—a "speed merchant," he was celebrated, whenever he was traded and compliments were required. No, Howie must be sending in Miranda to run for Jay Alcazar. "Move your ass," the manager said. "Run for Jay."

"*Por* Jay?"

"*Por* Jay. I don't see anybody else on base."

Alcazar was standing on second, resting, arms akimbo, when he saw Miranda emerge from the dugout. He did not even comprehend at first what was happening. It simply did not cross his mind that Howie Traveler—that anyone—would take him out of a tie game. Tie game? Jesus H. Christ, tie game, the seventh game of the league championship. As Miranda crossed the first-base foul line and Alcazar realized that, incredibly, that indeed was the case, he did not even quite know how to act. All his years playing baseball, this had never happened to him before, so he wasn't altogether sure of the diamond protocol. Should he stand on second until Miranda physically arrived there? Stunned as he was, he decided that he would wait, and instead of just touching Miranda's hand, as runners in a relay race, he patted the smaller man on the back. "Get home, Berto," he called out.

At home plate, Jorgenson watched Alcazar head to the dugout, out of the game. *You were right, Jay,* he thought, *the old fart will even manage a seventh game his way like it's the fuckin' bushes somewhere.*

Alcazar came into the dugout, slapping hands with several players who stepped up to greet him. He paused in front of Howie. "Nobody ever ran for me in my life," he said, getting that on the record.

Howie simply replied: "You never had a groin pull like this, either."

"For your sake…" Alcazar started, but he didn't say anymore. He only moved down the bench, but just before he sat down, he took off his batting helmet and hurled it hard against the rear dugout wall. It ricocheted back, and when it landed on the dugout floor, nobody dared pick it up. It just lay there, spinning a moment or so more. So, for good measure, Alcazar kicked the sonuvabitch. The television cameras caught the whole scene. It was good theater; America saw it all. The nation also saw Alcazar angrily mutter something, too. What it was was: "Goddamn injury." He was so terribly frustrated with his limitation. It really was the first time—the first time that mattered, anyway—when Jay Alcazar could not do what he told his body to do—in baseball, in bed, wherever.

In the television booth, the announcer said: "I've never seen Chief so worked up."

The director, in the truck outside Yankee Stadium, said: "Gimme a close-up on Traveler."

The camera found him, looking, really, quite contained, even assured. But the national indictment had been, implicitly, made.

The camera returned to Alcazar. Willis was standing over him, trying to calm him down, perhaps employing appropriate scripture.

Ollie Jorgenson dug in at the plate. Miranda inched off second. Serikawa threw a ball, outside. First base was open. He could pitch carefully, walk Ollie if he had to.

Miranda led off again. A little bit more, a little bit more. Suddenly, Serikawa whirled. The Yankee shortstop dashed at an acute angle toward the bag. Serikawa threw to the base. The shortstop arrived just in time, grabbed the throw and put the tag on Miranda. It wasn't all that close. He had made it back safely. But the Yankees had gained something from the transaction, for now Miranda was more cautious. Running the bases is really more about instinct than raw speed; the race isn't always to the swiftest. Sure enough, this time the lead Miranda negotiated wasn't quite so large, and when Jorgenson drove the next pitch up the middle, Miranda, who was still leaning cautiously the wrong way, hesitated for just an instant more before he overcame inertia and took off.

Howie said softly: "Go."

Miranda tore around third, as the coach there, Tatum, windmilled—keep going, go, go. The throw came in. He slid. He was out. But everyone knew: just a little bit longer lead, a better jump when Jorgenson made contact...

Alcazar himself thought: *He's faster, but I woulda scored.*

So the Indians didn't score. Neither did the Yankees, and the game moved into extra innings. Lauterbach came in and got Cleveland one-two-three in the tenth. But neither did the Yankees get a base runner in the home half. Then, in the eleventh, after Lauterbach retired the first two men easily, he walked Nakamura and Willis sent him winging to third with a bloop single. Two out, with the World Series a base away. It was Alcazar's time up, but, of course, he was out of the game, sitting there in his warm-up jacket on the bench next to Ty Baggio, which is where the television cameras found him again. Then they found Howie, arms akimbo. What could he do? He was out of right-handed pinch hitters.

"You gonna let him swing?" Westerfield asked.

"He's a major leaguer," Howie replied. "He's on the team, ain't he?" Westerfield kind of swallowed.

Only then did the TV camera follow Miranda to the plate.

He did not, as wise men are wont to say in assessing his performance, even hit a loud foul. Lauterbach struck him out on three pitches.

Howie said: "Well, Frosty, I guess my tit's in a ringer."

Sure enough, in their at bats, the Yankees won the game and the pennant and went onto the World Series.

After the victorious Yankee stars had entertained the press in the interview room, Howie was brought onto the little stage. Naturally, all anybody wanted to know was why he'd dared to take out Alcazar.

"Because I knew he was hurting, and I knew Miranda is fast, and I thought Berto had a better chance of scoring."

Was that the percentages, Howie? (That figured. People around baseball are always talking about the percentages. It is like people around the Supreme Court are always talking about litmus tests.)

Howie replied: "I'm sorry. There were no percentages here, because the situation had never come up before. If you're gonna have percentages, you've gotta have the situations to derive the percentages from."

So it was a gut decision, huh?

"No, it wasn't my gut. It was my head. Maybe my head was wrong, but it's the only head I got." He rapped his skull, and that got some laughs.

Did you ask Jay?

"You didn't see me run out to second base, did you—?"

No, but I mean like ahead of time, Howie, in case he got on—you know.

"No, I didn't ask him because I know Jay, and he would've just told me he didn't want to come out. Jeez, he didn't want to come out that time in Boston that nut almost shot him. It's like I learned from *Court*

TV. Don't ask a question unless you know you're gonna get the right answer."

Everybody snickered a little.

Greenberg of the Boston *Globe* asked: "What did Jay say to you when he came out of the game?"

Howie said, "Why don't you ask Jay that?"

Greenberg had been one of the pool reporters allowed into the Indians' clubhouse. He said: "I did. He said he didn't want to talk about it."

Howie thought for a moment. Then, straightforward, he said: "Well, I'll tell you what he told me. He told me nobody'd ever run for him before. It hurt him to have me sit him down. I knew that. But I was playing for the one run. And Jay was hurtin', and I'm the one who's the manager."

Sinister Dick turned to Mickey Huey, next to him, and whispered: "Not for long, you won't be, not after this."

THE
WALDORF

ALCAZAR SAT IN HIS ROOM at the Waldorf, looking out at Park Avenue, seeing nothing. Not just his groin—his whole body hurt now. It hadn't before the game. But then, if they'd made the Series, he wouldn't have felt the pain either. *Playing hurt* isn't really correct. If you care enough, if the games matter enough, you don't play hurt. Instead, you're still hurt, but somehow you forget that you hurt. That's the point. What you really do is, you *play dumb*. You don't allow your body to know the pain.

Now, though, the season was over, and all of a sudden, the little aches and the groin injury all began to manifest themselves. Alcazar's whole body throbbed. He dragged himself into the bathroom and threw down some pain pills and began to draw hot water into the tub. He'd taken a shower at the Stadium, of course, but he needed more soothing hot waters. That's all he could think of. He was amazed to find that, even the short distance to the tub, he was limping. Jesus, he wondered, how did I even play? Run? I can hardly walk.

He sat on the cover of the toilet seat and began to undress. It took excruciating minutes for him just to get his pants down over his feet and off. He had to endure terrible pain just to be able to reach down and take his socks off. Gingerly, then, he raised himself up, over to the tub where he slid his body down into the steaming hot waters. Only then, settling down, finding some comfort, did he begin to think about the game again, about how close the Indians had come to winning, to getting into the World Series.

He began, even, to get angry. One man was in the crosshairs of his wrath. How did the dumb sonuvabitch screw it up so badly? How did he cost them the pennant? "Goddamn Miranda," Alcazar muttered out loud. "Stupid fuckin' spic."

LINDSAY ARRIVES

EVEN BEFORE SHE TOOK HER RAINCOAT OFF, Howie reached for Lindsay, took her in his arms and held her. She could feel him shaking a little, but that only made her feel stronger. She had thought about this all the way up from Washington, the windshield wipers slashing back and forth on high, that thump-thump of a heart sound—and what she had decided was that she was going to take charge. She was going to be the parent. "Sit down, Daddy," she said, taking off her coat.

"I gotta tell, sweetie," he said, even before he did sit down.

"Why?"

"Just because it's the right thing to do. I always told you and Davey to do what was right. Now I gotta do what's right."

"But you don't know what's right."

He sighed. "Maybe I didn't. I do now. After she came to see me. Honey, lemme tell you, she was very believable." Howie gestured to the coffee table, where her business card lay. Lindsay picked it up and read it: Patricia Richmond, Assistant Vice President, Branch Manager. She said: "She's a *banker?*"

Howie smiled and said: "Yeah. You never know how you look till you get your picture took."

"So, what did she tell you?"

"That Jay altogether raped her."

"Well, Jay told you he didn't."

"Yeah, but honey, I *saw* the door open."

"Okay, but you don't know what happened when the door closed, Daddy. She's got her story, he's got his. That's why we've got juries."

"Well, yeah, but that's why the jury oughtta hear me say I saw her open the door and him grab her and kick it shut. Women don't open doors and try to get away if everything is, you know, hunky-dory."

"Come on, Daddy, maybe she was just kidding around."

He stared at her: "Like you?"

"I knew that had something to do with this."

"Whatdya expect?" he answered, and even with a bit of annoyance in his voice.

She reached out and took his hands. "Daddy, there wasn't anything you could do about that. It happened. It's over. It's past. Don't let that affect your thinking here."

"I've never forgotten it, honey."

"Well, I've never *forgotten* it either. But I can't go on letting it influence my life. So it's crazy for you to."

Howie turned away and began to pace. "I saw that woman's face, and I can't keep thinking it coulda been—"

"Mine?"

"Yeah."

"Well, it wasn't." For some reason Howie noticed at that point that she wasn't wearing any lipstick. She had left her place in such a hurry to come over to him. All Lindsay had on were jeans and a striped boat-neck shirt, with sneakers, no socks. She hadn't changed or anything.

That made him paternal all of a sudden. "Did you get any breakfast?" he asked.

"I'd had a roll when you called. I'm okay." She crossed her arms. "All right, you're gonna go to the police. Have you told Jay?" He shook his head. "You're going to, aren'tcha?"

"Yeah, 'course. I got to. I'm gonna tell Jay exactly what I saw and why I gotta tell, and then I'm gonna call up Moncrief and resign, and then I'm goin' to the police and then I'm gettin' the hell outta here. I think I'll go somewhere with Margo. If she wants."

"Well, if she doesn't, she's not worth your time anymore."

"Yeah, well…"

And then suddenly, it was the other way round, and Lindsay was the daughter again. "But why, Daddy? Why don't you just let it go? You'll never know the truth. They'll never get him on the evidence they've got. Can't he just pay her some hush money to make it go away?"

"I think maybe that's all she wants."

"There you go—and you'll still be manager of the Cleveland Indians."

"Nah, they'll bag me at the end of the season anyway."

"Maybe not."

"Yeah, well, if we make the playoffs." He made a little whistling noise. "That'll be the day."

Lindsay got her grown-up self back together. "Tell me. Is Jay still so pissed off at you for taking him out of the Yankee game? Is he still carrying a grudge?"

Howie shook his head, glancing up at the ceiling. "You know, he's never said word one to me about that. Not a word. Oh, he hasn't played worth a damn all year, and he's not hurt, but whether he's got it in for me, I don't know. Everybody says it. All the newspapers wrote it, and they keep bringing it up, so I just kinda live with it, but honest to God, I really don't think so."

"Really?"

"I just know he ain't been himself, not all season."

"Whatdya mean?"

"I mean, he seems distracted. Sometimes I think he doesn't even care." He shrugged. "I don't know. Jay's just different."

"Different enough to rape somebody?"

"Oh God, honey, I don't wanna think so, but—"

Impatiently, Lindsay said: "Where is he?"

"Jay?"

"Yeah, is he in the hotel?"

"Why?"

"Is he?"

"Yeah, he checked back in. I mean, different room, but he's right down the hall."

"I'm gonna go see him."

"What?"

"Yeah, I'm gonna go talk to him, Daddy."

"For God's sake, honey, why?"

"Because—okay, because I'm your lawyer."

"Come on."

"I am now." Howie shrugged. "And I'm gonna tell him myself what you're gonna do."

"That's crazy."

"No, it's not. If it's still so damned important to you, then let me do it. Let me ask him if he did it. Why not?" Lindsay shrugged. "Hey, I'm the one who got raped, Daddy, not you."

JULIO

FOR TWO WEEKS AFTER THE INDIANS lost in the seventh game to the Yankees, Alcazar sequestered himself at his house on Fisher Island. He entertained no women, and left but twice, once to see his doctor about his groin injury, once to have dinner with his parents. It was a desultory visit. He did not wish to talk about the defeat, nor was he prepared to talk about going to Cuba (and certainly neither did his father wish to discuss that), and so they made up subjects to chit-chat about over a cheerless meal. Jay had never been so distant, but they understood.

As he began to brood less, though, he made contact with the Cuban baseball agents he knew, and soon enough he was in touch with a man named Julio Baez. He was a Cuban American who carried two passports and was in the business of, for a good price, spiriting Cubans away to America in a high-powered speedboat. Not all Cubans who sought to escape to Florida tried to negotiate the waters in those desperate, rickety contraptions that always made such good standard Associated Press wire photos and spots on CNN when the Coast Guard apprehended them. The ones who had wealthy relatives in La Yuma—what the Cubans always call the United States—could arrange a much faster, more secure passage across the Straits of Florida.

Alcazar sought to strike a three-step deal with Baez—find Rita Garcia, escort him to her, and then convey her to freedom. The palaver did not, however, get off to a good start. Because in greeting: "Hey, Chief," Baez said, with a big smile.

Alcazar glared at him. "If I didn't need you, I'd tell you to get your ass outta here right now." Baez looked as wounded as baffled. "Don't you ever call me that name."

Baez bowed his head. *"Pardonome, senor."*

"And let's stick to English, *hombre*. My Spanish isn't all that good."

"Of course, Mr. Alcazar."

"In fact, I'll need a translator with me in Cuba. Just to be sure."

"No problem, sir."

"All right then, first you have to find the woman. Rita Garcia. I'll give you what information I have." He handed over an envelope; there wasn't much in it. "She's my mother."

Baez looked up, surprised.

"Okay, she's the woman who carried me. She was married to the man who was the younger brother to my father here—Victor Alcazar. He—my real father—was named Emilio."

"And may I ask where he is now?"

"He's dead. He died in prison down there."

"I'm sorry."

"Yeah, I never knew him. Victor became my father after they got me out."

"Do you have a picture of your mother?"

Alcazar shook his head. "I have no idea what she looks like, except I know she was pretty and she was dark. She must be, 'cause look at me." He pinched his own tan cheek. "And all the Alcazars are white."

Baez was still careful from his original *faux pas*. He spoke carefully now. "May I tell you something? What we say?"

"Say about what?"

"About the color of people."

"All right."

"We often describe people after coffee. You can see I'm very white, but still, just a little bit dark. They'll say, 'Baez, he's *leche con una got a de café.*' That's: he's milk with a drop of coffee."

Alcazar smiled. "I like that. And me?"

"You're darker. You'd be *café con leche*. Or maybe, since you've got your father's blue eyes: *leche con café*. We come in so many shades."

"And so my mother is just black coffee?"

"Or maybe *café con una gota de leche*. See? A drop of milk. But, in general, we divide black people into two groups. If you're *negro de pasas*—"

"What's that? *Pasas?*"

"Raisins. *Uno negro de pasas* means a black man with kinky hair. Looking at you, your mother, this Rita, she's probably what we call *una negra de pelos*.

That's a black woman with straight hair. Like yours."
He grinned. "They're the women we like the most."

"*Negra de pelos*," Alcazar said, enjoying hearing
himself repeat the colloquial phrases in Spanish.

"Yeah, and I can make sure some of them keep you
company when you're down there."

Alcazar held out his hands, palms out. "Hey, come
on, Julio, I'm there to see my *mother*."

They both laughed. "Well, let me know. There's
plenty. Unfortunately, pretty girls down there—what
can they be, but—" He shrugged. "*Jiniteras.* It's no
disgrace, not really. When you're pretty and poor and
there's no hope. Maybe you meet a tourist, a Canadian,
German, what have you. If you're a good-looking
negra de pelos—especially with blue eyes like you—
who knows? A *norteno* may take you home."

Alcazar bit his lip. "Goddamn," he said.

"Goddamn what?"

"Just goddamn that country. I gotta get my mother
out."

Baez waved a finger in the air. "If we can find her, I
guarantee it."

Alcazar said: "There's an extra $10,000 in it for you
the minute she gets here." Money was no object in this
case. But then, money was never much of an object
with Alcazar.

"Thank you," Baez said. After the initial misstep, he
was pleasing Alcazar very nicely. "Now, your
mother—Garcia. She and Emilio Alcazar—?" Delicately, he paused.

"No, I don't think they ever got married. I only
know he met her near this town named Cienfuegos

after he got out of jail the first time. They sent him there to cut sugar cane."

"Ah, *uno machetero*. Nasty work. Brutal."

"Yeah, I've heard."

"So," Baez explained, "she was Emilio's *marinovia*." Alcazar cocked his head that way he did, eyeing Baez curiously. "It's a good word we've made up. It's a combination of *marido*, which means 'spouse,' and *novia*, which means 'sweetheart, fiancée.'"

"*Marinovia?*"

"Yes, exactly. It sounds so much better than live-in girlfriend, doesn't it?"

Alcazar did like that. "If I ever move anybody in here, that's what she'll be," he said. "My *marinovia*."

"Ahh, famous as you are, you'll bring that word to La Yuma."

"No, just my mother, Julio. I just want to bring her here."

Julio got back on track. "But you know nothing of her since you left? Where she lives? What she does? Did she marry after your father died? Any more children?"

Alcazar shrugged, unknowing. "If there are any, get them all on the boat."

"And if there's a husband?"

"Of course. Him too. Just get her back here."

Baez said: "If she's alive, I'm sure we can locate her."

"Hey, she's alive. My mother's still alive down there. I sense that. I know that." Alcazar was never very mystical, but he felt absolutely sure in this one regard.

A
FAMILY
CHAT

SINCE HE WAS ENCOURAGED BY how well things had progressed—and, since, as well, his injury had completely healed—Alcazar began to put the sour thoughts of the season's end behind him. He resumed his usual discreet amorous activity, went fishing down in the Keys, and then even began working out some in the weightroom in his house. Always in his mind, though, he was waiting to hear back from Baez.

It was, in fact, only a matter of ten days before Baez reported that they had found the whereabouts of Rita Garcia. She was still living in Cienfuegos, working as a *torcedore,* rolling cheap cigars in a broken-down old factory. "But no one said anything to her?" Alcazar asked.

"You said not to approach her. My man didn't."

"Good. I'll go next week," Alcazar said. "Get the boat ready."

He was excited, in a hurry, but it was with trepidation that he revealed his plans to his parents.

"I'm leaving Tuesday," he told his mother.

"Have you told your father yet?" Cynthia asked. She was alone with her son in the large, light living room, sipping coffee, her bichon frise, Beaucoup, at her feet.

He shook his head. "I wanted to talk to you first."

"Oh?"

"Look, Mom," he said, "I've decided that if you don't want me to go, then I won't."

She was stunned, so terribly touched that she reached out and took his hand and squeezed it hard. "Oh, darling, that's so sweet, but I couldn't stop you. Even if I wanted to. Even if I had the right to. This is something you want so much. I know you must do it."

"Not if it'll hurt you."

She let go Jay's hand, and picked up the little dog and put it in her lap. This was diversionary. It kept her from crying. She patted Beaucoup. "When this first came up, I told you that it doesn't threaten me, darling. You're my only son, and I think I've been your only mother."

"That's right."

"If you can get this woman back here—"

"I know we can."

"Well then, I'll do everything I can to help her." She bowed her head, patting the little dog again. She looked back up, smiling. But now there was some mist in her eyes. "You see, the way I look at it, I owe her a great debt. She gave me you. So: what can I give her in return?"

Jay kneeled down by his mother's chair, and wrapped his arms around her. Her tears came for real now. His eyes clouded up some, too. When he leaned away slightly from her, she took her hand off the dog and touched his cheek. "You know, darling, as much as I love you, I never knew how much until I saw that madman holding the gun on you in Boston."

"I'm sorry you had to see that, Mom."

"Well, it was good in a way, because I think I died then, Jay."

"Died?"

"Yes, I was so frightened I honestly think I somehow died." She managed a smile. "And now that I've died, nothing can scare me anymore. Isn't that silly?"

"Oh, Mom." And he leaned forward and hugged her again, so hard that Beaucoup jumped from Cynthia's lap.

"Yes, that's how much I love you."

Victor Alcazar had come into the room, but he waited until Jay pulled back from the embrace before he announced himself. "So you're leaving," he said, for he certainly understood. As best he could manage, his voice was flat and carried no expression with it.

Jay rose. "On Tuesday, yes sir. Flying from Nassau."

"I take it they found her." Everyone was careful not to refer to Rita Garcia as the mother.

"In Cienfuegos."

"And what did she say?"

"No one's talked to her, Dad. I didn't want that till I got there myself."

"Of course." Victor moved into the middle of the room then. He was, as always, perfectly, fashionably dressed. It was nearing lunchtime, and he always wore a sportjacket when he ate with Cynthia. Usually, such as now, he also placed a boutonniere in his left lapel. Today's was a small yellow flower, perfectly round. As Victor drew closer he glanced at Cynthia. She nodded, and, without a word, reached down, gathered up her little dog, and left. Jay found that curious. His father beckoned him to take a chair. "Then I have something I must tell you," he said.

"What is this?" Jay asked.

"The circumstances."

"What circumstances?"

"The circumstances of when you left Cuba."

Jay sat down into a chair, but he did not settle there. He leaned forward. "Something I don't know?"

Victor kept his feet. Nervously, he played some with his hands as he began to recount the story. "I was able to speak to my sister before she and Jorge left. We had to be careful over the phone, you understand. I had no idea what sort of boat Olga was leaving in. God, had I only known, Jay. A rusty bucket, and packed to the gills with too many people."

"Yes sir. Would you like to sit, Dad?"

"No, I prefer to stand, thank you." Victor could be very formal, and he was now. "Had I only known, had we been able to speak more clearly, I would've demanded that she wait for something better. Time was not of the essence. Another week, another. But—" He shrugged. "In any event, not knowing the circumstances, I told her: bring the baby with you."

Jay's ears perked up. He rose up even more in his seat. "The baby? Just me?"

"No, Jay, no. Excuse me—the mother *and* the baby. Your father, as you know—Emilio was back in prison, and I was quite sure that this time they would never let him out. I was, however, still foolish enough to believe at that time that soon enough he would be overthrown, somehow." He paused. "You should know that, since you are going, Jay. Castro—they just call him…He. *El.* Like God. He. *El.*"

"Yes sir."

"So, there was nothing anyone could do for your poor father. Not till the day of reckoning. Of course, who knew they would never be able to get rid of Castro? Who knew Emilio would die first, so soon? They must have killed him. The bastards. They must have tortured him." Jay rested back a little. "He was a brave man, your father."

"Yes sir, I know."

"So foolish to fall for Fidel. But he was young, and that's what the best young people do. They're idealistic, and they can't be blamed if that leads them astray. Better man than I, your father was."

"No sir, come on."

"No, no, no, Jay. I never was caught up in that kind of fervor. I wasn't ever a good young man. I grew up too fast. I didn't have the time to be a romantic. It really isn't the Alcazar manner. But your father—when he realized how he'd been deceived by Castro, he was just as quick to work for a new revolution. And it cost him his life." He sighed. "But we didn't know that back then. We still believed freedom would come."

"Please sit down, Dad."

"All right." He chose a straight-backed chair, though, and crossed his legs at the ankles, as proper as any lady would. It wasn't effeminate, though; it merely seemed to ground him better, with his hands upon his thighs. "Perhaps that's why I'm so...unforgiving, why I cannot merely say, well, what's done is done." He waved an arm, as someone would be dismissive. "I believe I would dishonor your father, dishonor Emilio, if I were any less adamant. We find our rhythm in our lives. Emilio was a young romantic. I, perhaps, am now an old one. I'd like to think Emilio would enjoy that."

"You think I'm dishonoring him by going back?"

"Oh no, Jay, I would never say that. You have other demands upon your conscience. You have this woman there." He paused and made himself say it: "Your mother."

"Yes sir."

"But, to return to that time, when you were a baby. I knew Emilio would want his son out of there, away from Fidel."

"I'm sure that's true, Dad."

"Well, I was selfish, too. Nobody loves your two sisters as I do, but every man wants a son, and we knew then, your mother and I, that it would be unwise for her to bear any more children."

"I didn't know that, sir."

"It is not something we have discussed, nor really did we have to after you came into our family. Then, you see, yes, we had our girls, but here you were, you became my son...you understand: my son till Castro was removed and your father was released. I swear to you, Jay. That's what I thought. I would raise you for five, ten years, and then the happiest day of my life, Cuba would be free again, and I could give you back to Emilio. I swear to you, that was what I believed."

"And my mother? Rita? If she ever chose to come here?"

"Oh, if she came, we would welcome her into our house, Jay. We would make an apartment for her and you. Here. And your mother was as much for that as I was."

"But she decided not to come? To stay with Emilio."

"Yes, as you know."

Jay smiled sweetly. He said: "I always thought, for her to give me up, to give me my chance for freedom while she stayed there, waiting for Emilio. I've always thought how wonderful that was about her."

Victor lifted his hands up briefly, then laid them back in his lap, where he rubbed them together, nervously. "There, you see. It was not quite like that. This is what I must tell you." Jay only cocked his head at him, wary now. "A couple of days before the boat was to leave I was able to get through on the phone to Olga again. She said that she had gone to Cienfuegos, and spoken to Rita, and Rita did not want to come on the boat and...and she did not want you to go either."

"She didn't?"

"No. And so, Jay, I told Olga, whatever you do, bring the baby. Do not let another Alcazar grow up under that evil man. And that's what he is. He is the devil himself."

Jay rose slowly from his chair and approached his father. "Now wait, Dad. Castro isn't the subject here. We're talking about my mother. She wanted to keep me there?" Victor nodded. "So?"

"I could not tolerate that."

"So what then?"

"So I told Olga to get you."

"You had them kidnap me?"

"Really, Jay, I understand your feelings, but I believe that's too strong a word."

"Then how did Olga get me?"

"She and Jorge went to the house while Rita was at work, and the woman who was caring for the baby understood they were aunt and uncle, and she let them take you out for awhile."

"And then they just took off with me?"

"Yes. They left with you on the boat that night."

"You don't think that's kidnapping?"

"No. I think what it is, is it gave you a life of liberty. It gave you a chance to grow up here in the United States in freedom and to live the good life you have and to become the person you are. I would hope, when you balance the scales, Jay, that you would appreciate that."

"Yeah, but how much did my mother appreciate having her child taken from her?"

"She could have come, Jay. Olga said: come with us. Bring the baby. Come."

"But she wanted to stay, with Emilio."

"Yes, that was her decision."

"But your opinion counted more?"

Victor pondered for only a moment and then spoke very matter-of-factly. "Yes it did," he said. "For this family. After all, she wasn't married to Emilio."

"That's got nothing to do with this. She was his *marinovia.*" Victor looked up curiously when he heard his son speak such a colloquial Cuban word. "He loved her."

"Yes, and I'm sure Emilio loved his son, too, and would have wanted the best for you. If we could have spoken to him in prison, I'm sure that's what he would've wanted."

Alcazar glared at his father. "You had no right," he said, and he got up from the chair and, looking down at his father, he went on: "Maybe that's what broke his heart in prison, that he was taken from his *marinovia*, and then their baby was taken from them both. Maybe that broke his will."

"That's a hateful thing to say, Jay. Don't you dare ever say that again to me." He waggled a forefinger in his son's face.

Jay reached out and snatched the finger in his fist and held it there. "There won't be an again," was all he said, and then he let the finger go, and brushed by his father.

His mother was outside the room, listening. She was crying as he passed her, but Jay was so upset, so full of anger, that he did not even pause before her as he left his father's house, striding, the one long leg reaching out far beyond the other, until he was gone from her sight.

HAVANA

THE CUSTOMS OFFICER AT THE HAVANA airport immediately recognized Alcazar. "*El Jefe,*" he swooned, completely compromising that overbearing demeanor with which bureaucrats in impoverished or despotic countries invariably welcome visitors. He even started to call over to one of his colleagues, until Alcazar reached across the barrier there, whispered, "*Senor, por favor,*" then rested a finger upon his own lips. "I'm just here to visit Cuba, please," he went on in Spanish. "I want no attention." The officer, honored to be taken into the great player's confidence, settled for an autograph as the price for complicit silence.

Alcazar picked up his bag and met his guide. He was a hefty white man (with skin colored by a drop of milk, *gota un leche,* Alcazar thought, getting into the spirit). He had turtle eyes and a large, droopy mustache, but a manner not consonant with such a dispiriting countenance; in fact, he was an upbeat fellow, who, with the best Cuban outlook, chose to see the

empty glass as better than no glass at all. He introduced himself as Paco Acosta. Jay was immediately
pleased: Acosta spoke perfect, unaccented English; he
would make a fine translator whenever his own Spanish failed him. Acosta also explained that although he
had had no one to speak it to for many years, he was,
as well, fluent in Bulgarian, for he had been sent to
Sofia to study when Bulgaria was still another faithful
spoke in the Soviet wheel.

Outside the airport, which was almost bereft of
cars, Acosta escorted Alcazar to a Toyota van, intro-
ducing him there to Tomas, their driver. He welcomed
Jay with a warm abrazo. Tomas was younger and
somewhat darker than Julio, about the shade of
Alcazar, as a matter of fact, but bigger even than both
of the other large men. His hug enveloped Alcazar. It
was obvious that Tomas had been chosen as a driver
for physical attributes above and beyond his road
skills. He appeared to be a good man to have on your
side in a pinch.

Both men were officially in the tourist business,
having abandoned other, more prestigious professions
in order to work in an area where there was an association with foreigners (or, more to the point: the chance
of association with hard foreign currency). Paco had
been a history professor, Tomas a newspaper reporter.
The occasional undercover work they did for Julio
Baez, escorting the more fortuitous Cubans to their
maritime escapes, was dangerous but extremely boun-
tiful. Paco told Jay that he himself was seriously con-
sidering leaving on some speedboat run in the near
future; he'd get a cut rate. But there was a wife and

two children, and even with a family package deal, he still lacked sufficient funds.

"The trouble with *El Senor* is, he has the genes of an elephant," Paco explained, as Tomas drove the van away from the airport down the broad, empty highway. "Everyone in the whole damn family seems to live into their nineties. I tell my wife, we must go. Otherwise, Fidel will dance on my grave."

"You get my mother out safely, I'll get your family out," Alcazar promised, in casual response.

"You mean that?" Paco asked, incredulously.

"I mean it." Alcazar spoke that as blithely as if he was promising to buy him a round of drinks.

"Hey! And me?" Tomas chimed in from behind the wheel. "It's just me, no wife anymore, no children."

"You're a throw-in in the deal," Alcazar replied gaily. Whatever of their support he might not have had—and he was paying them generously, too—he now enjoyed it in spades. But, then, what was a few thousand more dollars when you made millions a year and didn't want to buy thirty-six cars or build a mansion the size of Delaware, the way other rich, young athletes did? All things considered, in fact, Alcazar was generous with the people he dealt with and lived rather prudently for a young man of his wealth. Among other things, he eschewed jewelry; even his ears were unadorned.

Tomas took him to his hotel in downtown Havana. the Santa Isabela, an old colonial palace that had been beautifully remodeled when Castro had been absolutely forced to let capitalist money in. The Santa Isabela lay by the Plaza de Armas, at the foot of

Obispo Street, the narrow shopping lane turned busy pedestrian boulevard that cut through the heart of Old Havana. In its bustle of commerce, Obispo gave to the city one thoroughfare which had the flavor of other, freer places.

It was tomorrow that the three men would travel the hundred and fifty miles or so to the southeast, where Cienfuegos lay by the bay. Alcazar was impatient. He would have gone right away, but Baez had convinced him that he should spend at least one day in Havana, catch his breath, see a little of the city.

So, after he got settled in his room, Paco and Tomas drove him about. In a way, what Alcazar saw—the dilapidated old buildings that had once been so majestic; the old cars held together by whatever passed for sealing wax these days; the semi-pro young girls, hitchhiking; the boys selling Che T-shirts (and whispering to sell cigars and/or their sisters, as well); the bulky, trucklike "camel" buses, overflowing with the sweaty multitudes—all seemed nearly familiar. After all, Alcazar had seen so many pictures and movies of Castro's Cuba. Then too, so many of his father's expatriate friends who had gone back to inspect their sad old home had returned with vivid descriptions of the place. So, for Jay, it was not sight-seeing so much as sight-confirming. He felt less a tourist than an intruder, peering at these poor people who could well have been him, in a wasted place that seemed, at last, simply and terribly disappointing.

He told Paco that he would like to walk about the old town himself. He had on sunglasses and a straw fedora and placed a cigar in his chops, so that he would not likely be recognized. Indeed, had he had a mustache as well he would have looked quite like a shady character from a *novela,* those Mexican television soap operas. "All right," Paco said, "but when you go down Obispo, just off the other end there is Parque Central."

"Central Park?"

"Not so much a park as a plaza. And whatever you do, Jay, don't go there." The admonition was offered in the same tone as in fairy tales, when the orphans are warned to stay out of the forest.

"Why?"

"Men gather there all day. And all they do, hour after hour, is talk about baseball. If they were to see you, I swear I do not believe they would let you go. We would never get to Cienfuegos."

So, naturally, like the little boy in the fairy tale, as soon as Alcazar had found his way down Obispo, he made directly for the Parque Central. And sure enough, there on one side, a swarm of men gathered about, shouting at each other on the singular subject of baseball. Alcazar stood in the back, in the shadows, under a palm tree, making sure to keep the brim of his hat well down over his forehead.

And there he listened. At first the men were arguing over some players on the Cuban national team, about which Alcazar knew almost nothing. But then, suddenly, he heard his own name, and the discussion of the seventh game of the Yankee series. He stepped back a little and tried to make himself even less conspicuous. He felt rather like Tom Sawyer, come back to town to find his own funeral in progress.

It was immediately evident, too, that the argument had the feel of liturgy. Obviously, Howie's removal of Alcazar from the game had been a subject of intense dispute for the whole month or so that had passed. Most of the boisterous assembled were convinced that it was madness to dare take out a player of Alcazar's stature. Howie was a fool, or worse. Only two men— one a grizzled old coot who wore a New York Mets cap, the other a scrawny young fellow who spoke with more assurance than all the others—loudly upheld the opinion that whatever Alcazar's intrinsic value, he was hurt, slowed at that time, so Howie was right to take the risk for the one, winning run. The others hooted at the two holdouts, but they would not back down and even appeared to pick up a little support on the fringes of the crowd.

There was a part of Alcazar that wanted to yank off his hat and sunglasses, hurl his cigar to the ground, and jump into the midst—ta, daa! He knew he would've been a veritable *deus ex machina*, god more than man, descending into the scrap. But the moment passed, and soon the men had moved on to discuss the World Series itself, wherein the Yankees had whipped the Braves. So, in time, Alcazar fell back, then passed away from the scene, drifting out of the plaza and back down Obispo to his hotel. There, he tried to nap, but was too keyed up to fall asleep, even when he made the room dark as pitch.

That evening, Paco and Tomas took him to the finest *palador* they knew, which was located through the harbor tunnel over by the Morro Castle. *Paladores,* Paco explained, were another of the concessions that Castro had made after the Soviet Union collapsed and Cuba lost its financial lifeline. The people were so desperate by 1994, even down to eating their pets, that *El* was forced to tolerate a certain amount of private enterprise. Thus were restaurants legalized in people's houses—*paladores*. Some of them quickly became, in fact, restaurants where the owners only incidentally also happened to live, but out of necessity they remained open and thrived on the tourist trade and amongst those few lucky Cubans who managed to find ways to accumulate real money, dollars and euros.

"It is better now," Paco said. "*El* had to loosen the ties some, or we all would have died—and what a bad advertisement for socialism starvation would have been."

"Still," said Tomas, looking over the rich menu, "we all know what the three great failures of the revolution are..." He paused for the old punchline. "Breakfast, lunch, and dinner."

The three men were sitting at a table in a corner of the courtyard, where Alcazar could best go unrecognized. There did not appear to be any Americans in the place, and, of course, the Europeans there would not know a baseball player from a Congressman, but a couple of Cubans spotted him and anxiously speculated on his identity. It couldn't be. But: the resemblance; it must be. They kept their distance, though. Cuba was not a place where you boldly inquired of strangers.

Alcazar ate well of the shrimp and roast pork, but he drank too many mojitos. That was unlike him; he was temperate with alcohol (and had never so much as even tried marijuana). But the sweet Havana Club rum, the mint, the sugar—he drank them like so much Mountain Dew and grew vague and tipsy, uncaring of whatever his two companions babbled on about. His mind was off. He was nervous of what the next day held for him, and it showed, never mind the liquor. Paco and Tomas understood; they made no more effort to take him out on the town. Alcazar gave them both hundred-dollar bills with thanks for taking such good care of him.

In his room at the Santa Isabela, Jay lay in the dark. The rum should have put him out at last, but it failed him, for too much still pressed on his mind. He wondered, as he had so often now, about this mother of his, Rita Garcia. What would he call her: *madre?* No, no, that would be foolish at first, however correct. Should he embrace her, kiss her? No, take both her hands—a gesture affectionate, but not too intimate—and wait to see how she reacted?

But she would be the one caught by surprise. He must be so understanding. Then too: would he see any of himself in her? Were there any half-brothers or -sisters? A husband? Whatever, they must all come with her when she departed in the boat for freedom. He would take care of them all in Florida. They would be, as indeed they were, his family. All the more so would he be their benefactor now that he had learned how he had been stolen from Rita.

Still, even now that he had somewhat accommodated the surprise of his father's revelation, Jay remained all twisted up. The trouble was that he knew his father was right. By kidnapping him, pirating him out of Cuba, Victor had given him a life, a joy—never mind the extraordinary success—that he could have never attained in this sad, awful place of his birth. And yet, he now knew that he had gained that wonderful world of his at the price of his mother's despair.

He had even begun to wonder: how does a man feel whose birth results in his mother's death? Wasn't that the equivalent of his situation? No, no it wasn't anymore his fault than the newborn whose birth means death for the mother, but it was just so: his glorious life had been fraudulently purchased from his mother. His life wasn't a lie, but neither was it any longer something that he could take at face value, because he knew that in fairness he should have lived that life here, in want and oppression. And with her.

Well, all right, now he would put it all back right. He would bring his mother to freedom—or more important, into his life, where he could give her all the love and everything else except the twenty-seven years he had been lost to her. Still, even with those sweet thoughts, Jay could not get to sleep. He turned over and over, and, an hour or so later he had to rush to the bathroom and throw up all that sweet rum and, with it, what he had eaten for dinner. It had been years since he had done that. But then, Jay knew that right now he was not himself. Tomorrow, though, tomorrow he was sure, he would be more himself than ever he had been. It was that thought that finally carried him off.

HOMETOWN

THE THREE OF THEM LEFT FOR Cienfuegos mid-day, in time to be there when Rita Garcia got off from work. "It's a little cigar factory," Paco explained. "The tobacco fields are east of there, near Remedios. It's not the best stuff. Nothing exported."

Alcazar was barely listening, as Paco went on with his tourist-guide spiel about how tobacco was harvested, rolled into cigars, distributed and so on and so forth. Alcazar was sitting in the front seat of the van, studying a map. He turned around to Paco, who was alone in the back seat, and interrupting him in the midst of his lengthy discussion about cigar commerce, he pointed to Cienfuegos, on the southern coast. "But the boat will leave from up here, won't it?" he asked, moving his finger to the north coast.

Paco touched a spot nearby. "Yes. See, right here—pretty much a straight run to the Keys," he said. "Or the mainland."

"It won't be hard to get her to the boat?"

"That's not difficult at all. The only real problem is avoiding the Coast Guard and landing. The problem isn't Castro, it's you guys. But"—he shrugged— "they never caught us yet."

"Never?"

"Not the baby we run. She's fast. And the captain, Oscar, he knows his stuff."

Alcazar nodded and sat back, pleased. After a moment, though, he asked: "When can we do it?"

"Anytime," Paco answered. "Right, Tomas?"

"Maybe not tomorrow night, but Thursday we could go, I'm sure."

"Really? That soon?"

"Whenever your mother says she's ready," Paco said. The only issue was money, and, of course, they knew Alcazar was good for the money.

Alcazar sat back again and watched the road go by. They were on the Autopista, the only real superhighway in Cuba, running from Havana down the spine of the island. They zipped along, overtaking only the odd car and authorized tourist bus. There was nothing much to see, not even any billboards. It all seemed so terribly out of place to Jay. He had no frame of reference for this.

By two-thirty they had turned off the highway and found their way to Cienfuegos. It was not unlike Havana in its dilapidation. The larger houses along the main streets were all tumbling down, if still showing the vestiges of how sturdy and attractive they must have been back when Cienfuegos styled itself as "The Pearl of the South Coast." Lots of places around the world were pearls of this-or-that once; surely, none had lost their gem status so thoroughly as had Cienfuegos. Tomas parked the van on a street in the middle of town, and they walked into the Parque Marti, passing by the statue of Jose Marti, Cuba's liberator.

Jay found there a fancy, wide-open place surrounded by large, handsome buildings—a cathedral, an old opera house, a museum—whose exteriors did not offer much evidence, from a distance, of how much they might actually be deteriorating inside. It must have been grand, once. "Caruso himself sang there," Paco announced, pointing over to the opera house, falling back into his guide motif. Alcazar nodded, even though he didn't know exactly who Caruso might be. As they walked across the plaza, without the benefit of any shade, he found it unbelievably hot— like walking onto the field in Texas in July for a day game Sunday. There must have been no breeze at all coming off the bay. The three men passed by the bandstand in the middle of the mall. There was almost no one else around, not even any children playing.

"Over there," Paco said, pointing to a little café, El Palatino. They went and sat inside, on rum casks, and drank beers under a ceiling fan.

Alcazar looked at his watch. It was past three. "Shouldn't you be going?" he asked.

"The factory doesn't let out work till—well, it's four-thirty by the time the rollers clean up. Don't worry, Jay, we'll be there."

"And you know what she looks like?"

"Hey, I saw her—remember?"

"Oh yeah. I'm sorry, I'm nervous." Alcazar took the cold beer bottle and rolled it across his forehead.

Paco patted him on the arm. "Hey, it's okay. You're meeting your mother. Any man would be nervous, yeah Tomas?"

"Any man."

Alcazar had carried one important thing from home, and now he took it out of his wallet and passed it over to Paco. It was a simple snapshot a girlfriend had taken of him a little while ago outside, in the back of his house. He liked the picture a lot. It was not some hokey posed baseball shot. On the back, he had written in Spanish: "I am your son, Juan Francisco Alcazar. I have come to see you. Please come with these men to see me. Love, Juan Francisco." Apart from tax forms and other official business, it was the only time he remembered signing his name that way.

Now, his baseball autograph—Jay Alcazar. That came with a tall swoop up of a "J" and then, in counterpoint, a big downward loop in the "y." His "Jay" was a formidable work. By contrast, his "Alcazar" was written out hurriedly, hardly more than a wavy horizontal line after the capital A, so that the last "a" and the "r" ran off to nothing. Well, there was only one Jay starring in any American sport. As long as the Jay was legible, it was quite enough for any lucky beneficiary of his signature. When, in his hotel room, he had written out Juan Francisco on the back of the photograph, it had felt labored and strange.

Paco looked at the photo: "Very nice." He flipped it over and read the message. "I wouldn't worry, Jay. I'm sure she'll believe us. Even if she isn't sure, she'll come." He shook his head and made a clucking noise. "To see her son."

"What mother would not come to see her son?" Tomas asked, shrugging, rhetorically. But:

"Giraffes," Jay answered.

They both looked at him. "Giraffes what?" Paco asked.

"Giraffes are horseshit mothers."

"Giraffes?" They both said in unison.

"Yeah, the worst." He said that with great conviction.

Paco and Tomas looked at each other. Finally, Paco said: "How do you know?"

Jay took a big swig of beer. "My parents. You know, in America. They have two daughters, their own, my sisters. When my oldest sister—Sarah—when she was getting married, I was eight years old. My mother. You know, my American mother—."

Paco said: "Yeah."

"She told my father that this would probably be the last time all five of us would be together, just the five of us, and she wanted to do something together. Not any crap like Disney World. Something special we'd all like. She decided we'd go to Africa on a safari."

With some surprise, Tomas asked: "You would shoot animals, the whole family?"

"No, no, no. On this safari you just look at animals. We went to Tanzania." The two Cubans nodded. "We saw all kinds of animals. Lions, leopards, cheetahs, zebras. Big old ostriches. And one day we saw a whole lot of giraffes, and this guide we had—Heinz was his name—Heinz told us that in the whole animal king-dom, giraffes were the worst mothers. Elephants, hip-pos, rhinos, whatever: you go after their babies, they'll fight you to the death. You go after a giraffe baby, the mother will just take off to save her own ass." He paused and breathed. "I never forgot that. I just see a giraffe on television or something, I think: what a horseshit mother. Never forgot."

Paco and Tomas didn't know what to say. Jay threw back a big swallow of beer. Finally, Paco said: "Well, that's giraffes."

Tomas said: "*Si*"—evidently in Spanish for emphasis.

Jay said: "Yeah, but it just goes to show, not all mothers."

The two Cubans found that very embarrassing, that he was worried his mother might be like a giraffe. So, Paco decided on a diversion. He made a big thing of getting out his mobile phone and handing it over to Jay. "It's on now. If there's any delay, Tomas'll call you on his phone. Okay?" Alcazar nodded. "It'll be an hour or more, Jay. Don't just sit here. Walk around." He wanted him to get giraffe mothers out of his mind. He pointed to the building at the southwest corner of the plaza. It was some kind of old palace, with a blue cupola. "You can walk up to the top, and see the town from there."

Paco and Tomas left for the cigar factory. Jay watched them cross the plaza, pass the statue, and disappear. He ordered another beer, but not long after he started to drink it, a whole slew of tourists poured into the plaza, disgorged from a bus. The tour guide steered them right toward the Palatino, so Alcazar paid the bill and left. He couldn't suffer their cacophony, and, besides, he feared they might be Canadians, who would recognize him and pester him. Right now, all he wanted was to be alone.

He took Paco's advice and walked down to the palace-like building, climbed up the steps and looked out over the town, to the port and the bay. Paco was right: it was a fine vista, especially since the poverty and filth was mostly hidden from this vantage on high. If it was Hawaii or Jamaica or the Bahamas, there would be fancy resort hotels and golf courses, and it would be called a paradise. Places with palm trees are always called paradise, even if they're dumps. Jay had no idea where the cigar factory was, but he searched for it anyway. Maybe it had a sign on the roof. Maybe he could spot Tomas' van. But foliage blocked his view of most of the streets. All he thought, then, as he looked down upon the houses, was this: this is where I was born. This is my hometown. Jesus: my *hometown*. And then he looked around some more and pondered where he might have lived as a boy, if his father, if Victor, had not had him stolen away from his mother.

Oh sure, had his mother reared him here, he would have been just as tall and agile, just as loved, just as good a ballplayer, and the Cuban scouts would have found him and taken him away from Cienfuegos to play for the national team. But never mind that. In this grim, dreary little place, he would have grown up as something apart, as Juan. And Juan would not be Jay. But I am me, he thought, because I am the only me. Everybody is who they are. But then: I would not have been *this* me. I would have been a different me, *altogether*. He smiled. Howie often used that word, altogether. He thought: well, even if I had been altogether the same baseball me, nothing else about me would have been the same.

It was scary to contemplate, and it bothered him all the more that he knew that his father had done an inexcusable thing, but he also knew in his heart that it was the best possible thing for him. That was so very conflicting. In fact, looking down on Cienfuegos now, it frightened him merely to consider how he might have spent his life here. Every day. Day after day, in this hellhole. He even had to catch his breath a little at that thought. What a capricious cocksucker life was. He hated the thought of what he almost had been, and he knew that was a terribly selfish thing to conclude just before he was going to meet his mother, who had lost him, unfairly.

Alcazar came down from the tower. Some tourists were heading up. He froze for an instant, but then he heard them talking, and it wasn't English, and he was sure it was German, so he didn't worry that they would recognize him, and he nodded politely as he passed them. He went back to El Palatino, but the place was jammed with more Germans, so he ordered another beer and took the bottle out to the bandstand in the middle of the plaza. It was a pretty, bright green, evocative of another time, although Jay wasn't quite sure what time—the nineteenth century or right before Castro or what exactly. He would ask Paco. He knew all this historical crap.

But now he realized he was really sweating again. There was not so much as a zephyr that blew this way, and although the sun had gone down some, it still managed to shine past the side of the blue cupola on the old palace and then slide directly under the roof of the gazebo onto him.

Still, even with all the tourists, none had come out here. Instead, the Germans were scurrying all around the edge of the plaza. There was nothing to distract Alcazar, so he kept glancing at his watch, so often that he told himself not to glance but every five minutes—although, of course, there was no way to live up to that regimen unless he looked at his watch to discover when the five minutes was up. Usually he did that every minute. Soon the sun fell down behind the buildings, and it grew a bit cooler. That was when he looked up from his watch and saw the three of them entering the Plaza, coming past the statue of Jose Marti.

The woman was in the middle, striding with them. She was obviously tall. He hadn't thought about that, what his mother's height might be. She was quite dark. Of course, he expected that. He could not tell how she looked, though, from the distance. Reflexively, Alcazar glanced down at his watch one more time. It was only a quarter to five. That made him smile. That meant that his mother had come right away when she had heard that her son was here to see her after all these years.

He went out on the steps of the bandstand and waved to the three, calling out to them where he was.

RITA

HOW OFTEN RECENTLY HAD JAY anticipated this scene? He had envisioned it so many times, hoping, perhaps, that the more he played it out—rehearsed it, if you will—the more relaxed and assured he would be. He depended on muscle memory to hit a baseball. Couldn't it be like that here with how he spoke and moved and acted?

Unfortunately, regardless of how often he had visualized what might happen, he was immediately thrown off. As Jay had imagined it, Rita Garcia would be a svelte, beautiful woman, a regular Latin siren—albeit, perhaps, of some fading glamour. She was, after all, he reckoned, in her late forties, perhaps fifty—no more. And she would surely be nervous and uncomfortable, still even in a certain shock that her long-lost son had suddenly dropped from the heavens before her. It would be his job to put her at ease, assure her. Just take her by the hands, speak tenderly.

But none of that was so. Even as Rita Garcia neared Jay, he could see that she was nothing as he had imagined. Well, yes, she was quite dark. But it was not the color of her skin he noticed. Rather, how weathered it was, furrowed. And there was a grayness to it, no shine—a dull, drab aspect. Her hair was gray, too, worn close-cropped and not at all attractive. Late forties or maybe fifty? Her face belied that; it seemed that she must be years older.

And yet, Rita Garcia held herself high, stepping confidently toward him in her long, shapeless pants. She kept an easy pace with the two big men who flanked her. If she was taller than Jay had expected, there was, too, no stoop to her. Neither did she display any timidity. In fact, far from appearing in any way discombobulated, Rita seemed merely curious, even bemused that she should finally be meeting her long-lost child. And as he came down the steps to the bandstand and walked toward her, she simply stopped, crossed her arms before herself, and even with a slight smile on her face, this, of all things, is what Jay Alcazar's mother said to him: "Ah, *El Jefe.*"

Naturally, he froze. He put a sick smile on his face, and completely forgot the business about taking her gently by the hands. *"Si, hola,"* was all he could manage.

"Hola," was all she said back.

"Everyone calls me Jay," he went on, in Spanish.

"Yes, of course. I've read so much about you."

And so they still stood there, facing each other at a divide of a few feet, her arms still akimbo, his hands fumbling before him. He was completely at sea, all his scenarios of this moment shattered by how contrary it had all gone. Paco and Tomas could see his confusion, and so as he kept standing there, at a loss, Paco prompted him. "Palacio del Valle," he said.

"Oh yes," Jay said quickly. "Would you like to go to the Palacio del Valle?" It was a grand old hotel, worn out now, but still the finest place in town. "We could talk there."

"No, this is fine," Rita said, shrugging her shoulders, stepping toward the bandstand. They had all figured that going to such a magnificent place would greatly please a poor worker in a cigar factory.

"Oh, sure, of course," Jay said, still so taken aback that he forgot and reverted back to English.

As Rita passed by she stopped in front of him, staring at his face. He held himself there, unsure. After a few moments, she reached up and touched one of his cheeks. "I could never quite see your father in you in the pictures. But now I can see some of Emilio."

"I'm glad."

She withdrew her hand, then, and, easily, casually, moved up the steps to take a seat on the bench that went round the inside of the gazebo. It was Rita now, in fact, who took the lead. She patted the seat beside her. "Come and sit. We'll chat."

Paco said: "Would you like drinks?"

"Sure," Rita said straightaway. "I'll have a Cuba *libre*."

"Another beer," Jay said, going up the stairs, taking his seat. Tomas headed over to El Palatino to fetch the drinks. Paco took his place at a slight remove from Jay. "I want Paco to stay," Jay explained. "In case. My Spanish isn't very good."

"You're doing all right. You could use some work on your tenses, that's all."

"Thanks."

"So," she said easily, "why did the great *El Jefe* come to see me?"

"Please, don't call me that."

"Oh? But it's in the newspapers, on the radio, TV."

"I know, but I don't like it. Jay, please."

She shrugged. "All right. I was the one who named you," she went on, easily, conversationally. "Juan Francisco was a friend of mine who had just been killed, fighting for freedom."

"I didn't know that."

"Of course. It's a very honorable name you bear."

"How was Juan Francisco killed?"

Rita looked over toward Paco. He understood right away. "You can say anything in front of me," he told her.

Rita decided she could trust him; she turned back. "Like your father, he was conspiring against Castro. Someone turned him in."

"Oh."

She crossed her legs, looking him straight in the face, and, rather abruptly, to the point: "So, why did you come to see me?"

"Well, I wanted to meet you, to talk to you."

"Yes, that's nice. But why now?"

"I don't know if you heard how last year someone tried to kill me."

"Yes, of course, in Boston. Everyone heard about that."

"Well, I guess when you go through something like

that, when you're afraid you're gonna die, it makes you think. I thought: it is time I went to find you."

She reached over and touched his hand. "That is very sweet. Of course, I've known all about you—the last few years, anyway. I've even seen you play on TV."

"You can watch American television?"

"Not supposed to, of course, but there are those with the dishes." She turned to Paco. "Right?"

"Oh yes," he said.

"So I've been very proud of you, Jay. Of course, only very few people know who I am to you."

"People don't know?"

"It's been so long. I had a baby, he was gone. The father died. After awhile, who remembers? Why bring it up?"

Jay saw an opening. "Did you…are there any other children?"

"Yes, I married a man a few years after your father was killed. His name is Ramon Moreno. But Ramon left—ah, we left each other—many years ago. Yet, my joy: there is a daughter."

"I have a sister?" Rita nodded. "Really? Can I meet her?" Jay grew excited, ready to tell Rita about the boat, how he was going to get her away—along with her daughter too, of course.

"Sure. Only she's in Havana. She's at the university."

"What's her name?"

"Eva," she said. "Eva Alcazar Moreno."

"Alcazar? After my father?"

"It was a way to remember him."

"But your husband—"

"Did Ramon mind? No, of course not. He knew Emilio. He was happy to give our child his name."

"That's so nice," Jay said. He was touched. He was even more excited now. There was so much he was curious about, and although he'd been initially disappointed by Rita's plain appearance, he very much did like her manner, her ease, her assurance. She was a strong woman, he could tell. So, Jay dared ask: "Do you know how my father died?"

"Oh, of course," she said. Tomas emerged from El Palatino, carrying the drinks, and so they paused in their conversation until he reached them. Jay raised his beer bottle to his mother.

"To you," he said.

She raised her rum in return. "And to you." Then she turned to Paco. "Please, if you will leave us alone for a moment. If he needs you, he'll call. All right?" she asked Jay.

"Sure."

Paco stepped outside the bandstand, joining Tomas. Rita turned back to Jay. "Your father was taken away just before you were born."

"So, he never saw me?"

She sipped her drink, then shook her head. "The same person who turned in Juan Francisco turned in your father. They executed Juan, but, for whatever reason, only left Emilio to waste his life in jail for twenty years. Who knows why they did that? Anyway, I would be allowed to visit him every few months. He would, of course, ask first about you, and I would tell him. But, then, you were still a baby, only nine, ten months old, when they stole you from me." Jay flinched a little with the verb she used—*roban,* stole. She noticed. "You do know the story, don't you?"

"Yes. My father—" he said, *"mi padre,"* but stopped himself and then substituted the name. "Victor told me."

A small smile creased Rita's lips. She went on: "I'm glad he told you the truth. It was a terrible thing." She looked directly at Jay to see his reaction.

"Yes," he said, and that obviously pleased her.

"So, it was about this time that Emilio began to ask me: 'Bring the baby next time, Rita. Let me see my boy, my Juanito.'"

"What did you do?"

"The first time, I said you were too young. Then I said you were teething. Then I said you were a little sick. But I knew then I couldn't go on and on that way. I had to tell Emilio the truth."

"And you did?"

"Yes." She took a big swallow from her glass. "This is very good. Thank you."

"And how did he take it?"

"How would you expect? He went into *una rabia.*"

Jay didn't know the word. *"Rabia?"* He screamed it at Paco. *"Rabia?"*

"Rage, berserk," Paco called back. Jay nodded.

"Loco," said Rita. "He went mad. As much as he had come to hate Fidel Castro, now he hated his brother more." The color vanished from Jay's face. He took his free hand and drew it across his brow, then took it down his cheeks, the thumb on one side, fingers on the other. "Emilio told me: 'Castro took me away from you, but since you had our child, I could stand it.

But now that Victor has taken Juanito from us—that I can't stand.' And so, he began to plot to escape. It was crazy. There was no way. But he was determined. He was going to escape and get to La Yuma and kill his brother."

"Kill Victor?"

"That was what he said he wanted to do. Then he would take you back. It was total madness. He would tell me, when I visited, and I would say, no, no, I'm all right. Juanito is surely all right. Don't be crazy. Maybe Castro will quit. Maybe he'll get killed. Maybe someone will make him free the political prisoners. The United Nations, someone. Something, you know. But from the moment Emilio learned about what had happened to you, he was so filled with anger, that…well, I think he truly lost his mind. There was so little to think about in that awful prison, and so, more and more, all he thought about was getting out and taking revenge on Victor."

"And he tried to escape?"

"Yes. But he had no chance at all." She even laughed when she said that. "It was hopeless. He didn't even get away."

"They killed him trying?"

"So they told me. I hope that was so. If not, it meant they caught him and tortured him before they killed him. So—" She held out her one hand, palms up, and shrugged, then drank more of her rum.

Jay stood up, turned his back, stared out. The German tourists had all been bundled back together and now were being steered, by their guide, inside the old opera house where Caruso once sang. Idly, without really seeing them, Jay watched them. Rita finished her drink and looked at him. When Jay turned back, she could see he was trying very hard not to cry. "So, in a way, I was responsible for my father's death?"

"Oh, Juan, no," Rita said, and she crossed over to him and took his hands (just as he had planned to take hers). "You were a baby. You did nothing."

"All right, so my second father was the one who killed my first father."

She didn't dismiss what he said, as she could have; she only qualified it. "Well, was responsible—yes, in a way, I suppose you could say that." Jay ducked his head, and Rita let go of his hand, reached up, and brushed away his tears. "But you mustn't cry, and you mustn't hate Victor."

"I don't know how you can..." He turned toward where Paco was. "Forgive, Paco, forgive."

"Perdonar."

"I don't know how you can forgive so easily."

"Oh, I don't know if I forgave him. But there was so much hate, and what did that give me? No, I just told myself that at least you were safe and free, that you were in La Yuma, and you had all that opportunity, and you would be fine. And I was right, wasn't I?"

"I guess."

"So, I went on, and I had another wonderful child who is mine."

Jay suddenly felt then that he had to embrace his mother. So he reached out and took her into his arms and held her tight to him. It pleased her, he could tell. She reached around him, too, and together they held on and rocked back and forth a little.

When he released her and stepped back, he smiled and took her hands in his and he said: "So, you've got to come with me."

"Come? Where?"

"To La Yuma. To America." She looked so puzzled. "Paco and Tomas, they—well, not them, but this guy—he has a boat. It's a fabulous boat, a speedboat. Absolutely safe. We'll take you tomorrow, the next night. Eva, too. Whoever you want."

Rita looked at him, her understanding replacing her wonder. "So that's why you came?"

"Yes, of course. To take you back."

"And where will I live?"

"Wherever you want. You can live with me. I have a big house in Miami. By the water. It's beautiful." Rita only nodded. So, quickly then: "Or I'll build a house. For you and Eva."

Rita reached up again and touched him on the cheek, as she had before. Only this time, she reached up with her left hand as well, and touched the other cheek, so that she framed his face between her hands. Then she said: "Oh, Juan, that is so nice of you, but, I'm sorry, I must say, no. No thank you."

No thank you. No gracias. The way she said it, the way it struck Jay, like, no thank you, I don't want another drink. No thank you, I don't need a receipt.

"No thank you?" Jay asked. "You don't want—"

"Juan..." She stopped. "No, no, Jay. You see, you *are* Jay, as you say. Whatever, you are not mine. Yes, yes, I gave birth to you, and I nursed you"—briefly, she touched a hand to her breast—" and yes, you have my blood, and Emilio's too, of course, but that is all.

Listen, listen, Victor's wife—I'm sorry..."

"Cynthia," Jay said.

"Yes, Cynthia—she is your mother. I ..."

"You don't have to live near her. You don't have to live near Victor. Listen, is it Victor? You don't have to ever see him. You don't have to live in Miami, in Florida. You can live wherever you want. I'll move myself. To be with you."

She waited till he was finished. He was struggling some with the language, and so sometimes she was fairly sure that she knew what he would say before he did, but patiently, she waited. And now, when he was finished, she touched his lips to silence.

"No, Jay. It can't be."

"Why?" he asked, brushing her finger away.

"Because things have gone one way, and they cannot be another."

"Of course things can be changed," he said.

"Yes, once," she said. "Not now."

"Ask Eva, please."

Rita shook her head. "No."

"But she's young."

"Yes, and Castro is old. She'll be able to make of Cuba what Emilio wanted."

"Victor wants that, too."

"Victor left."

Jay could see she was adamant. He didn't understand why. It made no sense to him that anyone could want to stay in this dreadful place when they could come to America, there to live in liberty and comfort. In absolute luxury. "Look, you can come back here when Castro dies."

"I want to *be* here when he dies." A small smile played across her face when she said that.

Jay slumped. He turned away, but then he feared that she would leave, and so quickly, he whirled back and held out his hands in supplication. "All right, all right. But Eva—maybe she *wants* to come. She can go to some college."

"No, now don't try to take Eva, like—" She was obviously going to say *like Victor took you from me.* But she stopped; he knew.

"Can't you talk with Eva?" Jay asked. Jay beseeched. "Maybe she'll feel differently."

"No. She stays with me here. I lost one child. No more."

"I mean, maybe she'll convince you to come. Both of you. Please." He paused. "Please, mother," Jay said. *Madre.*

She smiled as the word left his lips, but it didn't budge her. She only shook her head gently and said "No," softly. Rita could see he was going to argue more with her, so she waggled a finger in his face. "Understand, I'm so glad you came to see me. I wondered. You were so handsome, so rich, so famous—did you have a big head? And you don't. I can tell what a nice person you are. So that's enough. I couldn't have done a better job than Cynthia." She turned her head for just an instant and called out, "Paco, in a moment." Then she looked back to her son. "Go home and kiss your mother for me and learn to love your father again. Forget what happened when you were a baby. Hey, he gave you so very much."

Jay started once more to say something—who

knows what, just the something desperate people say to keep someone from leaving. Before he could, though, Rita put her finger back upon his lips and shook her head. Reluctantly, he nodded. She withdrew her finger, then, and moving closer, lifted her face to his and kissed him sweetly, part of her lips touching the side of his mouth, the rest touching his cheek. It was a dear kiss that he couldn't forget.

Then quickly, before another word, she turned and rushed away, across the floor of the bandstand, down the steps, striding toward the way out, past the statue of Jose Marti.

Paco looked up, and Jay rushed down to him, but only to thrust several large U.S. bills into his hands, to give to Rita. Paco and Tomas had to hurry to catch up with her, Rita was stepping away so briskly.

Jay looked, then, over the square. It was all but empty. The German tourists were still in the opera house. One person was crossing the last steps into El Paladino. The sun was all the way down now, behind the buildings. It was dusk in the middle of Cienfuegos, and it occurred to Jay Alcazar there, alone, in a gazebo, that he knew what it was like to lose his mother as she had once lost him. He couldn't help but keep thinking that part of it might have been because Rita thought that Emilio would have wanted it this way, to have nothing to do with the person Victor had stolen and raised as his own.

Perhaps sometimes, he decided, to gain the best, fair revenge you must spite yourself in the bargain.

LINDSAY

LINDSAY KNOCKED AT ALCAZAR'S HOTEL ROOM. She heard him yell something back, and then, in a moment, he opened the door. He'd pushed his breakfast cart toward there, figuring she was room service, ready to take it away. He drew back when he saw that, instead, standing there was some strange young woman wearing casual clothes.

"What is this?" he asked. He even almost started to close the door.

"Wait," Lindsay said, stepping forward, holding her hand up. "I'm Howie Traveler's daughter." He kept the door open then, looking her over. Dimly, he thought he could recognize her. They'd only met casually a couple of times—say hello to my daughter, hi, how're you, that sort of thing. "Lindsay. Remember?"

"Oh yeah." And then, the head cocked: "Howie okay?"

"Yeah, he's all right. But I gotta talk to you."

Alcazar pushed the breakfast cart past her into the

hall and nodded—albeit without any enthusiasm—that she could enter. "Jesus," he said, "I thought someone was settin' me up again."

"I understand," Lindsay said. The door closed behind her and she stepped in, but he made no more effort to welcome her, to offer her a seat, so she explained: "This is important."

"Yeah? Howie?"

"Maybe we oughtta sit down."

He shrugged. She took a chair, he slouched down on the couch. He was barefoot, wearing white slacks and a striped short-sleeved shirt from his own signature JC Penney line. "All right, what's up?"

"Jay, Daddy's gonna go to the police."

Alcazar sat up some. "Why?" he asked, but only out of general curiosity.

"Because, the other night—"

"What night?"

"You know."

"That night?"

"Yeah. When she opened the door."

Now Jay sat up. "How do you kn—…whatdya mean she opened the door?"

"Because you know she did, and when she did there was a man in the hall, and …" Alcazar's expression showed that he suddenly realized where this was going.

"Jesus," he said.

"Yeah, that was Daddy."

"Jesus Christ."

"Yeah."

"And he's gonna go to the cops?"

"Yeah."

Irritated, with asperity: "And he hasn't got the balls to tell me himself?"

"No, no, no, Jay—you know my father. You know Howie. He was comin'. He was comin' to see you first, and then he was gonna go straight to Moncrief and resign."

Alcazar slumped back down on the couch, flopped his head back, closed his eyes. Lindsay just let him lie out there. Finally, he opened his eyes and raised himself up some. "Why would he do that to me? He doesn't even know what happened."

"He just feels he ought to. It's his duty. Just to say what he saw. Just that. About the door."

Alcazar considered that. "So what the hell are you doin' here?"

Lindsay leaned forward. "I'm a lawyer. Okay, now I'm his lawyer. And…" Lindsay thought this over. Then very quickly she said: "And I wanna talk him out of it."

Alcazar looked at her quizzically. None of this was making any sense at all. That a manager would rat on his star. That was baffling enough. But now: his daughter is going to try and change his mind? "How?" was what Alcazar finally said.

"Well, convince me you didn't rape her."

Alcazar studied her. Now, absolutely everything seemed to be out of his control. Of all the damn things, his manager's daughter was taking charge of his fate. He eyed her. It's odd what you notice, even in a time of stress. And now what he noticed was that Lindsay didn't have on any makeup. The fact registered. He wasn't used to attractive young women showing up in

his presence without making every effort. In a per-
verse way, it gave Lindsay some substance. "Okay,"
was all he said, though.

Lindsay leaned in and very directly asked: "So you
didn't do it?"

"Hey, Howie's heard me say that enough. I have to
tell you too?"

"Yeah, tell me."

"Yeah, I swear. I didn't rape her." He crossed his
arms. He wasn't used to being on the defensive. And so,
petulantly then: "All right? Is that what you wanted?"

"Part of it."

"What else?"

"Well, come on, Jay, tell me why did she try to get
away?"

Alcazar stared at her. He was getting angry—
perhaps all the more so that she was running the show.
Finally he said: "I can't tell you that."

"Why not?"

"Because my lawyer said not to talk about it."

"Yeah, but your lawyer doesn't know what Daddy
saw."

Alcazar folded his arms. "Well, I can't tell you.
Jesus, isn't it enough that I swear to you I didn't do it?
Can't you tell Howie that?"

"Sure, I can tell 'im."

"Well then, do it."

Lindsay said, "Okay," but the way she said it made
plain that she thought Howie wouldn't be satisfied.

That irritated Alcazar all the more. "Hey, so now is
that all?"

"Actually, no."

"Yeah, what else?"

Lindsay leaned forward, and speaking very firmly and slowly, she told him: "I'll do my best with Daddy, but only if *you* make sure he gets another chance."

"Another chance at what?"

"Managing you guys. Another year."

Alcazar rolled his head. "Come on. You think I can do that?"

"Hey, don't play dumb, Jay," she said—and sharply. "You know damn good and well if you tell Moncrief you're signing somewhere else unless Howie Traveler stays, well then Howie Traveler stays." He didn't dispute that. "Just get Daddy one more year. That's all."

"And I agree to that, Howie forgets he saw the door open?"

"Well, there's a good chance."

"Wait a minute: I get him another year, and it's only 'just a good chance?'"

"I told you: he'll wanna know why she tried to get away. That's what he saw—with his own eyes. But I'll tell 'im you swore you didn't do it. Maybe that'll be enough." She shrugged, though: maybe not.

Jay leaned back on the couch again, thinking things over. Outside, there was a sudden gush of wind, blowing the rain so hard against the windows that they rattled. They both turned and looked. Then, sharply, he snapped: "Howie set you up for this?"

She shook her head. "No."

"He doesn't know you're here?"

"I told him I was coming, yeah, but no, as a matter of fact, he doesn't know what I'm talkin' to you about."

"Then why?"

"Why does it matter why?"

"Because it sounds like a crock, you know? Howie won't let anyone else tell him anything."

Lindsay turned away, then looked back at him. "Well, anyone else wasn't raped," is what she said.

Alcazar didn't get it right away. Only when Lindsay lowered her head and briefly put her fingers to the bridge of her nose, squeezing it there, did he appreciate her reference. He started to reach out to her, to touch her in some show of sympathy, but he thought better of that. He just said: "I'm sorry." He wanted to add her name, but if it had ever registered when she introduced herself, he'd forgotten it right away.

"It was in college."

"Hey, it's okay, you don't have to tell me."

"I've never really talked about it. I might as well."

"You never told anyone?"

"Just Daddy. Eventually."

"You didn't tell the cops?"

"No point. They wouldn't have believed me. Not in any court. It woulda just been a he said, she said thing."

"You sure?"

"Look, my brother had been killed just a few months before. On a motorcycle."

"I know. I've heard. I'm sorry."

"Yeah, well, I didn't think my parents could go through a thing like this so soon."

"So you mean maybe the cops could've pinned it on the guy?"

"Maybe. I fought. He was rough. There was probably some evidence. I don't know. I just knew my parents didn't deserve another thing like that. Not then."

"That was kinda tough on you, though, huh?"

"I guess. I left school. I made up an excuse. I went someplace else and, you know, tried to start fresh. It was a long time before I even told Daddy." She looked directly at Alcazar. "Look, it wasn't complicated. I'd gone out with him a couple times. We went to his room. We started making out. But I wasn't sure. I said no. I said no again. I pleaded with him. No good. He didn't stop. He said he knew I really wanted it." She paused for a moment. "He raped me. Yeah, now that I have said it, it is easy to tell. It's just hard telling what it *did* to me."

If the similarity between Lindsay's rape and the one which Alcazar was accused of hadn't occurred to her, it had to him. He stirred uneasily on the couch, his sympathy crossed now with some suspicion.

"So why'd you just tell me?"

"Because you wanted to know why Daddy would listen to me. Because he feels like, well, it's a rape case, and he can't just stand by. Because of what happened to me."

Alcazar shook his head. "No, that's not all of why you told me."

"It isn't?"

"No, it isn't, and you know it. You told me because you wanted to see how I'd react when you talked about getting raped. You wanted to see my face, didn't you?"

Lindsay pursed her lips and nodded slightly. "Maybe. Okay, maybe that was in the back of my mind."

"So, come on: how'd I do? Did I act all guilty?"

In fact, Lindsay thought he'd responded properly. But she didn't tell him that. Instead, she only said, "It doesn't matter what I think."

"Aw, cut it out," Alcazar snapped, and he got up from the sofa and looked down on her. "You got raped, and you don't care maybe I raped someone?"

"Look, dammit, this is about Daddy. I want him to keep this job. All his life he's wanted this. Okay?" She shrugged. "Sometimes you just have to deal with the—" She stopped.

"The devil. *I'm* the devil?"

"I'm sorry. Come on, I didn't mean that. It's only a figure of speech. I just mean sometimes you gotta work with what's given you. And right now, Jay, it's a two-way street, and you gotta work with me."

He leaned down so that his face was close to hers. "Yeah, and you're thinkin' that to keep your old man's job you gotta work with the hot-blooded spic who can't control himself when he's around a white woman." And for good measure: "We're all that way, right? All us beaners."

Lindsay didn't back off. She stared right back at him. "Fuck you," she said.

He was the one who blinked. He pulled his face back. "Oh, that's nice," he said, and then he walked away from her.

Lindsay got up and followed him. "Hey, Jay, what gives you the right to say things like that? What do you know about the way I think?" Now she had the edge on him; defensively, he only shrugged. "I know. I know. You're still just pissed off at Daddy for taking you out of that game last year."

Alcazar turned back sharply to her. "All right, now: fuck *you*." He said that right smack into her face, very plainly, and when she was the one who turned away this time, he reached out and grabbed her by the wrist—not hard, not with any strength, but grabbed her nonetheless. The point was obvious—and both of them immediately recognized that a man who was supposed to have grabbed someone and then raped her had just grabbed her, too. Lindsay looked down at where he grasped her. He kept hold of her wrist, though, and, then, if only gently, pulled her around. "What the hell do *you* know about what *I* was think-ing?" Only then did he let go his soft grip.

The remark stumped her. She didn't know what to think, let alone what to say.

"The truth is, lady, I never once got mad at Howie for that."

"Come on, Jay, you stormed into the dugout, you screamed at Daddy, you threw your helmet down. I saw it. The whole world saw it."

"Yeah, I did all that. But was I pissed at your old man? Was I?" Lindsay only looked back at him, blankly, confused. "Well, the answer is no. Okay, sure, I was goddamn frustrated that he had to take me out, because here was the biggest game of my life, and I couldn't run worth sh—…worth crap." Jay shook his head. "And Howie knew. Howie made the right call—and it took guts. Okay?" He waved a finger in her face. "So, like that. Sometimes what you see isn't what you see."

"Like the door opening."

"Uh-huh. Exactly. Like the door opening."

"So, all right: but it did open." He stopped and looked at her. "If you really didn't do it, why won't you tell me why she tried to get away?"

"What? Because you told me…about your rape?"

"Aw come on, Jay, this isn't truth or dare. You say you didn't do it, then tell me what the hell happened. Tell me so I can tell Daddy."

Alcazar considered that for a moment, then walked over to the minibar. He pulled out a Coke. "You want anything?"

"Got an orange juice?"

He grabbed one, took out two glasses, and put ice in his. Then he paused. "Oh, you want ice?"

"Sure." They were civil again. Sort of.

He fiddled with the ice, very properly and hygienically putting it in her glass with the tongs, and then when he turned back with her juice, he held it there and said, "What's your name?"

"What?"

"Look, I'm sorry, I really only met you a couple times, and when you introduced yourself here I wasn't listening and I didn't get it. I'd like to know your name."

"My name is Lindsay."

He handed her the glass. "Here, Lindsay."

The room was silent, then, for a long time. He reached for his Coke and drank a big gulp. Lindsay just sipped her juice and waited. Finally, Jay said: "Okay, so what're you gonna tell Howie?"

"I'm gonna tell him you swore you didn't do it, and so I don't want him to go to the cops."

"You believe me?"

"Maybe."

"Only maybe?"

"Yeah."

"But you're still gonna tell him not to talk?"

"I said I would."

"And then he won't go? To the cops."

"I told you: maybe. He'll be sympathetic to me, because…you know."

"Yeah."

"And I'll do the best I can, but if he asks me about what really happened…" She held out her hands.

"Yeah, but then you'll tell him I'm gonna tell Moncrief that I only sign with the Indians again if he gets another year."

Lindsay shook her head. "Oh no, Jay. Oh no. Daddy would kill me if he knew about that. That's just between you and me. I'll do my part, and if I get him to go along, *then* you gotta do your part. You gotta go to Moncrief. You know my father. You know he wouldn't take the job if you got it for him." She shook her head. "Not this way, anyhow."

Jay sipped his Coke. "Okay, then," he finally said. "Okay, it's a deal." He didn't stick out his hand, though. Instead, he just sort of gave her a little wave.

"Well, I'll do my best," Lindsay replied. She put her orange juice down and turned toward the door. Jay watched her go, but he wasn't thinking about her. He didn't know her. He only knew Howie, and right now Howie was the only sonuvabitch who mattered. Alcazar's mind was turning over. With each step she took, the more Jay figured that Howie wouldn't buy it. Okay, his daughter had been raped, but that was years ago.

Lindsay left the room, never looking back. The door closed behind her.

Howie, fucking Howie, would play every game his way. Didn't he tell Ollie that himself?

Alcazar jumped up and ran to the door and opened it. Lindsay was already way down the hall, almost to Howie's room, when she heard him call out to her, "Hey, Lindsay, come back."

JAY'S STORY

LINDSAY TURNED AROUND AND strode back toward him. He didn't move, just stood there, holding the door. As she came closer, two things occurred to her: how incredibly good-looking he really was, and how frightened he seemed. When she reached him, he said: "You really don't believe me, do you?"

"I don't know. No, I guess not." She stepped inside.

"I didn't think so." He followed her in. "You're a woman. You gotta side with her."

"No," Lindsay said. "It's just the door. You just have to explain that."

"Look, it's embarrassing."

"You think it's not embarrassing me talking about being raped?"

"All right. Sit down. I'll tell you what happened." She moved toward the couch. "I have to, don't I?"

"Probably."

He managed a smile. "Yeah this is like, whatdyacal-lit, where all those drunks sit around."

"Alcoholics Anonymous."

"Yeah, right, but they never tell anybody else—do they?" They were standing next to each other. "Do they?" She shook her head. "I'll never tell about what happened to you. And…you'll never tell?"

"If you don't want me to."

"You can't even tell Howie."

"Then what's the point?"

"Just listen to me. You believe me, he'll believe you."

"Okay," Lindsay said. He was right, too. She picked up her orange juice glass again and sat down.

"First. Can I ask you a question?"

"Sure."

"I don't know how to say this nicely, but don't you know I can pretty much get…you know, get…"

"Get laid. Yeah, I know that. But I also know you expect it."

That knocked Jay back a little. "You're not cuttin' me any slack, are you?" he asked, but with something of a smile.

"Hey, Jay, there's two people who told me never to go out with a ballplayer."

"Yeah, who?"

"My mother and my father."

Even Alcazar had to grin at that. "But," he said, "do you really think I'd rape someone? Just because a man raped you? Come on."

"A lot of men rape a lot of women."

Jay was still on his feet, and now he shook his head and rocked back and forth a little. More gently now, Lindsay went on: "Look, I don't know how to say this nicely, but my father says you haven't been yourself this year."

Alcazar nodded. "Well, Howie's right. I've had a bad season."

"Daddy's not talking about baseball, Jay. He says, somehow you're different."

"So I'd rape somebody? Jesus Christ, people are so stupid."

"Oh?"

"Not you." He chuckled. "Well, *maybe* not you. People—*people* think I got all bent out of shape because Howie took me outta that game, and the Yankees beat us. Sure, nobody likes to lose games. Sure, there's nothing I want more than to get into a World Series, but it's games. You play games, you lose some. You get the fuck over it. I'm sorry. Sorry."

"It's okay."

"No it isn't. I'm not supposed to use that language around ladies. That's the way I was brought up. It's common. I'm not common."

"I know that, Jay."

"Look, Lindsay, you're honest. Like your father. I don't meet a whole lot of honest women. Honest people."

"It's the circumstances. I'm not always this honest."

"Yeah, well, I want you to believe me. I want Howie to believe me. So I know I gotta be honest with you."

"Okay."

"Well, yeah, Howie's right. I have been screwed up. Not just losing a goddamn baseball game. It was afterwards. After the season."

"Jay, you don't have to tell me. Just tell me why she tried to get away."

"No, I'm gonna tell you. You're right. It is easy to tell. Maybe it'd be good to tell someone." He stopped and considered for a moment. Lindsay sipped her orange juice, but only so she didn't have to look at him. Suddenly, he blurted out: "I'm adopted. Most people don't know that."

"No, I didn't."

"See, my uncle—my father's brother—and his wife adopted me when I was a baby, so it's not a normal adoption like with strangers."

"I see."

"And last fall, what I found out is"—he paused so long, she thought he was going to stop—"…my adopted father actually stole me from my real mother. I found that out."

"Oh, God."

"Yeah. Then I found out that my real father…he was in jail then, in Cuba…he wanted to kill my father when he heard that, so he tried to escape and got killed himself."

Lindsay just shook her head. It was so sad. He was so sad. She stopped wondering why he was going through all of this instead of just recounting what happened with the woman. But, then, if she could tell him about her rape to see how he reacted, he could tell her about his troubles to win her sympathy. Two could play that game. Tit for tat. And if it was sympathy he was looking for, Jay was getting it.

He made some clicking noises with his mouth, then went on. "So I went to find my real mother. In Cuba."

"Did you?" Lindsay needed to say something.

"Yeah. Yeah. I met her, and guess what? Basically,"

— Jay shrugged — "basically my mother told me just to leave her alone."

"Oh, Jay." Now it was Lindsay who reached out her hand toward him, but he'd turned away and didn't see the gesture.

"I mean, I wanted to bring her over here. I even said bring your daughter, too. See, she'd married another guy and had a daughter." He shook his head, with what Lindsay thought was more confusion than despair. "But she just said no thank you. My mother just said now please take a hike. And, you know, it kinda breaks your heart when you finally find your mother, and she blows you off."

"Jay, I am sorry," Lindsay said.

But if he heard her, there was no indication. He was showing more agitation now, pacing a bit and running his hand through his hair. "It's funny. You go there, you stand in a place where you could've been all your life, maybe *should've* been, and it makes you wonder who you are."

"You're the same guy, Jay."

He shook his head. "No, I learned too much. I'll always be a different person now." He pursed his lips. "I can't change that. What I gotta do is, I just gotta get back to bein' the same ballplayer." Then, suddenly, he stopped and sat down across from her—but only on the arm of the easy chair. "Okay," he said briskly "So now here's what happened."

"All right."

"I come back to the hotel after dinner and there's my friend Ollie. You know, Ollie Jorgenson."

"I know."

"He's sitting there, having a beer with these two women. Tricia—you know her name?"

"I know."

"She's one, but Ollie's goin' after this other one. You can tell."

"I get it."

"Yeah. So, I join the party. Hey, it's a night game the next day. And you know how girls are."

"I'm a girl."

"Oh, yeah." He smiled. It was his first smile in a long while. "Well, you know, then, if Ollie's goin' after the one, they're both kinda uncomfortable. So, I'm gonna be a good guy and chat with the other one."

"Patricia."

"Yeah, Tricia, and she's nice—I mean, I thought that *then*—and she's not bad lookin', but I swear to you, Lindsay, I'm really not thinkin', you know."

"Yeah."

"I'm just being the good buddy, 'cause it's obvious to me Ollie's girl has decided, okay, she'll go up to his room. So, then they leave, and I stay to pick up the check, and what the hell, I ask Tricia if she wants to come up to my suite and have a drink. Frankly, I think it's a long shot. And yeah, sure enough she says, well, thanks, but she's had enough and she has to drive home."

"She says no thanks?"

"That's right. So, I say, well, come on up, and I'll make you a coffee." Jay pointed over to the cof-feemaker. "You know." He sighed. "Even then, I swear, Lindsay, I'm not really thinkin' I'm gonna, you know, score. In fact, I'm sort of pissed at myself. Now

I gotta sit there and have a coffee with this girl. But guess what?" Lindsay shrugged. "Soon as we get in the room she announces that she's changed her mind and would like a vodka. And I kinda turned to her, and she looks me right in the eye and smiles, and we kissed right there, standing up. I mean, we are hardly in the room." Jay sighed. "Okay. Christ, I hate telling you this."

"Why?"

"Because it's embarrassing, and you're, you know, a woman."

"Try to imagine I'm just a lawyer," Lindsay said.

"Yeah, sure. Okay: real quick. We sit down with our drinks, but pretty soon, we're making out, and we're gettin' pretty hot, and I, uh," Jay looked away, then turned back and quickly said: "And I asked her to give me a blow job."

Lindsay said "Oh."

Jay said: "Yeah, that's it." He looked back. "And, bingo, just like that, she jumps up and gives me this look like I'm disgusting, and she heads for the door. I mean: boom, like that. And that's when I lost it, Lindsay. I was so pissed off. I mean, come on: it's not like there's never been a girl ever gave a guy a blow job before. And so I just jumped up, and I ran after her, and just when she opens that door I grabbed her and brought her back in."

"And that's when Daddy saw you?"

"Yeah, I guess. I never saw anybody out there myself. In the hall. Obviously, she did, but I was just so pissed off. But I just said, very nicely, hey, I'm sorry, and lemme make amends. Please. So, I let go of her. I mean, she knew she coulda left then. But she didn't. She went back to the couch, and we were really very, uh, cordial and all, and we talked and we finished the drink, and then I, you know, made a little move on her again, and this time everything was okay, and we went into the bedroom and, you know, had sex like nothin' had happened."

Lindsay said: "So that was it?"

"Yeah. Then she said goodnight."

"And she left?"

"Well, first she got a little touchy again, but—"

"Wait a minute. How's that?"

"Well, I started to give her a little present."

"What kinda present?"

"You know, just some money. I told her to please go buy somethin' for herself. I even said, you know, I'm sorry about the mix-up in the beginning."

"And she got upset?"

"Yeah, she acted like I thought she was a pro. Jesus, Lindsay, I'm just givin' her a present. It's not like I got necklaces and stuff lyin' around to hand out."

Lindsay just said: "Look, Jay, I think she took it the wrong way."

"Yeah. And now she's taking me."

"Just a little misunderstanding between a man and a woman."

"I guess that's what I get for tryin' to be a gentleman," Jay said.

Lindsay didn't argue the point anymore. She just said: "You like my father, don't you?"

"Howie?" Jay asked. "What's that gotta do with anything?"

"You like him?"

"Well, yeah, I do. I like Howie. Matter of fact, he's the best guy I ever had as a manager."

"Okay," Lindsay said. And she thought to herself: if someone's got to profit from Jay's being so cocksure and guileless, it might as well be her father instead of some strange woman who just happened to waltz into Alcazar's bed one evening. Besides, she thought, Patricia Richmond had already gotten hers. She got to sleep with Jay Alcazar, which, all things considered, must be a pretty nice thing.

No, now it was Howie's turn.

THE DECISION

As soon as Howie let Lindsay back inside his room, this is what she said, straightaway: "Daddy, I don't want you to go to the police. He told me everything. He swore to me, and I believe him. I promise you: Jay didn't rape that woman."

"Lindsay, you sure, Lindsay? I mean, what she told me seemed awfully real."

"Trust me, Daddy. I was raped. *She's* kinda raping *him*—and it's not any nicer this way."

As curious as Howie was about what Alcazar had told Lindsay and what had really happened, he believed what his daughter told him. So he didn't go to the police. Instead, Howie never told another soul what he had seen in the hall that night when the door opened. He just altogether kept it to himself.

SPRING TRAINING

RIGHT AFTER THE FIRST OF THE YEAR, when the weather in Washington was dismal and she absolutely needed a change in her life, Lindsay let her hair grow. Howie hadn't been with her since Christmas, and so when he saw her in Florida in March when she traveled to Winter Haven, where the Indians held Spring Training, he was absolutely delighted.

"Get it straight, Daddy," Lindsay told him. "I didn't do this because you wanted me to. I just needed something different. It was either let my hair grow or get a nipple ring."

"You made a good choice," Howie said.

Lindsay went to the exhibition game that afternoon, against the Dodgers. She had a seat over the Indians dugout, in the first row, but Alcazar didn't notice her till he singled his second time up and was standing there on first, just idly looking back that way. He looked again, stared. It nagged at him how familiar she seemed, but he couldn't place her. Maybe the longer hair threw off his memory just enough. But, between pitches, he kept glancing back at her, squinting, canting his head the way he did when he was at bat, until finally it came to him who she was.

In the fifth inning, Alcazar doubled, and Casagrande, whom Moncrief had acquired in the off-season in a trade for Wyn'amo Willis, singled him in. He sprang up from his slide across the plate, headed back to the dugout, but, just before he went in, stopped and dusted himself off. Then, looking straight up at Lindsay, Jay winked.

Howie saw it, and he knew where Lindsay was sitting, so he knew who he had winked at. Lindsay had never told her father what she and Jay had talked about that rainy morning in Baltimore. Howie would always be curious as all hell—he was certainly not a don't-ask-don't-tell kind of guy—but she had told him never to ask about it, and he never did. So Howie didn't have a clue, either, when, out of the blue, Moncrief gave him his option year, even after the Indians failed to make the playoffs.

Lindsay had dinner with her father that night. It was the first time they'd eaten out together, just the two of them, since that evening at Cipparelli's in Baltimore. There weren't that many good restaurants in Winter Haven, but they got to Longhorn's around seven-thirty, because by then all the old people, the retirees, had eaten early, and, of course, the Cleveland Indians being the biggest thing in town, the esteemed veteran manager of the Cleveland Indians was ushered to a prime table.

They had just ordered their drinks—Howie's Old Grandad and water and Lindsay's Grey Goose and tonic, hold the lime—when there was a commotion. Even before he saw him, Howie knew. He said: "Jay's here." And sure enough, he swept into the room, cutting a swath. The woman with him was neither as glamorous nor mature as Howie was used to seeing with Jay. She was darker than his usual companions, too. But she was tall and wonderfully dressed and she seemed special to him, the way he walked in with her, the way he smiled.

Jay and the young woman were heading across the room when he spotted the Travelers. He said something to the *maitre d'* and guided his date over to their table. "Howie," he said, "I want you to meet my sister—well, my half-sister, Eva."

Sitting in a booth, it was hard for Howie to rise, but he did his best. "How do you do?" he said.

In English that was accented but obviously proficient, Eva said: "Very nice to meet you."

"And this is Howie's daughter..." Alcazar paused for just a second, as if he couldn't remember her name, and just before Lindsay started to volunteer her name, Jay said "Lindsay." He smiled and pointed a finger at her: gotcha.

"Hello, Jay," Lindsay said. "It's nice to meet you, Eva."

"I just got Eva outta Cuba," Jay explained. "Just last month."

Lindsay asked: "And your mother, Jay?"

Eva looked a little surprised at the reference. Well, even more so did Howie, who was completely in the dark. Jay gestured toward his sister: "I went to see

Eva. She's got a mind of her own. I got her out. And we're pretty sure now, our mother's gonna come next. She gotta come now. Right, Eva?"

She nodded, after a fashion.

They all four exchanged a few more pleasantries. Jay told Eva: "I was a free agent, but I signed again with the Indians because I knew we could win this year. Right, Howie?" Actually, though, Jay was looking more toward Lindsay when he said this.

Howie replied: "I altogether do not see why not."

And then Jay took his sister by the arm and ushered her back to his booth, where the *maitre'd* and the waiter were anxiously awaiting him. A camera flashed, and a few people applauded. Everybody was watching him.

The drinks came, an unwanted lime in Lindsay's vodka. "What's that about his mother?" Howie asked.

"Don't ask me, Dad. I told you: don't ask your lawyer about Jay." She decided that was too abrupt. She added: "He wants to get his mother out of Cuba."

"I thought his mother lived in Florida."

"Dad, don't ask."

It drove Howie nuts, but he just sighed and sipped his bourbon. "Well, guys like Jay, they usually get what they want."

Across the way, they heard Jay tell a little boy who was proferring a paper napkin, "I'm having dinner with this lovely lady now, but when we're finished I'll be delighted to sign."

Lindsay said: "Yes they do, Dad. They usually do get what they want." She fished the lime out of her drink. She just didn't care for limes. Then she raised her glass and said: "Here's to the best manager the Cleveland Indians have ever had."

"Well, anyway, I got the third year. The third year is when it's really my team."

As Lindsay was toasting her father, she glanced across the way and saw Alcazar looking back at her. He raised his hand to his eyebrow and gave her a sly little salute.

What Lindsay did then is she winked at him.

READING GROUP GUIDE

What parallels are drawn between the game of baseball and the game of life in this book? What parallels are there for Jay Alcazar specifically? For Howie?

Lindsay is the one who ultimately convinces Howie not to tell the police what he saw. Why do you think she does not want Howie to go to the police? Is it a personal motivation, or is it motivation for Howie's career?

Jay says, "Believe it or not, in a way, Howie's a lot like me." Would Howie agree with this sentiment? Do you agree that Howie and Jay are similar? In what ways?

The reader does not see much of Jay's relationships with women until the end of the story. How does Jay's interaction with his mother change your perception of him? How does his interaction with his sister change your perception of him?

Several times throughout the book someone will call Jay "entitled." Do you think that Jay feels as entitled to the things he has as other people make him out to be? What specific scenes make you feel that way?

Jay is very easily offended whenever anyone mentions race or anything that could be construed as a racial comment. Howie even tells Moncrief not to hire a Latino manager because it will anger Jay. Why is Jay so touchy about this topic?

When asked about injured players, "'I don't deal with the dead,' Howie would reply. That concluded the discussion. Ask me about the ones who could suit up." Howie believes himself to be one of the dead, but comes back to life at the end. What event makes this possible? Discuss the ethics surrounding that situation. What are the implications?

Early on in the book, Howie claims that he is not a racist, though he does exhibit some racist behavior. What racist behaviors does he exhibit? How do some of his views about different races help him in his career as a manager?

On page 16 we learn "when it came to the game of baseball, Howie was a connoisseur as much as he was a competitor." How does this differ from Jay's attitude?

We find out that Jay's "parents" are actually his aunt and uncle and that he was taken from his birth mother at his uncle's orders. His uncle believed that growing up in America would be what was best for Jay. Jay rebels against this idea, but eventually capitulates. Was Victor right or wrong to take Jay from his mother when she would not leave Cuba with the rest of the Alcazar family? What would you have wanted if it were your child?

After Jay has come all the way to Cuba to find his mother and bring her to the United States, she refuses and in fact spends very little time with Jay. What are her motivations? Who do you sympathize with in this situation?

What is Jay's attitude on the way to find his mother? How did his meeting with her and his trip to Cuba change his views about living in Cuba and what his uncle did when Jay was a baby?

The reader hears Jay's side of the story as he tells it to Lindsay and the story of Trish, the woman accusing him of rape, as she tells it to Howie. After hearing both of their explanations, who do you believe, Jay or his accuser? Who do you want to believe? Why?

Team management: Howie quotes Casey Stengal to Moncrief, saying, "The secret to managing is to keep the five guys who hate you away from the five who haven't made up their minds." He goes on to explain that you don't spend the bulk of your time with your stars, because they will play well regardless, but with the guys who don't play regularly because you want them to come through when they play for you. What does this say about the dynamic of a baseball team? Of any team?

Howie witnesses a woman apparently trying to escape from Jay's hotel room. When confronted by the authorities, Howie tells them that he saw nothing. Why does he lie to the detectives? Given the possible repercussions for Howie's career, what would you have done in the same situation?

ABOUT THE AUTHOR

Frank Deford is a six-time National Sportswriter of the Year, Senior Contributing Editor at *Sports Illustrated*, commentator on NPR's Morning Edition and a correspondent on the HBO show *RealSports with Bryant Gumbel*. In addition to being the author of more than a dozen books, he has been elected to the Hall of Fame of the National Association of Sportscasters and Sportswriters and has been awarded both an Emmy and a Peabody. Two of his books, *Everybody's All-American* and *Alex: The Life of a Child*, a memoir about his daughter who died of cystic fibrosis, have been made into movies. *Sporting News* describes Deford as "the most influential sports voice among members of the print media" and *GQ* simply calls him "the world's greatest sportswriter." Deford resides in Connecticut with his wife, Carol.